CHEM STRY

for Beginners

ANTHONY STRONG

A TOUCHSTONE BOOK
Published by Simon & Schuster

New York   London   Toronto   Sydney

Pages 176, 177, 185: *Lady Chatterley's Lover* by D. H. Lawrence published by Penguin and Cambridge University Press. Reproduced by permission of Pollinger Limited and the Estate of Frieda Lawrence Ravagli.

Page 237 SLOW HAND Words and Music by MICHAEL CLARK and JOHN BETTIS © 1981 WARNER-TAMERLANE PUBLISHING CORP. and SWEET HARMONY MUSIC, INC. All Rights for SWEET HARMONY MUSIC, INC. Administered by WB MUSIC CORP. All Rights Reserved

Touchstone
A Division of Simon & Schuster, Inc.
1230 Avenue of the Americas
New York, NY 10020

First Touchstone trade paperback edition September 2009

TOUCHSTONE and colophon are registered trademarks of Simon & Schuster, Inc.

For information about special discounts for bulk purchases, please contact Simon & Schuster Special Sales at 1-866-506-1949 or business@simonandschuster.com.

The Simon & Schuster Speakers Bureau can bring authors to your live event. For more information or to book an event contact the Simon & Schuster Speakers Bureau at 1-866-248-3049 or visit our website at www.simonspeakers.com.

Manufactured in the United States of America

1   3   5   7   9   10   8   6   4   2

Library of Congress Cataloging-in-Publication Data
Strong, Anthony.
Chemistry for beginners / by Anthony Strong.
p.   cm.
1. Biologists—Fiction. 2. Sexology—Research—Fiction. 3. Oxford (England)—Fiction. I. Title.
PR6119.T76C47 2009   823'.92—dc22   2009018873

ISBN 978-1-4391-0847-5
ISBN 978-1-4169-8718-5 (ebook)

Foreword

For a writer, the internet is a wonderful tool. If I want to research, say, folk customs in Seattle, or look up a Swedish train timetable from 1957, all I have to do is type in a few keywords and—hey presto—within moments the requisite facts are there in front of me, without my even having to leave my desk.

The downside is that sometimes there's just too much information. It can seem as if every last scrap of human knowledge, every random thought that has ever occurred to the human race, has been scanned in and uploaded somewhere, ready to snag the unwary author and divert him from his task. Sometimes I find myself wasting whole days transfixed by the scribblings of a gap-year backpacker in Tanzania, trawling through decade-old weather reports from Moscow, or simply drifting from link to link, propelled only by idle curiosity and a vague disinclination to do any proper work.

I can't now recall what I was researching when I stumbled across Dr. Steven Fisher's strange little paper about female sexual dysfunction. But as I read it, I soon realized that the story of the biochemist, the research subject identified only as Miss G. and the treatment known as KXC79 demanded a wider audience. I immediately saved a copy to my hard drive. It was lucky I did: later, when I went back to check, the paper and all references to it seemed to have vanished from the internet, as completely as if they had been deliberately removed.

I have made a few small changes to names and so on, mostly for legal reasons. Other than that, the text is as I found it. Meanwhile, several big pharmaceutical companies are reported to be "very close" to clinical trials of treatments for FSD. It seems safe to assume that, for reasons the reader is about to discover, KXC79 will not be among them.

Anthony Strong
England
April 2009

Female Sexual Dysfunction: Some Research Issues

by Dr. Steven J. Fisher, Department of Molecular Biology, University of Oxford.

International Journal of Sexual Biology 29 (May 2008): 701–50

ABSTRACT

BACKGROUND: Male sexual dysfunction has been well described in the literature. The compound sildenafil citrate, marketed by Pfizer under the brand name Viagra, has created a market estimated at over $1 billion annually. This has led to speculation that a drug targeted at female sexual dysfunction, or FSD, will be "the big pharmaceuticals' next miracle cure" (*Newsnight*, June 2007). However, the existence of FSD, and therefore of a treatment to combat it, remains controversial.

METHOD: The author describes a project to investigate a possible treatment for FSD, and cautions that some previously unconsidered factors may affect clinical outcomes. He describes in particular the case of Miss G., a research subject.

DISCUSSION: This paper was first presented at the conference Towards a Sexual-Dysfunction-Free Future 2008, sponsored by Trock Pharmaceuticals, where it provoked a lively response (see, for example, the correspondence pages of this journal, passim).

INTERESTS: The author acknowledges the generous funding of the Trock Research Foundation. This funding has since been withdrawn.

Twenty-eight women have now participated in the sexual dysfunction research project here at the Department of Molecular Biology, University of Oxford. Our approach is empirical: that is to say, the treatment, a synthetic enzyme code-named KXC79, is adjusted in response to each set of results. All the participants are volunteers and are assessed by my colleague Dr. Susan Minstock, using a number of standard evaluations (the Derogatis Sexual Functioning Inventory, the Locke-Wallace Marital Adjustment Test, the Female Sexual Function Index, etc.), before a decision is made as to whether they are suitable for inclusion. It is always explained to the volunteers exactly what the study will involve; to date, thirty-one potential subjects have declined to take part after these initial conversations. Nevertheless, early results have been encouraging; see, for example, S. J. Fisher and S. Minstock, "KXC79 and Female Sexual Dysfunction: Some Encouraging Early Results" (2007).

Miss G. was slightly unusual in that she was a postgraduate student here at the university who heard about the project from one of our research assistants.[1] Strictly speaking, this was a breach of our selection protocol. However, Miss G. worked in a completely different field, English literature, and in all other respects fulfilled our criteria: she was anorgasmic and had previously consulted a doctor "to make sure it wasn't just a virus." Notes were kept from initial

[1] The research assistant has since been terminated.

and subsequent interviews. She had also experienced relationship
problems:

> It wasn't just that I couldn't have orgasms—it was the fact that sex
> was such a big part of his life, and I couldn't share that. I simply
> had no interest in it. Almost as if I were going out with a football
> fan, but was bored by sports.

Based on this discussion and the questionnaires, Dr. Minstock
made a tentative diagnosis of Hypoactive Arousal Disorder and accepted her onto the study.

I myself met Miss G. for the first time when she came to the
lab for her induction. As this meeting, apparently so ordinary, was
in some ways the beginning of the whole sorry fiasco, I suppose I
should pause at this point to note my initial impressions of her—as
a person, I mean. The truth, though, is that I did not really have
any. If I may be allowed a small subjective observation, what I recall most is being somewhat annoyed that she was there at all: my
understanding was that the data-collection phase of our study was
completed, at least for the time being, whilst I prepared our latest
findings for publication. It was work that required a great deal of
concentration, and when Dr. Minstock showed someone into the
lab I did not, at first, look up from my computer.

"This is where the hands-on part happens," my colleague was
saying. "Well, when I say hands-on, of course, I don't necessarily
mean that literally—we've got toys to suit every taste."

Needless to say, I did not respond to this either. Dr. Minstock's
jocular manner, which she frequently assures me is simply a psychological stratagem to put test subjects and co-workers at their
ease, on occasion strays—it seems to me—into flippancy. Great
scientists from the past—men such as James Watson and Francis
Crick, say, when they were engaged in their revolutionary work on

DNA—never felt the need to be flippant. But Dr. Minstock, as a sexologist, does not always have quite the same regard for scientific method that I do.

"That's Dr. Fisher, who's in charge of the biochemical side," she added in a deafening whisper. "Don't worry, we won't disturb him if we're quiet. Over here's the photoplethagraph: basically it's like a little light we pop inside so we can see what's going on—"

"Photoplethysmograph," I said, still without raising my head.

"What?"

"That is a photople*thysmo*graph, not a photople*tha*graph. It calibrates reflected light. The darker the flush, the greater the vasodilation."

"Oh, yes," Dr. Minstock said brightly. "Photoplethysmograph. Of course."

"What's 'vasodilation'?"

I did look up then. There was something about the voice that had just spoken—something wry, ironic even, as if the speaker were somehow mocking herself for not knowing the answer.

Or—it occurred to me a fraction of a second later—as if she were somehow mocking *me* for knowing it.

In short, I thought I had discerned in the way the visitor had spoken a spark of real intelligence, an impression only partially dispelled by her appearance. I did not at that point know Miss G. was an arts graduate, but I could probably have deduced it. She was attractive, strikingly so—I might as well make that clear at the outset. But she was striking, if this makes sense, in an entirely unremarkable way. A pleasant face, torn jeans, a cashmere pullover, a book bag, a knitted cap—and, spilling out from under the cap, a fine mass of chestnut-brown hair, as squeaky-clean and glossy as a freshly peeled conker. One could imagine that if one were to touch it, the hair would be expensive and soft, just like the sweater. Clearly, she was not part of the university I inhabit, bounded as it is

by the Rutherford Laboratory on one side and the Science Park on
the other. Hers was another Oxford entirely, a city of drama societies and college balls and open-top sports cars roaring off for meals
in country pubs. In that Oxford, which overlaps mine whilst barely
impinging upon it, girls like her are . . . I almost want to say "two-
a-penny," but of course they are considerably more expensive than
that: their cashmere pullovers, their poise, and even their places at
Oxford are the products of costly private educations.

So I glanced at Miss G. and immediately thought that I knew
her type, a type which was both as familiar and as alien to me as if
she were a member of another species.

In this, as it later turned out, I was quite wrong.

"Vasodilation," I said, "relates to blood flow. Specifically, en-
gorgement of the surface capillaries due to physiological stimulation."

"Anything you want to know about the technical stuff, Steve's
your boy," Dr. Minstock said, with a little roll of the eyes which was
clearly meant to convey that knowing about the technical stuff was
a long way down her own list of priorities.

"Actually," Miss G. said, "there was one other thing—"

"I just need to check that file," my colleague said quickly. "I'll
only be a few minutes." As she left it seemed to me that she gave
the other woman a pitying look, as if to say "I warned you."

I sighed as I turned back to the visitor. "What did you want to
know?"

"I was just wondering," Miss G. said hesitantly, "if your treatment is something like Viagra."

I regret to say that even before she had finished this sentence
I was smiling slightly at its naiveté. "Not in the least, no. Viagra
would be completely the wrong approach for any problem you
might have."

"Why's that?"

"Well, I can tell you if you like," I said. "But I very much doubt you'll be able to grasp the answer."

She looked at me then in a rather level way, and I thought I detected a slight tightening of her jaw.

"Try me," she said.

1.2

My explanation will undoubtedly seem rather simplistic to my present audience, but for the sake of establishing exactly what I said to Miss G., I will repeat it here. "The active ingredient in sildenafil citrate, or Viagra, is a specific inhibitor of phosphodiesterase 5," I pointed out. "This cleaves the ring form of cyclic GMP, a cellular messenger very similar to cAMP. The inhibition of the phosphodiesterase thus allows for the persistence of cGMP, which in turn promotes the release of nitric oxide into the corpus cavernosa of the penis."

She nodded slowly. "You're quite right."

"Of course. The mechanism is relatively well understood." I turned back to my laptop.

"No, I meant you're right that I didn't understand. Not a word. Mind you," she went on, almost to herself, "it's got a sort of music to it, hasn't it, and I don't always understand a piece of Tennyson or Keats when I first hear it either. Sometimes you have to sort of . . . *feel* the meaning before you can work out the details. Let's see . . . so what you're saying is that once the phospho thingy, the phosphodiesterase, is taken out of the equation, and the cyclic GMP does its stuff, it's basically a question of nitric oxide, which must be a gas, so it's really just about hydraulics."

I must admit, I was quite surprised that she had managed to work out the gist of what I was saying from so little actual knowledge. "Approximately, yes. Women's sexual responses are rather more complicated."

"Ah. Now there, perhaps, I can correct *you*. You mean 'complex.'"

I frowned. "It's the same thing, surely."

She shook her head. "'Complicated' means something difficult but ultimately knowable. 'Complex' implies something which has so many variables and unknowns it can only be appreciated intuitively—something beyond the reach of rational analysis, like poetry or literature or love." And then, somewhat to my surprise, she recited what I took to be some lines of verse:

> "When two are stripped, long ere the course begin
> We wish that one should lose, the other win.
> And one especially do we affect
> Of two gold ingots, like in each respect:
>
> The reason, no man knows. Let it suffice,
> What we behold is censured by our eyes.
> Where both deliberate, the love is slight.
> Who ever loved, that loved not at first sight?"

My confusion must have been evident, because she added "Marlowe, Christopher, 1564 to 1593."

I bowed my head. "In that case, I stand corrected. But I still think I mean 'complicated.'"

And then she asked the question that started the landslide.

"Why?"

1.3

I rarely get the opportunity to talk about my work. Or rather, I get opportunities, but they tend not to be ones where the other person is really interested in the answer. Because of the various irrational taboos surrounding the physiology of sexual response, and the even greater taboo surrounding scientific discourse, I find that when I try to explain to people what I do, either their eyes glaze over or they become embarrassed. So when someone asks me a straightforward question I take the view that the more I can dispel their ignorance, the better.

"What you call love," I said, "by which I assume you actually mean romantic attraction, is a relatively simple phenomenon: cascades of a chemical called phenylethylamine gush through the central nervous system, inducing various emotional responses ranging from anxiety to a heightened need for touch. We know what it is, we know how it works, and, crucially, we know what it's *for*. Evolutionary theory, Miss G., teaches us that everything in the human body has a purpose. Our feet are shaped the way they are so that we can walk upright on the grassy savannah. Our thumbs work the way they do so that we can shape simple tools. Our hair is sleek and smooth and glossy so that our sweat glands can work more effectively. The male orgasm is another case in point. It has one purpose, and one purpose only: the continuation of the human race. Any pleasure we feel is simply the bribe by which nature induces us to spread our genes more widely.

"If you hook a man up to an MRI scanner during climax, you see a localized, muscular spasm lasting about six seconds: highly functional, but with little variation. A woman, on the other hand, gets pulled into it gradually, building up her orgasm in a series

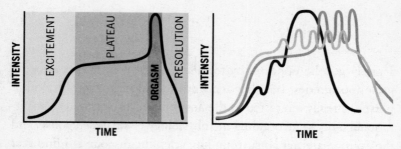

Figure 1: Typical male response.

Figure 2: Three different female responses.

of waves." At this point, I believe, I crossed to a whiteboard and sketched a brief illustration of the process, something along the lines of figures 1 and 2.

"First comes the excitement stage," I explained. "*Here.* There's a reddening of your chest, neck, and face, akin to a measles rash. A feeling of warmth pervades your pelvis. Your genitals engorge with blood; your pulse races, your limbs relax, you find it difficult to keep your mouth closed or control the sounds you make. A cocktail of stimulants, including dopamine and serotonin, are flooding your bloodstream, sensitizing your nerve endings and giving you a rushing sensation. Round about *here*"—I indicated the point with my dry marker—"your breathing becomes fast and shallow. Your capillaries dilate further, flushing your skin, which simultaneously becomes damp with perspiration. You are now at the stage scientists call the plateau, in which you feel as if you are being swept along on a rushing current of sensations. Synapses start firing in the right-hand side of your brain, the creative side, creating a flickering storm of electrical activity. Your nipples swell like berries. *Here* a chemical called oxytocin gushes from your pituitary gland, inducing an overwhelming feeling of euphoria.

You gasp, you bite your lover's neck, you shudder uncontrollably, and your lips contort.

"Yet all this has just been the curtain-raiser for the main event. *Here* your whole body stiffens. You have reached the point of no return, a feeling sometimes described as like being suspended at the top of a very high swing. You take a gulp of air and hold your breath, or grab your ankles and bellow. A pronounced frown—the so-called orgasm face—is a testament to the myotonic tension now building in your muscles."

I glanced at Miss G.'s face. She was frowning with concentration as she tried to follow what I was saying, but I could see that she was more or less keeping up, so I continued. "At around this point, *here,* the long tissues of the arms and legs also contract in involuntary spasms. A shower of electrical signals twangs up and down the vagus nerve, like vibrations bouncing along a tightrope. A fiendishly intricate chain of biochemical reactions, only recently understood by science,[2] lights up your brain like a switchboard. The central nervous system goes into overload; patterns dance behind your eyes; you feel yourself propelled, judderingly, as if traveling fast over rough ground in a flimsy vehicle.

"But only now, *here,* do you finally abandon yourself to what is happening. A cascade of muscular contractions—each one exactly 0.8 seconds long—pulses from your genitals, pushing outwards, until there is no part of your body, from the center of your hips to the tips of your fingers, that is not dancing to the same beat. And then at last, *here,* it lets you go, although you may find aftershocks occurring up to half an hour later. For around thirty seconds, Miss

[2] S. J. Fisher, "Neural Pathways in the Neurotransmitter Cascade During Climax of Human Females," *New Medical Chemistry* 3 (2006).

Figure 3: Excitement phase.   Figure 4: Plateau.

G.—perhaps for as long as three whole minutes—you have been in the grip of a sensation more intense, more extraordinary, than any male has ever felt."[3]

There was a brief silence. It occurred to me that the use of the word *you* might not be strictly accurate in this instance, since Miss G. would presumably not have been there in the first place unless she was having difficulty with some or all of this process.

---

[3] I should probably clarify that I was referring here only to the male and female of our own species. Amongst other mammals, the picture is more complex. Coitus between minks lasts approximately eight hours, though it is unclear how much of that is taken up by orgasm, as minks are notoriously irritable when sexually aroused and prone to biting researchers. However, it is known that a pig's orgasm lasts around thirty minutes, whilst the orgasms of the female bonobo ape are so frequent, and of such great duration, that two or more can sometimes overlap. S. J. Fisher, "Multiple Orgasm Amongst the Higher Primates," *Journal of Endocrinology* 74 (June 2002): 91–121.

"That is the how," I continued. "But the interesting question, the question which has perplexed scientists ever since we started looking at this area, is the one you asked just now."

" 'Why?' "

"Exactly. *What is it all for?* The clitoris appears to be the only organ in the body which has no function other than pleasure; the female orgasm is the only physiological mechanism for which we can find no evolutionary purpose. It isn't necessary for conception; it isn't needed for eating, or sleeping, or raising young; it confers no advantage that can be passed on to the next generation. According to all the principles of natural selection, it shouldn't exist. But it does. And even more fascinatingly, it sometimes goes wrong, for reasons we still cannot entirely fathom.

"That is the great mystery—and the great prize. In an age when we know almost everything there is to know about almost everything, the female orgasm is one of the few remaining puzzles. Your genitalia, Miss G., are the final frontier of scientific knowledge, the last unexplored territory. Indeed, I would go so far as to say scientists know more about the woolly mammoth than we do about your climaxes—and the mammoth is extinct! But all that's changing now. Little by little, the bright light of research is illuminating the dark recesses of ignorance, and soon there will be no problem or glitch caused by nature for which science does not have a solution."

I stopped, aware that I had spoken at rather greater length, and with rather more passion, than I had intended.

"Goodness," Miss G. said, and once again I had the feeling that she might be mocking me, just a little. "You make it sound like so much fun, as well. So when do I start?"

1.4

I explained, of course, what the actual tests would involve—that she would be connected to instruments measuring blood flow, muscular activity, pH, and so on. So that she would fully understand what I was talking about, I even took her to the testing room and showed her the couch, with its hygienic paper cover, its lines of tiny plastic crocodile clips, and its electroconductive pads. It is at this point that many volunteers back out. Miss G., however, took it all in stride, asking several intelligent questions about the different pieces of equipment, such as the Schuster balloon and the Geer gauge, and—somewhat to my surprise—observing that the software which linked them was based not on Windows or Apple but on Linux.[4]

"I'm a part-time programmer for the Tennysonline project," she explained. "The coding would be a nightmare if we didn't use open-source."

I noticed her looking rather anxiously, though, at the array of devices by means of which arousal is induced. These range from a small monitor, on which we can play video clips, to various kinds of transcutaneous electromechanical apparatus. The latter devices are necessarily rather more industrial in appearance than their High Street equivalents (figure 5), something which our subjects can find rather daunting. I tried to reassure her by explaining that the difference stemmed partly from the fact that we had to be able to vary the input from the control room next door.

"So basically you can change what's happening to me just by pushing some buttons in there?"

---

[4] Miss G., quite unusually in my experience, even pronounced the name correctly, i.e., "Linnucks" not "Lie-nux." See www.paul.sladen.org/pronunciation.

Figure 5: Some High Street stimulators (top) and their laboratory equivalents (below).

"Exactly. Which in turn means that when we compare the measurements from one session with those from another, we can tell whether it's taking more or less stimulation to produce the same result—in other words, whether the treatment is working."

"And how many times will I have to do all this? Before I'm cured, I mean?"

"I don't think you quite understand," I said, a little stiffly. "This is a research project, not a doctor's office. There are no guarantees of improvement."

"But I thought you had seen some encouraging results? Or was that paper you published last year overstating?"

"Ah." I had never before been confronted with a research subject who had actually read one of my own papers on the research in question, and for a moment I was at a loss as to the proper way to respond. "The paper was sound," I said at last. "But the science is highly advanced. I very much doubt whether you understood it properly."

This seemed to satisfy her—although she opened her mouth as if to comment further, she closed it again without speaking.

I turned to indicate Dr. Minstock, who was by now loitering ostentatiously. "Now, unless you have any more questions," I said, "I will leave you in Susan's capable hands. I should explain, by the way, that she is a sexologist, while I am a neurobiologist. But we get along perfectly well." That, of course, is a joke, though admittedly not one which many people outside the fields of sexology or neurobiology would appreciate. As they left the room Susan said something to Miss G., something too low for me to catch. It was followed by a barely suppressed cackle of laughter. Generally I am immune to my colleague's so-called empathy-building remarks at my expense, but on this occasion—I suppose because, somewhat unexpectedly, I had actually quite enjoyed talking to Miss G.—it annoyed me. I went into the control room and poured myself a beaker of water, staying there until I had regained my composure.

1.5

When I told Miss G. that Susan and I got along, that was true, generally speaking. When I was first given funding by Trock—really substantial funding, funding that transformed my little theory about primate populations into a full-scale human research project almost overnight—the firm imposed only one condition: that I was to bring a female sexologist on board. It wasn't easy, at first, sharing my project. But eventually Susan and I got used to each other—one of our research assistants remarked that it was almost like a marriage, but with more sex—and in any case, excitement about what we were doing helped to smooth any difficulties between us.

I need hardly tell this paper's audience that, in the great race to bring a successful treatment for female sexual dysfunction, or FSD, to market, a race currently taking place in clinics and laboratories all over the world, our little team is widely considered to be amongst the frontrunners. Oh, others may have reached the clinical phase before us; some may even have filed patents. By comparison, our progress has been slow but steady. While our rivals rushed to publish wild conjecture masquerading as research, we preferred to test and refine, test and refine; methodically exploring every avenue, no matter how unpromising; eliminating every false trail, no matter how seductive; checking and replicating every tiny success, in order that our method would eventually be seen to be as sound as our results. And now the prize was almost within our grasp. I do not mean money, although for our backers that must surely follow; I mean *acclaim*: the chance to have our names spoken in the same breath as those of the great scientific pioneers of the last century, people such as Chadwick, Townes, and Koch, or even—I may dare to believe—James Watson and Francis Crick. Under that sort of pressure, a few small personality clashes with one's colleagues are almost inevitable.

But there have also been occasions when I have become aware that Susan—how can I put this?—thinks that I am a bit *staid*. I suppose this shouldn't have come as a surprise: sexologists are by the nature of their profession a rather wilder bunch than we neurobiologists are. There was one occasion in particular, at last year's Sexual Endocrinology conference, when I had to go to her hotel room to collect some papers I wanted to look at before the following morning's session. I had already got ready for bed, and rather than get dressed again I simply put the hotel dressing gown on over my nightclothes. I thought as I knocked at her door I could hear voices, but if I assumed anything it was simply that she had the TV on. Then the door was pulled open. Susan was dressed in a loose

toweling robe herself—but she, I couldn't help but notice, was not
wearing nightclothes underneath. In one hand she held a tumbler
of drink. From inside the room drifted the herby odor of what I
took to be marijuana. On the bed behind her I caught a sudden,
shocking glimpse of writhing naked bodies, and I heard a woman's
voice—I am fairly sure it was that of Heather Jackson, a strikingly
attractive research student who had recently started working for
us—laugh throatily. A man's voice, somewhat muffled, growled
something in response.

Susan quickly stepped forward into the corridor so that my view
was blocked. I explained what I wanted and she went to get me the
papers, closing the door again until she returned.

She handed the papers over and I started to walk away. Then, as
if on an impulse, she called after me, in a voice that slurred slightly,
"Steve?"

I turned.

"You know," she said, "you should lighten up a bit."

I said nothing. I took the papers back to my room, but for
once my mind was incapable of processing the formulae in them.
I found myself realizing, almost for the first time, that what I was
reading—the complex interplay of neurotransmitters and secre-
tions, hormones and platelets, desire and arousal, my life's work—
was all about *sex:* actual, flesh-and-blood bodies, writhing together
like that knot of sexologists cavorting on Susan's bed. It may sound
odd, but it wasn't something that had ever really occurred to me
before—or at least, if I had acknowledged it, it had only been on an
intellectual level. And I was disappointed too with Heather, whom
I had believed to be a more serious academic than her behavior
that evening had revealed her to be. That night I did not sleep well,
and my paper next day on the climax of the female pygmy chim-

panzee was one of the worst delivered I have ever given.[5] I kept hearing that throaty female laugh coming from the bed, and the muffled deeper voice answering it.

Nevertheless, it was sensible of Trock to insist on my partner's being a woman. Susan takes care of the difficult part, the interaction with our volunteers: attaching all the tiny plastic clips, explaining how to use the mechanical devices, carrying out psychological counseling, and so on. Now that I think about it, it is perhaps a good thing that the volunteers remained unaware of the omnivorous nature of her own tastes, as revealed by that glimpse into her hotel room. But whatever her other failings, I really cannot fault her manner with the subjects, with whom she never seemed less than totally professional.

[5] A pity, as it remains one of the very few studies of its kind.

The testing room, as I have explained, is separate from the rest of the lab. The privacy is more psychological than actual, given the presence of so many monitoring devices, but we find it helps our subjects to relax. In the control room, I opened the microphone channels and heard my colleague's voice say, "So that one just eases in there—whoops—a little closer to the couch, if you could, the lead won't reach that far. That one's a snapper. Great."

I brought up Startle on my laptop. This showed a view of Miss G.'s left eye, magnified a hundred times. I adjusted the focus: on my screen the giant disembodied iris also adjusted itself, the pupil opening and closing as Miss G. settled herself (figure 6). She had unusually light eyes for a brunette; the bluey-grey-brown double-recessive must have been present in both her parents.

"So what happens now?" her voice said, breaking into my reverie.

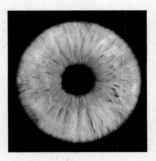

Figure 6: Miss G.'s left iris.

I activated my own microphone. "We wait. KXC79—that pill Susan gave you—takes around fifteen minutes to pass into your bloodstream."[1]

There was a short silence, during which Susan joined me in the control room and began going through the pretest checks. Visitors have occasionally likened our little booth to the cockpit of a 747 before takeoff; crammed into the tiny space are more than thirty different monitoring devices, all of which need to be primed and readied before the tests begin.

"Annie, I'm going to start a very gentle stimulation device," Susan said, pressing some buttons. "At this stage we're not looking to do any more than relax you. Later on you'll notice it getting rather more intense." By her elbow an oscillograph came to life, its flowerlike pattern opening and closing in time to the neurostimulator's output.

Out of the corner of my eye I saw my colleague looking puzzled as she checked her instruments. She pulled off her headset. "This is odd," she whispered. "The vibration meter is showing quite intense activity, but my inputs are set almost at zero."

I looked at the readouts. Sure enough, they appeared to show that Miss G. was oscillating at a steady 14 Hz. It was most perplexing.

---

[1] We have been criticized, I believe, for providing KXC79 in pill form, rather than as a faster-acting nasal spray. Our reasons for this had largely to do with patient acceptability: we believed that nasal sprays are inherently anerotic. Others disagree. According to one newspaper report, "Palatin, an American drug company, is in clinical trials of a melatonin-based drug that can be taken as a nasal spray before sex." Melatonin is the chemical responsible for changes in skin pigmentation during exposure to sunlight; it is also thought to increase libido. The report concludes: "Researchers think it unlikely that such sprays would lead to people becoming tanned as they would not be used every day. However, those using the implants to get a tan could experience frequent sexual arousal." Jonathan Leake, "Superdrug for a Dark, Lean Love Machine," *Sunday Times,* April 11, 2004.

"Whatever it is, it's not responding to any of my controls," Susan said, twisting a knob at random. "Could she have brought her own stimulator? I didn't think to ask—"

Then I realized what was causing the instruments to read as they were. For all her apparent self-assurance, the woman on the testing couch was trembling—trembling like a leaf.

This, of course, was something of a problem: the data would be worthless if we were unable to distinguish between the different stimuli that had generated it. Turning to the CD player, I pressed Play. In our headsets swooping, melodic sine waves and polytones collided, reacted, and reemerged as something completely different—an extraordinary mixture of music and mathematics.

"What's *this*?" Susan asked.

"Tomita—his arrangement of Mussorgsky's *Pictures at an Exhibition*. I was listening to it earlier."

Susan made a face. "It's hardly going to put her in the mood, though, is it?"

I watched as Miss G.'s shaking gradually subsided. "On the contrary. It already appears to be having the desired effect."

Susan shrugged and reached for the controls. "Let's get started then, shall we?"

"Dr. Fisher?" Miss G.'s voice said, suddenly loud in our ears.

"Yes?"

"Could you tell me a bit more about that pill? How it's going to affect me?"

"Of course," I said. "Though it's pretty complex—complicated, I mean."

On my left, Susan pointed urgently at the clock and shook her head.

"First," I said, ignoring her, "you need to understand what a neurotransmitter is. Think of your body as a kind of biochemical

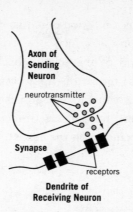

Figure 7: How a neurotransmitter works.

computer. Instead of using cables and wires, different parts of the body communicate with each other by sending messages through the cells. Although there are big gaps, called synapses, between the cells, each cell also has a little transmitter station known as the presynaptic nerve terminal." (See figure 7.)

Susan was by now waving one painted fingernail vigorously back and forth across her throat.

"The terminal beams out messages in the form of chemicals, which are accepted by the neuron of the next cell at a specialized site called a receptor," I went on. "So—"

Susan pulled her headphones off. "We need to start these tests, Steve. Now. We're about to miss our window."

"*So*," I said firmly, "the action that follows activation of a receptor site can be either depolarization, which means it has what we call an excitatory postsynaptic potential, or hyperpolarization, which means it has an inhibitory postsynaptic potential."

"Finally," Susan muttered, reaching for the controls.

"To put that in layman's terms," I added, "a depolarization

makes it more likely that an action potential will fire, while a hyper-polarization has the opposite effect."

"And that's the end of the science bit," Susan said quickly. "Annie, we're going to move this up a notch. Try to think some nice erotic thoughts, if you can." She pushed some buttons, and the familiar background hum of electromechanical devices whir-ring into life began to crackle on the headsets.

2.2

We sat in silence for a few minutes, looking at the readouts.

"This is looking surprisingly positive," Susan murmured. "I'm going to go to four."

The hum intensified.

"The KXC79 should just about be peaking," Susan said. "I'll see if we can't—" She pushed some more buttons. "And a bit more of *this,*" she muttered, twisting a knob. "Okay. Let's see what's cooking."

I switched to the heat-sensitive thermograph, looking for the telltale pattern spreading across Miss G.'s chest and neck that would indicate an arousal flush. So far, nothing. There was little I could usefully do to help now, so I got on with plotting the data from previous test subjects on a spreadsheet according to their ethnicity.

After another four minutes Susan pushed another switch. "We seem to be losing the . . . but perhaps . . ." She twisted a dial to-wards the maximum.

I glanced at Startle. The screen was completely blank. Then I realized that this was because Miss G.'s eye was in fact now closed. She was breathing deeply and regularly—almost as if she were fast asleep.

To my astonishment, a delicate snore began to make itself heard on our headsets.

"Is she *asleep*?" Susan said.

"It appears so."

"How extraordinary. Well, there's not much point in continuing with this." My colleague began briskly flicking switches to their off positions. "Annie? Annie, wake up."

"Was that okay?" Miss G.'s voice asked, a little groggily.

"You did fine. I'm just sorry it wasn't more eventful for you." Susan went through to the testing room and began unhooking Miss G. from the devices.

"Oh, it was nice." Miss G. said. "Nicer than—well, than usual, anyway."

"To be honest, we're hoping to make it a lot more exciting than that," Susan said sternly. "Perhaps Dr. Fisher made it all just a bit *too* relaxing. Or perhaps it's some little problem we haven't spotted with the treatment."

"I'm sorry that wasn't much use, Dr. Fisher," Miss G. called.

I hastened to reassure her. "Oh, no, that isn't the case at all. An experiment that doesn't work often tells you much more than one that does. That's the whole basis of scientific investigation. And, anyway, that was only a very mild dose. I'm going to give you a skin patch to wear for a week or so. It's just like a nicotine patch, really, except that it'll be raising your background levels of KXC79. Hopefully next time you come back we'll see a marked difference in your responses."

2.3

Sometimes our subjects like to chat after a session, so Susan has evolved a debriefing procedure that gathers more feedback in the

post-test period. In Miss G.'s case, however, there had been so little
reaction it was barely necessary, and it was only a few minutes before my colleague rejoined me in the control room.

She picked up a readout from the EMG and began to cross-
check the results. "Interesting girl," she commented.

"Yes."

"I wonder why she didn't—"

Suddenly we were talking over each other. "You must have mis-
judged—"

"If you had prepared her properly—"

"You actually bored her to sleep. To sleep! I mean, that has to
be a first. Even for you."

We worked in a furious silence for a while.

"That's odd." Susan was studying the printout.

"What is?"

"There's a small escalation about seven minutes in. Then, by
seven minutes twenty, the line's gone flat again."

"What happened at seven minutes? Is that when we increased
the stimulation?"

"That's what I'm checking." Susan was running her finger down
the list of Stimulation Events. "No. According to this, seven minutes was before the actual tests had started."

"Play the tape," I said. But Susan, ahead of me, was already
winding the audiotape back towards the start of the session.

"Here we are. Six minutes fifty," she said, pressing Play. I heard
my own voice saying:

*"So the action that follows activation of a receptor site can be
either depolarization, which means it has an excitatory postsynaptic
potential, or hyperpolarization, which is an inhibitory postsynaptic
potential."*

Susan pressed Stop. "Must be an RAE."

RAEs—random arousal events—are a recurrent difficulty in our

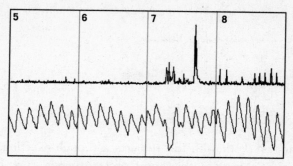

Figure 8: EMG showing Miss G.'s random arousal event at
07.00 (top). The lower line is just me talking.

line of work (figure 8). To put it simply, people sometimes react in
odd ways, and at odd moments, for reasons neither they nor we can
fully explain. We tend to exclude RAEs from our data, because if
we didn't, nothing would ever make any sense.

"Another one?" I said. "That's the third this month." And we
carried on packing up the equipment.

The hands-on work with test subjects, although exacting, is only the tip of the research iceberg on a project such as ours. For help with the number crunching we employ assistants, usually graduates who work in exchange for supervision on their theses. At the time of Miss G.'s inclusion in the program there were just three of these: Heather Jackson, keeping a low profile after her lapse at Sexual Endocrinology; there is Evans, a Welsh girl whose real passion lay in the genetic mutation of fruit flies; and Wulf Sederholm, a brilliant young theoretician whose work on sexual chaos theory was so esoteric and possibly so groundbreaking that I doubt there were more than three or four people in the world who were capable of understanding it.[1]

The week following Miss G.'s visit was an especially exciting one for our little team. After many delays my application for more equipment had been approved and we took delivery of several new instruments, including a state-of-the-art Medoc genitosensory analyzer (figure 9). It was not cheap, but it was purpose-built for this kind of work and, as I had pointed out to the funding board, getting one was a clear sign that we were now competing with the big boys.

Susan had also taken delivery of a new piece of apparatus—something she described as "the last word in stimulators." It went by the name of the Sybian, and was a fearsome-looking device

[1] Unfortunately, neither Wulf nor I was among them.

not unlike one of those bucking bronco machines that people try to ride at fairgrounds before the operator turns up the speed so much they get thrown off. I mentioned this to my colleague, who laughed and said, "That's 'bucking' with an *f,* Steve. And believe me, once you're pinned in place by the attachments on this baby, there's no way you're being thrown anywhere." She has a coarseness of expression, sometimes, that I find quite distasteful. (And I particularly loathe it when she calls me Steve.) However, I could see by the gleam in her eye that she too was excited about her new acquisition, so I left her to it and got on with installing the software for the GSA.

I was not so busy, though, that I didn't have time to think about Miss G. In fact, I found myself thinking about her quite a lot. KXC79 had never caused drowsiness in our test subjects before—quite the reverse. Although this was potentially quite a worrying development, I hypothesized that the problem was in all likelihood a simple anomaly, caused by a combination of Miss G.'s unfamiliarity with the process and a lack of engagement with Susan's stimulation program. But this, in turn, set me wondering how we might prevent it from happening again. Frankly, I couldn't imagine Miss G. getting much out of Susan's extensive repertoire

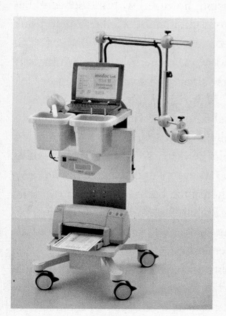

Figure 9: The Medoc GSA, a state-of-the-art genitosensory analyzer.

of pornographic videos (most of which, I had noticed, consisted of what my colleague liked to call, with an American growl in her voice that was probably meant to be ironic, "hot chick-on-chick action"). But equally, if she was to stay awake in future sessions, something a little less soothing than Tomita might be required. I reasoned that, being a literature student, she might prefer erotica in the written form; so, finding myself outside the university book-shop one lunchtime, I went in, with the intention of buying some appropriate material.

3.2

I was distracted from this mission, however, by the discovery that at long last my preordered copy of Richard Collins's new book *Enzymes and Influences: How Biochemistry Built Our Brains* (2008) had arrived. Those of you who work in the fields of neurobiology and endocrinology will of course already be aware of Professor Collins's work, and indeed of my high regard for it. It is true that he is still a somewhat controversial figure. But to those who call him a popularizer, or sniff disdainfully at "media science," I say this: If a man can make evolutionary biochemistry so simple, so accessible, that almost anyone with a PhD or even a good degree in engineering can understand it, then where's the harm in that? I myself had the great good fortune to have Richard as my supervisor when I became a postgraduate eight years ago, and to say that he inspired me is an understatement. I still remember that momentous day when I went to him with my thoughts on oxytocin and primate popula-tions. Of course, he grasped what I was getting at instantly, and saw much more clearly than I did the whole difficulty of the posterior pituitary. But his words of encouragement stay with me still, and whenever I read his books some of that idealistic excitement comes back to me—the heady sense that, by understanding science, we are understanding and changing our world. Sadly, he and I are in touch less than we once were; as well as his media appearances, there are his teaching duties at the Universities of Toronto and Adelaide and at Harvard, not to mention his demanding schedule as the Trock Ambassador for the Physical Sciences. Some years, we only seem to bump into each other at the big international conferences. But I have his most famous saying—"For every action there is a chemical reaction"—pinned up in my bathroom above the mirror, where it is the first thing I see each morning; it seems to me to be not only a witty aphorism about enzymes but also a valid principle by which to live one's life.

It was with some reluctance, therefore, that I tore myself away from the pages of *Enzymes and Influences* and went in search of erotic literature. I had been worried that works in this category might prove hard to track down, but fortunately the shop had decided that sex warranted a bookcase to itself. (What determines these things? I found myself wondering. Clearly there were no consistent principles of classification at work here, such as the Linnean system, or there would also have to be separate bookcases for fiction about fruit, fiction about birds, fiction about trees, and so on.) Erotica, for reasons which were not entirely clear to me, was positioned between Humor and Occult, and contained a substantial number of titles. But which to choose? The titles, in fact, were not much use. Was a book called *Dirty Laundry* (Birch, P., 2002) likely to be more or less erotic than one entitled *Punished in Pink* (Celbridge, Y., 2005)? It occurred to me that Miss G. might prefer a book written by a woman. But that didn't make things much easier—almost every volume seemed to be the work of a female author. In the end I chose half-a-dozen at random, and I was making my way back to the till when I saw her—that is, Miss G.

The university bookshop is the sort of place which likes to pretend it isn't actually a shop at all, but a cross between a library and a vast café, with armchairs scattered around the stacks and various drinks and snacks available. This hospitality is enthusiastically abused by the students, who go there to write their essays, consulting the books on the shelves without paying for them. (I say "abused," but I was recently informed by Wulf that a bookshop actually makes more profit from selling a cup of coffee than it does from selling a book, so perhaps it is simply a sound business strategy.) Miss G. was sprawled sideways across an armchair, her legs over one of the arms and a pile of texts precariously balanced on her lap. In her right hand was a pen, around which she was idly curling a stray tendril of hair. She looked, if anything, even more striking than on the last occasion we had met.

Unfortunately, as I looked at her another customer bumped into me, sending my own purchases crashing to the floor. Miss G. glanced up.

"Oh, it's, um, Dr. Fisher," she said. "How nice to see you." She retrieved the copy of *Dirty Laundry* that had skidded under her chair and handed it to me.

"Hello," I replied. Then, unexpectedly, I found myself blushing.

3.3

Blushing—or subcutaneous peripheral vasodilation, to give it its proper name—is actually a rather intriguing phenomenon. The physical mechanism is relatively well understood: the facial vein that supplies the small blood vessels in the face is responsive to beta-adrenergic stimulation, a property unusual in venous tissue. But the reason why some people blush and others do not is more obscure. Researchers in my own field have tried to link it to the vasodilation that occurs during sexual arousal, leading to the oft-repeated observation "After the blush, the orgasm." Personally, I think this a red herring—an early batch of KXC79 which caused our subjects to blush furiously, for example, had little effect on their sexual response.

My own susceptibility to this functionless physiological quirk is, as you can imagine, a source of great annoyance. Over the past few years I have trained myself not to go red in the face whilst discussing sexual responses in the laboratory, yet it seems that if you put me in a bookshop with an attractive girl and a dropped pile of pornographic books this is no longer the case.

Another curious thing about blushes: sometimes they can be contagious, just like yawns, sneezes, and, in certain circumstances, orgasms.[2] Certainly this is what seemed to happen that day; no sooner had I greeted Miss G. than she too turned a faint shade of pink.

"What are you up to?" I eventually managed to ask. It was not the most imaginative question, given that there are only so many things one can be up to in a bookshop, but it got the conversation going.

"Oh, just reading some idiot who thinks that romantic literature is inherently disposed to the semicolon. How about you?"

"I'm picking up some books," I said, demonstrating the literal truth of this as I plucked *Deviant Desires* (Anonymous, 2008) from the floor at her feet.

Miss G. peered at the volumes scattered around her, and I felt myself going an even deeper shade of red. She ignored the erotica, though; it was the Collins she picked up, with an exclamation of "*This* looks interesting. What's it about?"

---

[2] This, of course, is a joke, though it occurs to me that my work would be very much easier if it were not.

And then, somehow, without my even being aware of quite how it happened, we were sitting in the café with two cartons of steaming Fair Trade coffee in front of us, and I was telling her about Richard Collins and his visionary insights into the biochemical basis of human society, the words tumbling out of my mouth as I struggled to explain as much as possible before she got bored—as surely she must—and left.

But she didn't leave. She sat there, her bluey-grey-brown eyes fixed on mine with an expression of furrowed concentration, interjecting occasional comments and questions as I described for her that mysterious, post-Darwinian bioverse where the enzyme, not the atom, is king, and where love quite literally makes the world go round.[3] Eventually I paused, and she looked at me with such fascination that I flushed again, this time with pleasure.

" 'Beauty is truth, truth beauty,'" she murmured.

I frowned.

"Keats, John; 1795 to 1821," she added. "A poet."

"Oh," I said, considering. "Well, it's not a verifiable equation, is it? But it's a very compelling one."

There was a moment's silence.

"So what your professor—Richard Collins—what he's saying, basically, is that chemistry is inescapable," she said.

"Not just inescapable. Chemistry is *everything*—the whole world we live in. Take that coffee of yours. Have you ever asked yourself why it doesn't stay hot?"

She glanced down. "Because they put more in the cup than any human being could feasibly drink in a week?"

---

[3] I was grossly simplifying Professor Collins's theories, of course, and I refer the interested reader to the great man's own publications, where he or she will find them explained much better than I ever could. Also, I am aware that the world does not literally go "round," being an oblate spheroid.

"It's because the universe is dying."

Her eyes widened as she took in this statement.

"Entropy," I explained. "The second law of thermodynamics. Everything that exists—every person, every galaxy, every cup of liquid—is in a gradual transition from hot to cold, from unstable to stable, from disorder to order. In this brief interval of disequilibrium we have human life—and hot coffee."

She nodded thoughtfully.

"Or take this spoon." I picked up a plastic teaspoon from the table. "If I rub it on my sleeve—like *this*—I can fill it with the building blocks of existence."

I held out the spoon and she peered inside. "But there's nothing there!"

I moved the spoon towards her hair, and one of the fine chestnut strands reached forward to meet it. I raised the spoon higher, and the hair moved too, following my gesture. Like a snake charmer I made it dance—up, down, from side to side, adding more, giving her first a fuzzy halo, then a wimple of stretching filaments . . .

"Oh!" she said, and there was a note in her voice that hadn't been there before.

"Negatively charged particles," I explained. "The building blocks of life."

"Let me—" She reached for the spoon. As our hands touched there was a tiny crackle. On the table, a few grains of sugar lay scattered around an open paper packet. They jumped, attracted to her skin by the charge that had been transferred from me to her.

"Chemistry can show you how to blow up the world, or it can tell you the best way to dunk a biscuit in your coffee," I said as she sucked sugar grains from her fingers. "It can cure incurable diseases, or feed the hungry millions. Even the mysteries of sexual attraction—*especially* the mysteries of sexual attraction—are now shown to be nothing more than the result of an endless series of evolutionary experiments. The whole process of affection and desire, our family life, the way we organize our society, our hopes and dreams, the differences between male and female—they are all the consequence of a billion irreversible reactions, and we, their byproducts, are merely organic suspensions of salts and minerals in a temporary state of agitation."

"What a remarkable thought," she said. A single rhomboid crystal, remaining on her upper lip, trembled as she spoke. After a moment the end of her tongue came out and licked it away.

"Yes." I tapped the volume on the table. "The words are Richard's, actually, from his book *God Is a Biochemist,* but the sentiment is one with which I am in complete agreement."

3.4

And now I must come to the part of this encounter which, for a number of reasons, I find the most difficult to relate.

We were by now discussing the issue of bioevolutionary imperatives, as described by Professor Collins in *The Genius of the Gene.* "But if that's the case—if sex is simply a delivery mechanism for the evolutionary advantage," Miss G. was saying, "how do you explain sexual behaviors that *don't* give us any benefit?"

"Such as?"

"Well . . . kissing, for example."

"Kissing?"

"Yes. I was just wondering," she said, dropping her eyes, "why we sometimes get an urge to kiss another person. Even someone completely *random*. Where's the evolutionary imperative in *that*?"

"It's a good question," I conceded. "And one to which we

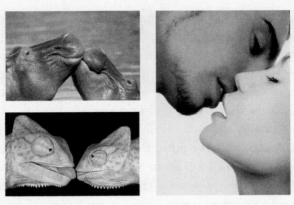

Figure 10: Three species which kiss. Counterclockwise: African hippopotamus, *Chamaeleo jacksonii*, *Homo sapiens*.

don't yet have the full answer. The issue, you see, is whether kissing is an instinctive, inherited behavior at all, or something we learn. Bonobo apes kiss, and some birds, and even a few species of gourami fish, which suggests that it's instinctive. But, equally, there are some human societies where kissing is completely unknown: Mangaia Island, for example, in the South Pacific, where no one kissed at all until Europeans arrived in the 1700s."

"So it must be something we learn from seeing others do it?"

I held up a finger to forestall her. "As it happens, there is a third possibility. Some recent studies have suggested kissing could be a way of exchanging invisible chemical messengers in order to test the suitability of a potential mate—the so-called histocompatibility theory. But that's an unproven hypothesis, I'm afraid, and there are plenty of people—Richard Collins amongst them—who think it overly sentimental."

"Well, quite," she said.

There was a brief silence. For my part, it was because I suddenly found myself wondering what it would be like to kiss Miss G.

While we had been talking, our natural wish to avoid disturbing those at neighboring tables had caused us to lean our heads increasingly close together. Now, in this slight pause in the conversation, I happened to glance down from her eyes—her clear, intelligent eyes, each bluey-grey-brown iris like a galaxy of gas and stars suspended in space—to her lips. She was, as I have already said, physically not unattractive, and her lips were no exception: rose-pink, slightly parted, and bare of any makeup. For a very brief moment I felt an extraordinary urge to press my own lips against them. The feeling—the *compulsion*—was so powerful it was almost hypersensory: I could actually imagine the scent of her breath, the soft feel of her skin, the warmth of her tongue, and the sweet sugary residue still remaining on her lips.

And then something even odder happened. As—purely in my imagination—our lips touched, I had a sensation of vertigo, as if I were looking over the side of a very tall building. The next moment, I was falling—falling through time. A series of unconnected images crashed into my brain. Two hominids, both covered in sleek brown hair, catching sight of each other across a grassy savannah; two monkeys in a tree, tenderly grooming each other for mites; two warthogs, grunting as they rutted; two tapirlike creatures, early mammals, curled up together in a Mesozoic burrow with their hairless warm-blooded young, while the ground around them shook from the stamping feet of a herd of diplodocus overhead, and the sky rumbled with falling meteor showers. . . .

I shook my head and the curious images receded. I must have betrayed my confusion, however, because the bluey-grey-brown eyes were now looking at me with a somewhat quizzical expression.

"Sorry," I said. "Miles away. Where were we?"

3.5

Soon after that, Miss G. had to go and finish her essay. As we got to our feet, though, she picked up *Enzymes and Influences*.

"Where would I find this? I'd love to read some more about—what did you call it?"

"Submolecular sexuality. But I very much doubt you'll be able to—" I caught myself. Miss G. was looking at me in that level, rather steely way again. And although of course I had been looking forward to reading Richard's book, it occurred to me that if Miss G. *did* read it, and *did* manage to understand it, there was no one with whom I would rather discuss its contents. "I had that copy on special order," I said. "But if you'd like to borrow it . . ."

"But you can't have read it yourself yet."

"It's no problem, really. Please, take it. Here."

"Well, if you're sure. I'll give you my contact details in case you change your mind." She pulled out a pen. Not having any paper, I offered her the back page of *Over the Knee* (Locke, F., 2006) and she scribbled something on it. "That's my Hotmail. And my snail mail. Or I could just bring it back next time I'm at the lab."

"Oh—yes. The lab." In the excitement of our conversation, I had somehow forgotten that she was actually a research subject. I muttered something about hoping there had been no adverse effects from her last visit.

"Not adverse, no. But I'd say there's definitely been some kind of effect." She frowned. "Quite a marked one, actually."

"Good. Well, I suppose we'll find out on Thursday."

As I turned to go she said, "Oh, and by the way, I'd recommend *Lady Chatterley's Lover,* if you're after something erotic. It's much better written than most of that stuff."

I believe I may even have blushed again.

3.6

As you can no doubt imagine, I went back to the lab that day in a
somewhat disturbed frame of mind. On the one hand, I had spent
an enjoyable couple of hours talking about matters of science with
an intelligent and attractive woman—an unusual, not to say unprecedented, event. On the other, I had come dangerously close to
having inappropriate thoughts about a research subject—thoughts,
moreover, of a most bizarre nature. What had caused them? After
all, I had conversed with attractive women before, often in circumstances far more intimate than my having a cup of coffee with Miss
G., and nothing of the kind had happened then. But a moment's
thought soon supplied the answer.

It is at this point that I need to reveal a small piece of personal
information. At the time I am describing, I was without a sexual
partner. In fact, I had been without a sexual partner for over three
years—almost as long as I had been engaged on the FSD project.
And although it is true that I had been extremely busy, my single
status was not entirely because of lack of opportunity. At various
conferences and so on, female colleagues had made it clear that
they would not be averse to seeing me in a more informal context.
But I had never followed those invitations up.

The real problem, if I am to be completely honest, is that I find
women rather boring. This is not misogyny, I hasten to add: I find
men boring as well. Compared to my work, people are just not
very interesting. Of course, I am aware of the irony in this: I can be
fascinated by the intricacies of a woman's pituitary gland or brain,
while at the same time finding her actual thoughts and emotions
somewhat mundane.

In short, it was undoubtedly simple sexual frustration which
had prompted those strange, almost hallucinogenic fantasies.

Fortunately I did not believe Miss G. had noticed anything amiss. As far as she was concerned, one could simply go on as if nothing had happened.

All the same, I made a mental resolution that I would not place myself in temptation's way again. After Miss G. had come in for her second session I would get Susan to explain that she should never have been recruited in the first place, and that she should in future seek help for her sexual problems elsewhere.

4.1

Time is an interesting phenomenon, isn't it? Normally, it flows from A to B, and thus to C and so on, in a pretty straight line.[1] And this, frankly, is the way we scientists like it. For all our talk of wormholes and relativity and the space-time continuum, we prefer our time quite classical. When we describe a discovery, especially, we tend to relate the events and experiments that led up to it in the order in which they happened, rather than in the order in which we became aware of them. Thus do we give the impression of a planned, methodical progression towards an inevitable truth, rather than the chaos of half-glimpsed solutions, blind alleys, false dawns, and wild guesses that—if we are honest—actually occurred.

All of which is a roundabout way of saying that the document I am now going to quote from was one with which I became familiar only much later. Needless to say, events might have turned out very differently had I been made aware of its contents at the time.

Ladies and gentlemen, may I draw your attention to Miss G.'s private diary.

---

[1] I mean C as in the third letter of the alphabet here, of course, and not c as in the letter Einstein used to denote the speed of light (299,792,458 meters per second) in the equation $E = mc^2$, since that does all sorts of strange things to time. In fact, it would be completely untrue to say of Einstein's c that time goes from A to B to C and so on—one would have to say that time goes from A to B, approaches C, and then gets stuck.

4.2

Ugh! I still can't believe that I'm going to write a blog—sorry, *diary*—about my sex life. Or lack of it.

But apparently it's a necessary part of the study that I keep a record of how sexy I feel. Dr. Minstock—Susan—says it's all part of learning to be intimate with myself and that it'll liberate my inner feminine or something. (Random question: Why does "intimate" mean sexual, when "intimation" means a thought or idea? Must look that up later.) Susan, I suspect, would prefer me to pen this by candlelight in some scented leather-bound notebook scattered with rose petals. I told her no way am I putting anything on paper. Quite apart from the environmental cost, what if someone finds it? At least this computer is password protected. No one will ever read these words except me.

Another weird thought.

So here goes.

This whole thing started when Simon decided I had a problem. It seems my lack of enthusiasm in bed was making him unhappy.

"So do you want to stop having sex with me?" I asked.

"Of course not," he said, a little tetchily. "Making love to you is utterly sublime, my darling. I'm just wondering what we can do to make it even better."

"I wouldn't mind stopping," I said. "In fact, that probably *would* make it better, for me. Plenty of people are having celibate relationships now, you know. I read an article."

Wrong answer. Recriminations, shouting, followed by the mother (father?) of all sulks. Believe me, no one knows how to sulk like a male academic with a bruised ego. By the end of it I've (a) had sex with him (again! That's the second time this month), and (b) promised to go to the doctor to see if there's anything that can be done.

Basically, it's not enough that I do it occasionally. I have to enjoy it too.

The disloyal thought occurs to me that Simon would be perfectly happy with someone who faked it, so long as she faked convincingly enough. Like that girl we used to call the Shrieker, who had the ground-floor room at Bristol. After a year of keeping us awake with her screams of pleasure, she and her boyfriend split up. She confessed it had been a kind of Method acting all along: if she gave a good enough performance, she was able to persuade herself she was getting something out of it.

Not that Simon would like me to shriek. That would be Distasteful. And Simon has very good taste. This is evidenced by the beautiful art on his walls, the beautiful clothes on his body, and the beautiful thoughts about the Nature of the Romantic Sublime in his head. (So heaven knows what he's doing with me, since I'm clearly not in his league beauty-wise. Perhaps it's just the forbidden thrill of seducing one of his students.)

Goodness, what a lot of disloyal thoughts seem to be spilling out! Maybe Susan's right after all—this is actually quite therapeutic.

More later, then.

UrlGirl67 ☺
"When the only tool you have is a hammer,
you tend to treat every problem as if it's a nail."

Anyway—to continue with the backstory—after we had the row I did what I usually do when confronted by a problem: I went on the internet. And, feeling faintly silly, I typed in "female + can't have orgasms + can't seem to get excited about boyfriend + not sure if really fancy him."

No exact matches, but removing the quotes and some extraneous words brought up 200,964,237 results. Mostly stuff that I *don't* want to look at, thanks very much. So I added the magic words "peer-reviewed."

And this strange little paper appeared. Or rather, three papers appeared, but two were about monkeys. The one that wasn't was cited as:

S. J. Fisher, and S. Minstock, "KXC79 and Female Sexual Dysfunction: Some Encouraging Early Results" (Department of Molecular Biology, Oxford University, 2007).

In other words, just up the road. I'd never heard of an academic called Fisher, or one called Minstock, but arts and sciences tend not to mix much here, so that was hardly surprising.

There was a lot of science stuff I didn't fully understand, even with the aid of a dictionary, but the gist of it seemed to be that they were working on a treatment for female sexual dysfunction that was going to be as straightforward as popping a pill. It wouldn't be available on the open market for a while, because of the time it takes to get government approval, but reading between the lines, I could see they were pretty confident they'd cracked it.

Which started me thinking.

If I could solve all these problems with Simon, a little voice inside me was saying—*if I could just take a pill and turn into the happy, orgasmic, randy little unit he so desperately wants me to be—wouldn't that be nice?*

Well, no, actually, another little voice was saying. *Who wants to be Simon's drugged-up sex puppet?*

Ah, but that's the Female Sexual Dysfunction talking, another voice pointed out. (And it was pretty impressive, incidentally, to suddenly have a proper medical label for what I thought was just a low sex drive. Not to mention a whole chorus of voices popping up in my head to talk about it.) *It's only because you have this problem in the first place that you aren't keen on the drugged-up sex,* the voice said. (That's the third voice, of course, not the second—try to keep up.) *Look at everyone else,* the voice said, *at it like rabbits. That's what's normal.*

In fact, the more me and my voices discussed it, the more we decided it was a pity I couldn't give something like KXC79 a go.

I mentioned the article to Simon. I hadn't planned to, actually, but he was getting grumpy again and I thought it might help if he knew that I had at least done a bit of research.

"Fisher," he said thoughtfully. "Fisher . . . I do seem to remember some ghastly pointy-head with that name skulking round the place. Not the most likely person to have solved your little problem."

(That is so typical of Simon, by the way. Whilst he will happily tell you that he has an IQ of 170 and is therefore a near-genius, anyone who works in a different discipline is just a pointy-head.)

(And another thing I've noticed: he always talks about the discrepancy in our sex drives as being *my* problem, not his. Of course, according to all the magazines, TV programs, books, and so on, he's right, so I suppose it must be me. It's just that no one has ever really convinced me that sex isn't, well, a waste of good reading time. Not to mention rather messy.)

(Since I seem to be complaining about Simon rather more than I meant to, let me just say for the record that of course I do love him. Not in the he-makes-my-heart-beat-faster-every-time-I-see-him sort of way—because, let's face it, that doesn't really happen, or at least not to me—but I know I'm so lucky to have him. He's one of the cleverest, most amazing people I've ever met. And he's going to be a professor soon. And . . .

And he's my supervisor.

Which makes it rather hard for us to break up, actually, without causing a whole load of problems and recriminations I'd rather do without. Plus, The Role of the Mythical Feminine in *The Idylls of the King* and Certain Other Poems by Tennyson is tedious enough already without having to explain it to a new supervisor who'd probably tell me to start again from scratch.

And after all, who wants to be single?

So, basically, although I'm unlikely to end up as the next Mrs. Frampton, this is fine.

For now.)

UrlGirl67 ☺
"When the only tool you have is a hammer,
you tend to treat every problem as if it's a nail."

The funny thing was that although Simon had initially been sniffy about Fisher and his "dodgy little pills," as he called them, after he'd spoken to a couple of people in the Senior Common Room he came back quite excited. "Apparently the man's on to something," he reported. "He's got backing from one of the big pharma companies—there's a whole laboratory up there on South Parks Road stuffed full of strange buzzing little machines. Porn, too. They have a special dispensation from the university authorities to store some of the most filthy film clips ever made." He paused significantly. "You never know, you might enjoy it."

"Enjoy what?"

"Being part of his study."

I stared at him. "What do you mean?"

"It's obvious, isn't it? You can't get these pills on the open market yet, but if you become one of his test subjects, you'll get them straightaway."

"What makes you think he's recruiting test subjects?"

"Oh, it's well known," he said evasively. "Actually, I think I might have spotted an ad. Where was it? Ah, yes." And he handed me a copy of the *Oxford Mail* with a small ad circled in red pen.

"Are you sexually dysfunctional?" it said. "Female? Would you like to earn extra cash by helping out with medical research?" There was a phone number, and then, in smaller print: "Oxford University is an Equal Opportunity Employer."

"You never know," he said persuasively. "It might be fun."

I shuddered. "Fun? *Fun?* Normal sex is depressing enough. Why on earth would I want to go and have my bits poked about with by some weirdo scientist?"

Another tactical error.

"Because you love me, of course," Simon said stiffly.

And that was the beginning of his campaign to get me to ring the number in the ad. Although he was pretending to be matter-of-fact about it, the idea of me being wired up to all the weird machines he'd heard about and made to watch dirty movies was clearly exciting to him— almost as if he thought it would somehow jump-start me into becoming more enthusiastic in bed.

So what with his nagging on the one hand, and a feeling that I really ought to do something about this missing piece I seem to have on the other, I thought I should probably give it a go. But I still wouldn't have done anything if I hadn't met this Welsh girl at a party. She was telling me about her supervisor, who she described as "a total goof"—but she said it with a fond smile on her face, and I could tell she actually liked her goof quite a lot. Then she said his name.

"You work for Steven Fisher?" I said. "The sexual dysfunction man?"

"That's right." She gave me a funny look. "He's a bit of a genius, actually. You know he was the youngest scientist ever to win the Johann Kurtis Award?"

I didn't. Nor did I have the faintest idea what the Johann Kurtis Award was, but I could tell it was something I should have been impressed by. The next day I phoned the number in the ad.

There was an initial interview with Susan, which I evidently passed, and then I had to come in for the first session. By this time it was seeming oddly normal to be discussing my orgasms, or rather the lack of them, with complete strangers, and I found myself becoming quite interested in what these people did. I mean, it's all very well to find traces of myth in the poems of Tennyson, but this lot were actually *discovering* stuff. Stuff that might change people's lives.

And then I met Dr. Fisher.

Let me just say that I loathed him the moment I set eyes on him. I'd been expecting . . . oh, I don't know, some spotty, dandruff-ridden, odiferous technician. Like the person who comes to mend the photocopier, only smarter. But the person I met in the lab was much, much worse than that. Because he was shy and good-looking and clever and just unbelievably, fantastically, condescending.

"What's vasodilation?" I say, just to make conversation—well, just to remind him that I'm there at all, actually: he was having some tetchy argument with Susan about whether they really needed any more data. I mean, hello? The data is standing right here, and she has a name.

And he smirked—he actually smiled at the question! As if I were some dumb blonde asking what the carburetor did!

All right, smartarse, I thought, I'll show you. So I rather pointedly asked some intelligent graduate-student-type questions. You don't get to do a PhD without learning how to deal with male academics and their overdeveloped egos. Tell me about your specialist subject, ooh please why don't you, while I open my eyes very wide and look impressed.

Unfortunately, he smirked even harder, and told me in so many words that there wasn't much point, as I couldn't possibly understand.

Try me, says I, through gritted incisors.

But the bastard was right. I realized too late I had simply demonstrated the appalling depths of my ignorance.

And then—a funny thing—instead of just walking away, I actually started to try to puzzle out what he was on about. He was talking about orgasms by now—why they're such a mystery, and how by studying them he hopes to find out more about other species or something. I couldn't follow it all. But I realized that for these people it isn't just about who's got more publications to their name, or being able to boast about your TV appearances like Simon does. These people are *driven*. They want to solve the mystery. And suddenly I wanted to be part of it. To be in the clever club, like them.

Christ, I even dropped into the conversation that I run Linux on my laptop. Talk about showing off! But I think Dr. Fisher was impressed, just a little.

And then, once the tests had begun, the oddest thing happened. I found myself getting—no, I can't write this down. Oh, all right then, I'll try. (As it says on the log-in page: AUTHORIZED USERS ONLY. If you do not have permission to access this information, please exit now.) To try to take my mind off what they were about to do to me, I started talking to Dr. Fisher. And suddenly I felt myself reacting to the sound of his voice through the headphones. I mean *physically*. It was so ridiculous it was almost funny. There I was, trying to have a serious conversation (and trying to prove to Dr. Fisher that I'm not just some ditzy Eng Lit airhead), when—*whoosh*—my body starts behaving as if I'm some lovestruck teenager in the presence of a rock god.

Of course, I realize straightaway that it must be the KXC79. But that doesn't make it any less embarrassing. I mean, Dr. Fisher's hardly going to have any respect for me if I start gasping and moaning before the tests have even started.

Something else I start to think about: How come Simon has never made me feel like this?

Bugger.

Because the time to consider questions like these is probably not when you're hooked up to at least a dozen different measuring devices, including something called a napkin-ring myograph which is positioned several inches beyond where the sun usually shines, and two pointyheads are monitoring every aspect of your sexual responses.

I assume it's just some sort of reflex reaction—Dr. Fisher being a man, and the KXC79 making me extraresponsive. But I don't want to ask him if that's the case, because I know he'll just say I'm too dumb to understand.

All in all, it seems easier just to do what I usually do when Simon gets amorous—i.e., pretend to be asleep. I seem to get away with it too, so perhaps those machines aren't as sensitive as they make out.

UrlGirl67 ☺

"When the only tool you have is a hammer,
you tend to treat every problem as if it's a nail."

Simon, of course, wants details. He seems obscurely disappointed that I haven't been participating in some wild orgy.

"Look," I explain patiently, "it's the least erotic experience you can imagine. You're wired up, there are people scrutinizing every sound, every movement you make—would you be able to perform under those conditions?"

He frowns. "Mmm. I see your point." Then he brightens up. "But they play porn clips?"

"Actually," I tell him, "they played music. To relax me." I've been humming Tomita's *Pictures* ever since, in fact, but I don't tell Simon that. Then something makes me add: "It's very hard work. I certainly won't be up to having sex normally until the study is over."

For a moment he looks furious. Then: "Well, I suppose if it eventually solves your little problem it'll be worth it," he says grumpily. "Perhaps you could remember to ask them about those porn clips, though."

UrlGirl67 ☺

"When the only tool you have is a hammer,
you tend to treat every problem as if it's a nail."

A couple of days later I go to the bookshop to check out a couple of new studies on Tennysonian punctuation (yes, really). And I suddenly realize that I am completely and utterly bored. Bored with my thesis, bored with my subject, bored with my life.

I put *Sense and Sentences: The Semiotics of the Victorian Semicolon* back on the shelf and go up to Information.

"Excuse me," I say to the person behind the desk, who looks as if he'd be more at home on a skateboard. "Where's science?"

He looks at me a bit strangely and says, "Downstairs, where it always was."

Turns out that underneath this tiny medieval bookshop there's a whole vast modern basement I didn't know anything about. It's like a spaceship down there—the hum of air conditioning, bright lights, modern stacks stretching away into the distance. I pluck a volume off a shelf at random. It's called something like *New Developments in Crystallography*. It's full of odd diagrams and strange formulae that mean absolutely nothing to me.

I glance at the guy browsing next to me. A spotty, odiferous smart aleck. He's reading the same book with every sign of enjoyment. Christ, at one point he even *chuckles*.

Is he really any cleverer than me?

I think not.

I hunt along the shelves until I find something called *Chemistry for Beginners* and take it back upstairs.

I'm on page 15 when someone says hello and I realize that it's Steven Fisher. I quickly drop *Chemistry for Beginners* behind my chair. Then I turn bright red with embarrassment. Luckily he doesn't seem to notice.

He insists on buying me coffee and explaining this book he's just bought. And I realize that he isn't actually patronizing at all, just incredibly passionate. For him, the world is an amazing place, and he wants to understand it. It's hardly his fault if everyone else exists on a lower level of knowledge than he does.

He even lends me the book. Though, to be honest, it makes much more sense when he explains it. (In fact, when I'm reading the book afterwards I keep imagining his voice speaking the technical passages, and somehow it helps.)

There's an odd moment when he starts talking about why people kiss. I've always thought of kissing as a rather pointless thing to do, actually, but he tells me this theory that it's all about two bodies exchanging chemical messengers to see if they're compatible. And I find myself wondering what would happen if he and I were to kiss—whether our pheromones and submolecules or whatever they're called would get on and pronounce us a match. In fact, the image of the two of us kissing is so vivid, and so nice, that it's all I can do not to swoon into his arms like some stupid Victorian heroine.

Of course, there's still all that KXC79 sloshing through my system from Tuesday's tests and the patch he's made me wear. So perhaps it's no wonder I'm getting these thoughts every now and again. It's not entirely nice—I mean, is this what normal women have to go through, women without FSD? Are they constantly imagining themselves kissing every attractive stranger they meet? That must be so weird. . . . Admittedly it's only happened with Dr. Fisher so far, but I'm clearly going to have to be careful.

UrlGirl67 ☺
"When the only tool you have is a hammer,
you tend to treat every problem as if it's a nail."

Back in the lab, I looked up "kissing" in the index of Richard Collins's book *The Evolution Revolution* (2004). It was not a subject to which he had given much attention. There was only one brief reference:

> For another example of the terrible deception our genes play on us, we need look no farther than kissing. As men, we are all programmed to think we have to find the most beautiful woman in the world and make her fall in love with us—youth and beauty being nature's way of telling us we've hit on a nice healthy gene pool to mix with our own. But the truth is that the most beautiful woman in the world is already taken—or else, as described earlier, she's busy looking for the highest-status man. So, little by little, we learn to lower our standards. At some point, whom we want and whom we can achieve finally intersect. And at that moment, just to make sure we don't mess things up by taking a long, hard look at our potential partner and running a mile in the opposite direction, nature helps us along by giving us a narcotic—a bit like having an epidural during the pain of childbirth, except that in our case we're blinded by the cocktail of aphrodisiacs, mood enhancers, and other mind-altering chemicals we call falling in love. Kissing, along with all the other forms of mutual self-stimulation common in courtship, is just nature's way of slipping us the pill.

There was nothing about hypersensory hallucinations. Not that I had expected there would be. Richard, as a serious scientist, would hardly have devoted space to so subjective a phenomenon.

Meanwhile I decided I had better do something about my single status before it interfered with my work any further. The simplest solution, I realized after a few moments' thought, would be to join a dating site. After a brief search on the internet I found one that only took eight minutes to register with. I simply had to complete a short personality profile and upload a photograph, and then I was done. It was actually rather fascinating—I could immediately see how the data from such an enterprise might provide an interesting basis with which to substantiate a number of Richard's more controversial theories. And although it has to be said that none of the women the computer initially offered me as potential dates seemed like people I would want to meet, let alone have a physical relationship with, at least there were plenty of them, and it was only when an internal phone call came through from Professor Noble's secretary that I remembered I was meant to be elsewhere, at a meeting with him and Kes Riley.

5.2

Julian Noble, I should explain, is our Head of Department. Scientists are not much given to jokes, but I sometimes think whoever appointed him must have had a sense of humor, since a less likely leader in an exciting field like experimental neurobiology you could hardly imagine. Nor is he even much of a scientist. Many years ago, as a young man, he made some interesting observations about wing mutations in Malaysian moon moths that garnered him a fellowship and, in a lean year for discoveries, even a prestigious medal or two. Since then he has clung on, limpetlike, to both his tenure and his reputation. As he has never been distracted by the demands of any research worth the name, he has gradually been given more and more of the administrative responsibilities no one else wanted; the Department, and a chair bearing the name of some equally fusty and forgotten forebear that went with it, eventually fell into his lap as well. Retirement, and even greater obscurity, now beckon, but in the meantime he runs the Department as if it were a small British preparatory school and we a group of troublesome schoolboys, instead of the internationally renowned cutting-edge think tank that we actually are.

Kes Riley is no academic. But I sometimes think that Trock's director of marketing is smarter than almost anyone I have ever met—it is simply a different kind of intelligence, a drive to succeed. He is no older than I am, and to be on the board of one of the biggest pharmaceutical companies in the world at his age is just as remarkable as anything I have achieved. There is absolutely no doubt that were it not for him, and the vast research budgets he scatters around the world seemingly at whim, there would be no KXC79 project.

"Steven!" Kes got to his feet and gave me a complicated handshake. We sat down around Julian's ancient desk, and the professor made us instant coffee in mismatched tannin-stained mugs. I saw Kes take a sip and put his to one side.

"Steven!" Kes said again, and I saw that he had the most recent draft of my new results in front of him. "What can I say? I'm speechless." He tapped the pages. "Are we sure? The numbers work? No side effects? No psychotic episodes or feelings of depression? And—most important of all—no acne? The occasional psychosis we can live with, but nobody wants a sex pill that gives you bad skin." He smiled, but his shrewd eyes remained fixed on mine.

"No acne," I said firmly. "Absolutely none. As for other side effects—well, we'll have to wait for the data from a proper clinical trial, of course, but I'm reasonably confident. Twenty-seven sexually dysfunctional women have taken part in the study; twenty-seven women are now sexually functional again."

Nodding, he picked up the paper and began to leaf through it. I saw that the margins were covered with his annotations. "Remarkably thorough," he said at last. "Steven, I salute you. You've done a brilliant job. As ever."

"Of course, it's only preliminary," I said modestly. "There are months—possibly years—more work to be done yet."

Kes slapped the paper back down on the table. He seemed expectant: excited, even.

Julian Noble sighed.

"Tell him," Kes said impatiently. "Or shall I?"

Julian waved his hand and gazed out of the window. Kes leaned forward. "Steven, it's good news. We're giving the Department Preferred Partner status on the FSD project."

"Really?" I said eagerly. "But what about Tokyo? The Higachi program?"

"You hadn't heard?" His face clouded. "As you know, Professor Higachi's treatment is—was—derived from the testes of the sperm whale. Supplies have been difficult to come by—it was always a worry for us. Anyway, it seems last week the professor was on board a Japanese research vessel when they finally caught one. In his excitement, and his efforts to direct the whalers where to cut, he leaned too far over the rail. He was crushed against the ship's side by the death throes. He's alive, just, but it seems unlikely his project will survive."

"I see. Poor Higachi. As you know, I disagreed with his approach, but there was no doubting his commitment."

"Yes. But still, science marches on." Kes picked up my paper again. "Can you have this ready to deliver at the conference?"

I stared at him. I did not have to ask which conference he was referring to. In less than a month's time Trock was sponsoring a major symposium in London. All the big players in FSD would be flying in to take part.

"I'm talking about a keynote address," he added. "Quite apart from anything else, it'll help bury the Higachi fiasco." He slapped my paper with the back of his free hand. "And 'Oxford University' still looks good on a press release, at least to the general public. Why not? It will look as if we planned the whole thing—stage-managed it to launch Desiree to the world."

I was so astounded that, of the many responses I could have given to this proposal, I selected completely the wrong one.

"'Desiree'?"

"Well, we can hardly go on calling it KXC79 now. I've had my team brainstorming some ideas. Desiree's the current favorite."

"But it sounds—"

"It's a name, Steven," he said impatiently. "*This* is what matters." He pointed at my paper. "Well? Can you be ready? I need hardly tell you what an honor it is."

He did not. To give such a paper, to such an audience—and in such circumstances too: the launch of my discovery, to my peers, with the support of my backers plain for all to see! I have read many accounts of the first readings of famous papers, from what would become *On the Origin of Species* to the Watson and Crick paper on DNA.[1] For a moment I dared to think that the first reading of the KXC79 study might rank alongside them.

---

[1] J. D. Watson and F.H.C. Crick, "A Structure for Deoxyribose Nucleic Acid," *Nature* 171 (1953): 737–738. "It has not escaped our notice that the specific pairing we have postulated suggests a possible copying mechanism for the genetic material," Watson and Crick wrote. When they walked into the Eagle pub at lunchtime, they were less circumspect. "We've just found the secret of life," they announced. But it is the former statement, surely—in all its elegant understatement—which deserves its place in the annals of science.

Then I came to my senses.

"I'm afraid it's out of the question," I said. "I'm sorry, Kes. It's much too soon."

Julian Noble sighed. Kes Riley frowned—but it was Julian he turned on, not me. "Now, wait a minute, Julian. If *Steven Fisher* is telling me there's a good reason why this paper, which is apparently so watertight and which only needs a few little spelling corrections—and, if I may so, Steve, a few more color illustrations and rather fewer equations and footnotes and so on—if *he* says there's a reason why it can't be ready in time, then I personally think we ought to hear him out. Because although it may sound colossally dumb to let such an opportunity go by, and although it may well have knock-on effects in terms of your department's Preferred Partner status—we might even have to devolve the funding into next year's fiscal—those sorts of issues are secondary to the science, right? Whatever happens, we at Trock always want to do good science. And if this opportunity has to be let go, and the whole project sinks into obscurity, and some other approach gets into trials first—well, that's just too bad. The important thing is that we never, ever make our scientist partners do anything they aren't completely comfortable with. At Trock, scientific integrity is always our number one, two, and three priority."

Then he turned and looked expectantly at me.

I said hesitantly, "It's just that I'd want to double-check—"

"According to *this*"—he held up my paper—"you've already triple-checked."

"Quadruple-check, then."

"Steven," he said impatiently, "it's very simple. Are you a hundred percent confident in this paper or are you not?"

"Oh, yes. The paper is fine."

"Well, then." His eyes narrowed. "Unless there's something you haven't told me? Something that's been niggling you—some result

that didn't look so good, so you quite reasonably decided to omit
it . . . ?"

I shook my head. "Nothing like that."

And then I remembered Miss G.

5.3

The paper which I had sent in draft form to Kes—"KXC79 and Female Sexual Dysfunction: More Encouraging Results"—had been
written before Miss G. walked into my lab. There was not a word
or a figure in that paper which was not true. But, equally, there was
a particular tone of voice which spoke, to those able to decipher
such things, even more eloquently than the data. It was a kind of
scientists' code: despite all the *possibly's* and the *might's* and the
should-be-investigated-further's, my tone was one of quiet, under-
stated triumph. And why would it not be? I had developed a treatment for a distressing disorder which afflicted, according to some
reports, up to 56 percent of all women.[2] I had tested it, refined and
reformulated it, then trialed it on twenty-seven volunteers—and in
every single case it had worked. My success rate was 100 percent.

But then a twenty-eighth woman with FSD had walked into the
lab, and it had not worked on her. Indeed, it appeared to have sent
her to sleep.

I stared at the table, wondering if I should say something.

Kes Riley and Julian Noble were negotiating budgets. I was
barely listening—it was all just figures. So far as I could tell, Trock
was offering to pay 150 percent of the costs of the project, as well

---

[2] I am of course aware that, to a statistician, this means FSD is not a "disorder" at all,
since by definition a disorder must affect less than half the population. I do not propose
to get into that debate now, as it seems to me to be principally a matter of semantics.

as the salaries of all persons involved, along with various bonuses and royalties. I continued to agonize.

The fact of the matter was, twenty-seven women is not actually a very big sample, and in the early days of the study we experienced some fairly disparate results. To begin with, our subjects experienced at the crucial moment instead of an orgasm an overwhelming desire to sneeze. It was massively encouraging—it proved that KXC55, as it was then, was doing *something*—but our efforts to replace the sneeze with a more appropriate reaction were initially unsuccessful. We were very pleased when two participants, instead of sneezing, suffered from violent nosebleeds—again, it proved we were able to eliminate the sneezing—but the rate at which we were now losing our volunteers was, as you can imagine, quite rapid, and it was some time before an opportunity to test a new formulation presented itself. Then came the phase when our subjects started blushing furiously. After that we had a difficulty with hiccups, and although on several occasions they were also accompanied by orgasms, the EMG data showed that the hiccups had been, if anything, more eventful. We managed to cure *that* problem, but the unexpected side effect was that our subjects experienced extreme arousal every time they got an attack of the hiccups. And so on.[3]

It was one balmy Oxford evening the previous summer, whilst strolling on the water meadows, that I hit on a radical way of reformulating the treatment: KXC79, in other words. So far, as I have said, the results from that had been nothing short of spectacular. But twenty-seven good results, statistically speaking, means almost

---

[3] At least we never had the problem recounted by Y. C. Chuang et al. in "Tooth-Brushing Epilepsy with Ictal Orgasms," *Seizure* 13, no. 3 (2004): 179–182. "We report a 41-year-old woman with complex reflex epilepsy in which seizures were induced exclusively by the act of tooth brushing. All the attacks occurred with a specific sensation of sexual arousal and orgasm-like euphoria that were followed by a period of impairment of consciousness."

nothing, particularly if accompanied by another result that you can't explain.

Reluctantly I said, "Actually, there is one thing I should mention."

5.4

"The issue," Kes said, "is not the bloody paper."

It was twenty minutes later, and we were still going round in circles.

"We are all agreed we should exclude this woman from the paper, yes?" he demanded, looking from one to the other of us. "For all we know, she simply stayed up too late partying and doing Class A drugs. In fact, it would probably be more irresponsible to *include* the dopey cow than it would be to exclude her."

I frowned, and he held up a finger. "That's the public line, any-way. But—privately—neither can we afford to ignore her. Are there side effects we hadn't anticipated? Interactions with other medica-tions? Steven, I know you're confident you've got the depression angle covered, and I'm very reassured that you say this girl's got good skin, but this is completely new territory for Trock—there could be angles to this stuff that we haven't even thought of. It'll all come out in the clinical trials, sure, but the bottom line is, I don't want to go to clinicals and spend a shedload of cash just to end up with egg on our face. Or acne, for that matter." He shuddered. "So we proceed, but with caution. We continue to prepare this paper for launch at SexDys, just as if nothing had happened. But we also prepare a plan B—another paper, something noncommittal."

"And what, pray, decides whether you go with paper A or paper B?" Julian Noble inquired.

"Isn't it obvious?" Kes said. "If by the time of the conference this girl's problem is sorted, then so is ours. Equally, if we know what the issue is and it's something we can deal with, fine. We can quietly omit it from the paper and no one will be any the wiser. But if in three weeks' time we're still in the dark, we'll have to present paper B. And in the meantime we'll keep talking up the Higachi method in our PR, just in case."

There was a long silence. There seemed to me to be a flaw in this plan somewhere, but my head was spinning and I could not for the life of me think what it was.

"Steven, is there anything you need to get this sorted in time?" Kes demanded. "More funds, more equipment, more people? Whatever it is, just let me know."

I shook my head. "My team know what they're doing."

"Good. Well, I've gotta go," he said, looking at his watch. "But I'll leave it with you, yes? We have a plan?"

Julian nodded. Kes zipped his papers into a small black case. "One other thing," he said, his hand on the door. "Now this project is live, our competitors will be getting curious. Make sure those pills are kept securely locked up. Understood?"

With a wave he was gone.

5.5

There was another long silence. Julian Noble was staring out of the rather grimy window at the small square of grey Oxford sky it revealed.

"Perhaps we shouldn't do it," I said.

Julian snorted faintly.

"I mean, I'm still not a hundred percent convinced this plan is good science," I added.

He sighed. Reaching into the top pocket of his tweed jacket, he
brought out a small tin of mints. He popped one in his mouth and
replaced the tin, without offering it to me.

"I'll phone him back," I said. "Tell him KXC79 needs more
time."

Julian swiveled his gaze at me. His eyes were rheumy and liquid,
as brown and threadbare as his jacket. "You will do no such thing,
you fucking little fool."

"I'm sorry?" I said, taken aback.

"For twenty years," he said, "I have managed, by hook and
by crook, to prevent the university from closing this department
down. I did this, not in the hope that any useful research would
ever get done here, but because it was the only department I was
likely to get. When I arrived, it was the Department of Applied Zo-
ology. Now it is the Department of Molecular Biology. I did that—I
changed the name. And do you know why?"

I shook my head.

"I did it in the hope that, one day, some idiot sponsor would
come along, be impressed by the humiliatingly trendy moniker,
and throw some money at me. It didn't work, of course—not at
first. I had to watch charlatans—media scientists like your friend
Collins—getting the attention and the budgets. I even took on his
cast-offs." He pointed a long finger, so bony and emaciated it re-
sembled the end of a malacca walking stick, at my chest. "It wasn't
until after I'd agreed to give you house room that I discovered what
you were really up to—that my department was effectively now a
knocking shop."

I opened my mouth to protest, but he ignored me. "They laugh
at me, you know. The other heads. I'd give up going to High Table
completely, if I could afford to. "Afternoon, Julian. Anything to
report from the love lab?" "Any news from your nymphos?" And
now—finally!—all the years of biting my tongue have paid off. It

couldn't have come at a better time, as it happens. Lowther on the first floor has just produced some very promising work on the varying lengths of earthworms. No funding, of course: the commercial world isn't interested in earthworms. But that doesn't matter now, does it? Your nymphos are going to pay for his *Lumbrici*. Not to mention my retirement home in the Pyrenees. So let me tell you this, young man: When you sit there and squeak that you aren't sure whether your sordid little project is good science—frankly, I couldn't give a monkey's."

"Ah," I said.

He nodded, and popped another mint in his mouth. There seemed to be no more to say.

"I want those pills locked in my safe," he said as I got to my feet. "Every last one of them. If those are Trock's conditions for getting Precious Partner status, or whatever they call it, then we follow them to the letter. Do I make myself understood?"

5.6

I did not give him the satisfaction of seeing how angry he had made me. I went back to the lab. There I mixed up a hundred grams of chalk powder with 20 cc of water and put the mixture into the pill press, along with a little food dye.

One of the ways we double-check our findings is to alternate the real treatment—KXC79—with a placebo, a dummy pill made of nothing but chalk. I therefore had all the ingredients for making dummy pills on hand. In fact, the only difference between the dummies and the real thing was a few drops of concentrated KXC79.

Leaving the real pills locked in my own cupboard, I took the dummies upstairs and placed them on Julian Noble's desk.

That afternoon I gathered my team together.

"I have good news," I said. "Kes Riley of Trock has informed me that, thanks to the work you have all done on KXC79, we are now gaining Preferred Partner status."

There was a smattering of applause.

"Which means, amongst other things"—I paused—"that I will be making the keynote presentation at SexDys, to which you will of course all now be invited."

This time there was a moment's stunned silence before they applauded wildly. I called over the noise, "I need hardly tell you how much still has to be done in the next three weeks. But on top of everything else, we have a small anomaly with one of our research subjects to clear up." I explained briefly about Miss G. "The upshot is that we're going to have to go back over every single test session and look for indications of drowsiness," I concluded. "Heart rate, blood pressure, but especially Startle—check them all. And we need to retest every result we aren't a hundred percent confident about."

"Even the Ukrainians?" Rhona asked.

"Especially the Ukranians," I said firmly. Looking around the room, I could see they all understood how much I was asking of them.

As they dispersed, talking excitedly amongst themselves, Susan came over.

"Steve?"

"What is it, Susan?"

"These new tests. Will they involve Lucy?"

"You know perfectly well that's out of the question."

"But Lucy's available. And she's more than willing," she argued. "Tracking down the other test subjects could take forever."

"Susan, how many times do I have to tell you? That's exactly the kind of slipshod thinking that could cause problems when our results are scrutinized. There can be no cutting of corners."

"Very well," she said calmly. "In that case, can I take it she'll be leaving us soon?"

I hesitated. "It's not quite as straightforward as that."

"Steve, last week she threw a radio at one of the cleaners. The poor woman was frightened out of her wits."

"I heard about that incident. Lucy had simply run out of batteries. She needs company, that's all."

"And who's going to give it to her?" she demanded. "We're all busy, and we'll be even busier now. Steve, isn't it time we sorted this out? You say we mustn't cut corners, but in that case, what's she doing here?"

I sighed. "I understand what you're saying. Look, I'll go and have a word with her. Maybe I can do something."

Susan nodded, although I could tell she was unconvinced. I took a deep breath and headed for the staircase.

6.2

I followed the stairs down to the basement. As I pushed open the heavy rubber-insulated door I heard the sound of people arguing. There was a shout, gunfire, then dramatic music. I looked at my watch. *Emmerdale*. Lucy never missed an episode.

Down there, amongst all the outmoded scientific junk that had somehow never been thrown away—the jars of Victorian fetuses preserved in formaldehyde, the boards of pinned butterflies, the moth-eaten stuffed civet cats and the rusting Tesla coils—down there, the smell of perishing rubber and evaporating formaldehyde was overlaid by another smell: the faint but pungent scent of urine on straw. At the back of the room was a line of built-in cages, their rusting bars running all the way from ceiling to floor. Most were empty now, their concrete floors swept bare, only a few stains and discolored patches remaining as evidence of a scientific past that was either glorious or shaming, depending on your point of view.

When Lucy saw me she bared her teeth and made a rude gesture.

"I know, I know," I said. "Far too long. But something came up."

For a moment she sulked. Then, springing to the bars, she rattled them forcefully and signed "tree."

"I'm sorry," I said reluctantly. "I don't have time to take you out today."

She chattered angrily and gestured at the door.

"Sometime soon, I promise."

She turned her back on me, even more sulkily. I had been expecting that, and in any case it was no more than I deserved. I checked her food and water and made sure she had some toys to keep her amused. But in my heart I knew that it was all completely inadequate. The simple truth was that Susan had been right. Lucy should not have been there.

Bonobos, for any of you who are not familiar with these remarkable primates, are an offshoot of the chimpanzee family—*Pan paniscus*, to be precise. In the wild, they survive only in one small area of the African Congo, in an area devastated by civil war, poaching, illegal logging, and climate change. It seems almost certain that at some point in this century we will drive them into extinction. The loss of any species is a catastrophe, but in the case of the bonobo it would be a kind of genocide.

What makes bonobos so special is that their society is organized almost entirely along sexual lines. Unusually amongst primates, they have sex for pleasure as well as for procreation. But it goes much further than that: they trade sexual favors amongst themselves in a kind of barter economy, and use sexual prowess as a way of establishing pecking orders. Their simian flexibility helps, of course, but an exuberant willingness on the part of every bonobo to throw itself without hesitation into the nearest gang bang counts for even more.

When I first met Lucy she was living in the basement with nine other bonobos, doing what bonobos do best—eating, sleeping, and having energetic sex of every hue and description. For two years I studied them, writing up my observations in a succession of papers that, amongst other things, helped to establish my own reputation.[1] In particular I studied Lucy—the name I gave to the matriarch of one particular social group. Then the ban on laboratory experiments with apes was introduced.

Whatever you think of this ban—and it is still a subject of controversy amongst scientists—its motives were undoubtedly benign. And yet its effects were terrible. Almost overnight, in Oxford alone, hundreds of animals—those too old to be returned to the wild—were put down. Amongst those scheduled for termination were the bonobos—all of them. Imagine it: a species that was almost extinct, whose natural environment was inaccessible because of war, whose numbers were in free fall . . . and we were going to kill them.

---

[1] S. J. Fisher, "Singultus and the Orgasm of the Female Bonobo: A Possible Mechanism for Future Investigation," winner of the Peter Beaconsfield Prize for the most outstanding postgraduate thesis; and "Neural Pathways of the Female Bonobo," which won the Johann Kurtis Most Promising Young Scientist award; etc.

By then Lucy had become a favorite of mine. She was easily the most intelligent primate I had ever met, able to communicate in simple sign language and completely housebroken. I asked the authorities if I could keep her. They said no: regulations were regulations. So, the night before the bonobos were due to be put down, I smuggled Lucy out of the colony and hid her.

My life has been spent in the service of the scientific method. Logic and reason are my watchwords. But what I did that night was scarcely rational. To this day, I do not even know if it was the right thing to do. I was taking a highly social animal, an animal for whom sexual interaction with her peers was the greatest happiness she knew, and condemning her to a life of solitary, sexless misery. Perhaps if Lucy herself had been able to say what she wanted, she might have told me to leave her with the others.

All I knew is that I could not abandon her to die. For once in my life I did not stop to think. I acted on instinct, and I have half-regretted it ever since. One day, I knew, I was going to have to deal with the consequences of my actions. But for now, Lucy would have to wait, while I addressed myself to the more pressing problem of Miss G.

I do not mind admitting that I spent the days leading up to Miss G.'s next visit in a somewhat apprehensive state. I had made what preparations I could—in addition to the new equipment, the testing room now contained two scented candles and a stack of crisp new paperbacks, and I had added the entire repertoire of Jean Michel Jarre to our music library—but the truth was that there was little I could do other than run the tests again and hope that this time the outcome would be different. If it was, I would be able to dismiss Miss G. from both the study and my thoughts, writing off the previous results as an unexplained but allowable glitch. The launch could go ahead, and triumph and acclaim would once more be mine.

I wondered if Miss G. might mention our chance meeting to Susan, and it was this, as well as my own nerves, which prompted me to keep one ear on their conversation via the intercom as I prepared the tests.

"So, Annie. Anything to report?" I heard Susan's voice ask. "Any erotic feelings, fantasies . . . ?"

"Um," Miss G. said hesitantly.

"Go on," my colleague demanded.

"Well, yesterday I did have a sort of daydream about— But it's embarrassing."

I heard Susan laugh. "I'm a professional sexologist, Annie. I can assure you there's nothing you can tell me that I won't have heard many, many times before."

"Well, all right, then. It was about snails."

"Snails?" Susan said. "I must admit, that is a bit . . . So what happened in this fantasy of yours?"

"I'd been reading about these snails, you see," Miss G.'s voice said. "Giant African snails. Which are huge—almost as big as guinea pigs. And I was just drifting off when I began imagining about six of them, slithering all over me." (See figure 11.)

"And this was . . . *erotic*?"

"Just for a second. Then I felt really stupid."

"Nothing's stupid in fantasy, Annie," Susan said sternly. "You have to go with the flow. Even if it's snails. Anything else?"

"Not really. There was someone I— But no, that definitely doesn't count."

"Okay." I heard the sound of Susan snapping shut her clip file. "Annie, last time you got a little too relaxed, so today we're going to sit you on this piece of apparatus here." I heard a thump as she patted the Sybian.

Miss G. sounded doubtful. "Do I have to? It looks a bit brutal."

"It's certainly a powerful machine. But that may be just what we need, wouldn't you say? Now, let's see if Dr. Fisher has managed to find his little pink pills." I turned the microphone down. By the time Susan entered the control room I was busy measuring the correct dosage of KXC79 into a plastic cup, and trying to remember where I had come across a reference to African snails before.

7.2

Soon the various devices were primed and ready, and my colleague had joined me in the control room. While we waited for the treatment to do its work I put on *Oxygene Parts 1–7*. Miss G., meanwhile, leafed through *Dirty Laundry* (Birch, P., 2002) briefly before putting it to one side with a sigh.

"Dr. Fisher?"

I leaned forward to the mike. "Yes?"

"Sorry I didn't bring your book back. I haven't quite finished it."

Susan's head swiveled to look at me. But I had no intention of explaining which book Miss G. was referring to. "Are you enjoying it?"

"Very much. Though some of the science is a bit beyond me."

"If there's anything you'd like me to explain . . ."

"Well, I wish I could get my head round the difference between a hormone and a pheromone."

"That's an easy one," I said. "In fact, I'm teaching this to the second-year undergraduates this very term. A hormone is a chemical messenger within the body; a pheromone is a chemical transmitted by an animal, usually as an odor, which has a specific effect, such as sexual excitement, on another animal. The way that pheromones work between organisms is *analogous* to the way hormones send chemical signals around the body, but otherwise quite different."

I suddenly remembered where I had seen a reference to giant African snails. Professor Collins used them as an illustration of this very point.

"As it happens," I said, "there's a very simple example of pheromones at work in the case of the giant African snail, *Achatina immaculata*, where the slime one snail leaves behind contains a substance that inhibits sexual activity in other snails."

"Well, if she wasn't anerotic before . . . ," Susan muttered.

Miss G.'s voice interrupted.

Figure 11: *Achatina immaculata.*

"Okay, except by that definition I can't see there's any difference between a hormone and a neurotransmitter."

"Exactly!" I said. Miss G. had put her finger on one of the most important points in neurobiology. It is an insight second-year undergraduates often fail to grasp—and she had understood it almost intuitively. "We call them pheromones when they travel from one organism to another, hormones when they're released into the bloodstream, and neurotransmitters when they're released from a cell. But essentially they're all the same process."

"I thought so," Miss G. said excitedly. "I thought, Those snails are like great big black cells—"

"Firing their slime at the next cell along," I agreed.

Miss G. sighed—and it seemed to me, listening, that it was a sigh of wonder. "It must be great to be a scientist," she said, a little wistfully. "You know all this incredible *stuff*."

"Now I need you both to shut up," Susan said firmly. "Annie, try to concentrate on sexy thoughts, if you can." She twisted a knob on the control panel in front of her.

7.3

We waited, studying the machines. I was still hopeful that the previous session was going to turn out to be a statistical blip, but with so much riding on the results it was hard not to be a little anxious. I was particularly interested in the output from the GSA, which was giving me a level of detail I had never had access to before. I pushed a button and brought up Miss G.'s face through the heat-sensitive camera. Her lips were almost white; the lobes of her ears were a dark purple; and her exposed, thrown-back throat was a shifting vermillion (figure 12).

I cross-checked with the graphical information from the GSA.

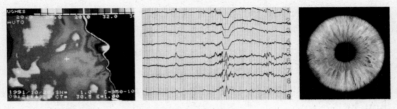

Figure 12: Real-time comparison of data streams.

This is excellent, I was thinking. Real-time comparison of data streams.

Suddenly there was a little tremor in the readout, like the first tiny shivers of an earthquake. I switched back to the thermograph. Before my eyes, orange shaded through to yellow as warmth spread up Miss G.'s throat.

I went to Startle. Miss G.'s eye was blank and unfocused. But the GSA readout was flickering insistently, a scribble of tiny but persistent zigzags that, as I watched, grew in intensity.

"Go on," I whispered under my breath. "Go on. . . ."

Like a kite taking off in the wind, the line shot up . . . peaked . . . dipped . . . peaked again, but higher this time, . . . hesitated briefly . . . then finally soared into a series of dizzying, undulating peaks and troughs that lasted fully thirty seconds, almost touching the roof of the graph, before drifting back towards the baseline in a long, lazy decline. In all this time Miss G. made hardly a sound, but what I was seeing left no room for doubt. KCX79 had done it. Miss G. was anorgasmic no longer.

I let out a long, relieved exhalation, and a knot of tension in my shoulders, previously unnoticed, eased perceptibly. The paper . . . the conference . . . triumph and acclaim . . . Everything was back on track.

Susan's voice cut across my thoughts. "Annie? Are you getting anything from this?"

I stared at her. Hadn't she noticed what had just happened? It appeared that, intent as she was on her own equipment, she hadn't seen the evidence I was seeing. I opened my mouth to say something, but Miss G.'s voice forestalled me.

"I—uh—no, not much," she said, rather breathlessly, I thought.

"Oh." Susan flicked a switch, and the hum of the machines died. "In that case—"

I leant towards the mike. "Annie?"

"Yes?"

"Did you feel *nothing at all* just now?"

"Well, it was perfectly pleasant, but— No, nothing special."

I didn't answer. I knew for a fact that Miss G. had just experienced an orgasm (figure 13). How could she not be aware of it? It just didn't make any sense.

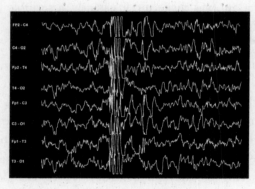

Figure 13: It doesn't look like "not much" to me!

. . . The big embarrassment is that when I go back to the lab for my next appointment I only have to hear Steven Fisher explaining the difference between a peptide and a pheromone and I just seem to *melt*. And when they rig me up to their machines—well, let's just say something happens that hasn't happened for a very long time.

My God, that KXC79 must be powerful stuff.

I think Susan may suspect something. I threw her off the scent with some random stuff I made up about snails. But I ask you—snails? Where the hell did that come from?

UrlGirl67 ☺
"When the only tool you have is a hammer,
you tend to treat every problem as if it's a nail."

That night in bed I read some more of the book Steven lent me, with Simon tossing and turning beside me—well, more turning than tossing, actually, which might be the problem. I'm seriously thinking of giving him a blow job just so he'll go to sleep and I can get on with *Enzymes and Influences*. This stuff is dense—you need to concentrate on every line, or you miss some vital piece of information and whole chapters become incomprehensible.

Eventually Simon says, "What on earth are you reading?"

"It's a science book."

"Science!" From the way he says it you'd have thought I was reading Jilly Cooper. He grabs it from me and flicks through the pages with a supercilious sneer on his face. "Well, well," he says, handing it back. "I always thought you were a bit of a geek."

And I know he's just being catty because he's pissed off about the whole no-sex thing, but for some reason this remark makes me so cross that I mentally withdraw the offer of a blow job, even though it means I lie there pretending to turn the pages but actually unable to concentrate at all.

Am I a geek?

Well, it's true I like making lists. Such as:

Five Signs You're a Geek

5. Think Leela is cooler than Lieutenant Uhura
4. Know who Leela and Lieutenant Uhura are
3. Know my computer's IP address
2. Know the IP address of everyone else in the department and can solve most network problems quicker than the system administrator—admittedly not difficult because Bruce, the sys admin, is Really Not That Bright
1. Make lists the correct way, i.e., in descending order

Five Signs You Can't Be a Geek

5. Have first-class degree in English literature
4. Am a girl
3. No spots
2. No dandruff
1. No B.O. (God, I hope)

Oh, on the minus side I should probably mention that I'm the secretary of the College's S & S Society. But being into S & S doesn't make me a geek. It just happens to be something that a lot of geeks are into. Coincidence.

Hmm. Is it possible, as Dr. Minstock would say, that I'm blocking something here?

UrlGirl67 ☺

"When the only tool you have is a hammer,
you tend to treat every problem as if it's a nail."

It is my habit, when confronted by a particularly difficult problem, to mull it over during my weekly attendance at the University's Campanology Society—that is, while bell ringing. Whether it is the noise (a sound so massive it seems to reverberate through your very bones), the feel of the woolen sally as it slips through your hands, the venerable smell of cassocks and candle wax, the way all eight of us stand in a solemn circle, our only communication nods and smiles as the Tower Captain ritually bellows the changes—"Eight to two: four to one"—or the simple mathematical elegance of the ringing patterns themselves as my tenor bell moves up and down the peals, I don't know, but for whatever reason I find bell ringing an activity especially conducive to thought. I have unraveled some of the most complex difficulties of sexual function whilst ringing a Clifford's Pleasure, Plain Bob Minor, or Cambridge Surprise, and on the rare occasions when the Society is able to pull a complete peal of five thousand and forty changes I almost always gain some new insight or understanding of my work.

That night, at our midweek practice, I once again found my thoughts returning to Miss G. Clearly, resolving the mystery of her anomalous results was now both crucial and pressing. Yet the mystery seemed only to be deepening. I could conceive of no biochemical reason why Miss G. should suffer from drowsiness, on the one hand, or be unaware of having an orgasm, on the other. I could not even be certain whether they were two separate problems, or if there was a link—some connection between them I was currently unable to discern.

It was exactly the sort of problem which, in my postgraduate days, I would have taken to Richard Collins. He has a remarkable ability to cut through the complexities of a situation. I can still hear the advice he gave me when one of my bonobos started to behave strangely. "Every problem of science," he pointed out, "is ultimately a problem of logic. And every problem of logic is ultimately a problem of biology. The world is physics, Steven, but brains are biochemistry."

It was just that sort of inspirational steer I needed now. I had already tried e-mailing him, but there had been no reply. So I did what I sometimes do in these situations: I tried to imagine what he would suggest if he were with me.

And I seemed to hear his voice, quite clearly, saying, "Don't guess: investigate. Stick to the science, Steven. First establish the facts, and only then develop your hypothesis."

As ever, he was quite right. I decided I should not jump to any conclusions until I had double-checked my findings.

9.2

On the following Tuesday Miss G. returned to the lab for her third session. Unfortunately on this occasion there was a delay in the proceedings caused by a computer incompatibility between the Medoc and Susan's laptop. What the incompatibility was did not become clear for some time, owing to the fact that Susan's response to any software problem is to press all the keys at random, causing her machine to lock up completely. Miss G. was already wired up to the measuring devices, so the delay was ill-timed to say the least, but after rerouting the biothesiometer to my laptop and—Miss G.'s suggestion, this—running a workaround by porting Susan's laptop to my slave drive, we were able to proceed.

Susan was by this time rather flustered, and she muttered to me that we should probably abandon the session altogether. But Miss G. said she was happy to continue, so we did.

At four minutes twenty, a series of thirty-eight internal muscular contractions at 0.8-second intervals commenced. This was accompanied by an increase in skin galvanicity of ± 6.5 µV and a rise in temperature of 0.8°. During this time Miss G. did not make any sound, although admittedly if she had done so it might have been drowned out by the music she had chosen (*The Well-Tempered Synthesizer*, Wendy Carlos).

At five minutes ten, the contractions subsided.

At seven minutes thirty Miss G. said through the intercom, "You know, we could also have tried checking for an IRQ conflict on the LAN ports."

At nine minutes eighteen, a series of twenty-four internal contractions at 0.8-second intervals commenced. This was accompanied by a similar increase in galvanicity and temperature.

It seemed to me that Miss G. twice moaned involuntarily, but on both occasions she quickly turned it into a cough.

At nine minutes forty the contractions subsided.

At twelve minutes exactly, Dr. Minstock asked Miss G. over the intercom, "Annie, is this doing anything for you?"

On receiving a negative response, she terminated the test session at twelve minutes twenty seconds.

What on earth was going on?

Another session. Similar result. TWICE. That's never happened in my life.

Okay, so here's the thing: I really, really do not want Dr. Fisher to know what is happening to me at the lab.

First, because it's only a teeny-weeny stupid physical attraction for someone who—let's face it—I barely know from Adam.

Second, because he is very clever and may work out what effect he has on me. In which case I think I will die of embarrassment.

Third, because he already thinks I'm some lightweight fluffy arts slut who is completely at the mercy of her out-of-control hormones.

Fourth, because—oh, admit it—I don't want to give him the satisfaction of thinking he's right. Yet again. (I can almost see the look of supercilious satisfaction on his face as he ticks me off his to-do list.)

Fifth, because once I tell him that his treatment has worked and I'm cured, that'll be it—there won't be any reason for me to go to the lab after that. And, well, I quite enjoy it. Not just in the obvious way (though that has been a revelation—just as Dr. F. described at the beginning) but also because I actually quite like talking to him, despite the supercilious sneers. In fact, the thought of never seeing him again is really quite unnerving.

And sixth, because—oh, God—what if my reaction wasn't only down to the KXC79? What if I never really was anorgasmic, or whatever they call it, after all?

What if I'm just with the Wrong Man?

Gulp. Don't go there.

UrlGirl67
"When the only tool you have is a hammer,
you tend to treat every problem as if it's a nail."

___

And then I'm reading *Enzymes and Influences* and I suddenly have this complete and utter moment of epiphany.

It's not that I'm with the Wrong Man. I'm just doing the Wrong Subject.

UrlGirl67 ☺
"When the only tool you have is a hammer,
you tend to treat every problem as if it's a nail."

___

"Ah, Wulf," I said, catching up with Dr. Sederholm on the stairs of the Department building next day. "I'm glad I've run into you. I need to pick your brains about this girl on the study. I think she's having orgasms but she's saying she isn't and I don't know why."

My colleague considered this for a while. "The first time Rhona and I slept together," he said thoughtfully, "she was not having orgasms either. But she did not want to seem rude. So she pretended that she did have them. Now there is no problem, and she doesn't need to pretend anymore."

"How do you know?"

"Know what?"

"That she isn't pretending anymore."

"Oh." His brow, which had furrowed momentarily, cleared again. "She told me."

"Unless she's just saying that because she thinks you might be asking yourself if she's still pretending, and saying that she was pretending before makes her pretending now more believable," I pointed out. Something else occurred to me. "The *a priori* of this, I cannot help but observe, is that you have slept with Rhona, and on more than one occasion."

"Oh. Yes. It's been almost two months now. Didn't you know?"

Now that I thought about it, I had seen the two of them together, holding hands, on several occasions, although I had not drawn any specific conclusions from this. I shook my head.

"Anyway," he continued, "what I am suggesting is that it doesn't really matter if someone is faking or not. Not in the long run."

"Although it does make our results rather problematic," I said. "The whole point of our research being to establish whether or not KXC79 actually *works*."

"Hmm." He pondered for a moment. "Perhaps you need to think of your experiments as being like Schrödinger's cat," he suggested. "You know, the hypothetical cat shut in a box which would somehow either be killed or not, depending on the state of a single subatomic particle. Schrödinger's point was that at any one moment the cat would be either alive, or dead, but on average it would be half dead and half alive all the time. This is the whole basis of my own work, actually, and of submolecular chaos theory generally."[1]

"Wulf," I said, "I am familiar with the conundrum of Schrödinger's cat. I'm just struggling to see how it helps. In this particular instance."

He held up a finger. "Or there's the 'tomato effect.'"

"What's the tomato effect?"

"When the tomato was first introduced to North America, scientists thought it must be poisonous, owing to its coming from the same family as deadly nightshade. It was only when people started cooking with it that they began to reconsider." He brightened. "Perhaps you even have a Schrödinger's tomato. That would be very interesting, actually. Something very obvious, but also unpredictable."

"Wulf," I said, "I think I see what you're getting at now."

---

[1] Dr. Sederholm has asked me to point out that this is in fact a very approximate summation of his work, in which he is attempting to bring together Schrödinger's cat, Gödel's undecidability theorem, fuzzy logic, quantum incompleteness physics, and Heisenberg's uncertainty principle into a Unified Theory of Bafflement.

"You do?"

"You're telling me I shouldn't jump to any conclusions until I know much more about her."

"Exactly," he said, sounding a little relieved. "On a submolecular level, that's almost certainly what I'm saying."

11.2

I got out Miss G.'s file, hoping some simple explanation would leap out at me.

She was, as I had surmised, extremely well educated. At school she had acquired a large number of A-levels in the arts subjects, subsequently taking up a place at Bristol University. Graduating with a first in English literature, she had moved to Oxford to do her doctorate, where she was supervised by a Professor Frampton.

After this brief CV came the standard questionnaires—standard for our line of research, that is. Miss G. had had her first sexual experience at the age of seventeen, an event she described as "satisfactory." (We were into a multiple-choice format by now, so perhaps she simply meant more "satisfactory" than "excellent" or "unpleasant," those being the other two choices.) In all, she'd had six sexual relationships. One of these she rated as "excellent," though under "Duration" she'd selected "one night." One she rated "unpleasant"—that, oddly, had lasted a year. The others were rated mostly "satisfactory," although in one case I noticed she'd ticked both "excellent" *and* "unpleasant."

Then came a section relating to current relationship. From the choices "Are you (a) single, (b) dating, (c) in a relationship, (d) co-habiting, (e) married, or (f) promiscuous," Miss G. had ticked (c), although, mysteriously, she had left the box relating to quality for that relationship blank. I felt a brief stab of curiosity about what sort of man had managed to gain Miss G.'s affection. Doubtless someone just like her: some floppy-haired, poetry-spouting fop.[2]

From the data on "sexual confidence" I learned that a man's eyes were more attractive to her than his buttocks; that she had been unfaithful once (Was that, I couldn't help but wonder, the episode that had been both "excellent" and "unpleasant"?); that she thought her thighs unattractive (from my recollection of her, not actually the case); that she "slightly agreed" that "the best part of sex is the cuddling afterwards"; that she preferred coition to be relaxed, playful, romantic, with the lights on, clean, regular, and conversational (as opposed to energetic, serious, in the dark, messy, spontaneous, and noisy); that she usually slept in a T-shirt; and that she preferred mornings.

According to her Myers-Briggs, she was an INFJ, or Idealistic Introvert, who preferred Thinking to Feelings, Judgments to Perceptions, and Intuition to Sensation. According to her Derogatis, her ideal frequency of intercourse would be once every three months. She agreed with the statement that "human genitals are not generally attractive," and disagreed with "sex rarely goes on long enough," thus placing herself towards the conservative end of the sexual spectrum. According to her Minnesota Multiphasic Personality Inventory, she was not sociopathic, psychopathic, dissociative, bipolar, depressive, anxious, or obsessive. Her Female Sexual Function Index never really got off the ground after a poor start with question one ("Over the last four weeks, how often did you feel sexual

---

[2] The subject of what women look for in a partner is ripe for further research. For example, in surveys 72 percent of women claim that "a good sense of humor" is the most important factor. Yet one High Street chain of sex shops now reports sales of over two million vibrators a year (Ann Summers Press & Marketing Pack, January 19, 2005). Assuming an average product life span of seven years, by 2015 there will be more vibrators in the UK than there are men. Presumably they are not all being bought for their ability to make women laugh.

desire or interest?" Answer: "Never"), thus making follow-ups such as question three ("Over the past four weeks, how would you rate your level of arousal during sexual activity or intercourse?") largely irrelevant, although it certainly made her answer to question sixteen rather intriguing ("Over the past four weeks, how satisfied have you been with your overall sexual life?" Answer: "Fairly satisfied").

I sighed. Interesting as all this was, it was of no help in solving the problem.

I flicked through the transcript of her interviews with Susan. There seemed to be large gaps; presumably Susan had not yet typed up all her notes. Towards the end, a section headed "Fantasy" caught my eye.

Susan: You don't seem terribly interested in some of these questions, Annie.

Miss G.: Don't I? Sorry. I just don't find sex very interesting, I suppose. But I know that's the whole problem. . . . I'll try to concentrate.

Susan: I want to talk to you now about fantasy.

Miss G.: Fantasy! [*Sits forward*] Now there's a subject I *am* interested in.

Susan: Ah! I sense we're getting somewhere at last. Tell me about your favorite fantasy.

Miss G.: My favorite fantasy?

Susan: Yes. What sort of scenario is it, what are you doing, who's there with you.

Miss G.: There are so many. . . .

Susan: I'm getting a sense that this is important to you. Am I right?

Miss G.: Definitely.

Susan: Well, let's just pick a recent one. Something hot, please.

Miss G.: Hot? Okay. I should warn you, though, it's kind of complicated.

Susan: No problem.

Miss G.: Okay. I'm in the Gorge of Darkwind. It's pitch-black, and there are poisonous miasmas all around me, swirling, burning everything they touch. I'm at the head of a band of fearless warriors—

Susan: What are they wearing?

Miss G.: What? Oh, leather stuff, I guess. And one of them has the helmet of Azeroth. That's Nor, the leader of my troop of battle-hardened swordsmen. As I stand there, blasted by the fiery Azerothian winds, he moves to my side. "Lady Maud," he says respectfully, "I think we should turn east." I look east, and my heart almost fails, for to the east lie the lands of ancient lost lore, where the spirits of the tormented wander freely, preying on unwary travelers!

Susan: Go on.

Miss G.: So then we move east.

Susan: And at what point does it become sexual?

Miss G.: Sexual?

Susan: Yes. This is all very fascinating, Annie, but I'm wondering if we could jump to the point where you and Nor have sex.

Miss G.: Me and Nor have sex! You must be joking!

Susan: What's so funny? This is your fantasy, not mine.

Miss G.: But in real life Nor is a spotty historian called Willem, with a goatee.

[Pause on tape]

Susan: What do you mean, in real life?

Miss G.: I mean, outside the fantasy. Nor is only his character—and believe me, it's taken a lot of Experience Points for him to get this far.

Susan: I think we may be talking at cross-purposes here, Annie. What sort of fantasy is this?

Miss G.: A Level-3 Swamps and Sorcerers multiplayer scenario. It's the one the College's S & S society is playing at the moment—we meet every Friday in term time. I'm the secretary.

Susan: Ah.

Miss G.: Do you want to come along? We always need more Orcs.

Susan: No. Could you describe a sexual fantasy, please?

[Pause on tape]

Miss G.: I don't really have any.

Susan: You must have fantasies. Everyone has fantasies.

Miss G.: No, sorry.

Susan: [*sighs*] Why do you want to take part in this project, Annie?

Miss G.: It sounds interesting, I suppose.

Susan: But you do want to become sexually functional?

Miss G.: Oh. Yes. Of course. That too.

Susan: Well, you'd better start keeping a diary of your sexual fantasies. That's definitely an area we'll need to work on.

I could not help smiling, partly at Susan's annoyance when Miss G. refused to divulge her fantasies—my colleague has a penchant for eliciting details of what she likes to call "bi-curiosity" in our subjects—but also at the surprising image of someone as poised as Miss G. playing something as, well, *uncool* as Swamps and Sorcerers. I mean, I used to play a bit myself when I was a teenager, but it had been many years since I personally rolled the polyhedral dice and took an LR-3 on Probability.

The last thing in the file was a summary from Susan:

Miss G. is a slightly built young woman who presents as somewhat dreamy in manner. She contacted us via one of our lab assistants, who apparently told Miss G. about the project at a party. There is absolutely no doubt that she has a sexual function disorder—indeed, by most diagnostic criteria she could be said to have several different disorders. However, when asked the standard question "What are you hoping to get out of your participation in this study?" Miss G. gave the impression she wasn't really sure. Expectation management was therefore less of an issue than usual,

although of course I impressed on her the standard caveats. At the
end of this conversation Miss G. professed herself still keen. Conclusion: recommend acceptance.

I put the papers down, unsatisfied. Clearly, Miss G. was emo-
tionally inconsistent and sexually somewhat confused. She dif-
fered from the vast majority of the population only in that she was
getting—and wanting—less sex. It hardly explained what had happened in the lab.[3]

And then I had a sudden moment of clarity. I saw that everything I had read—the questionnaires, the statistics, the interview—
these were not the real Miss G. They were simply a trail of data left
behind her in the physical world. In the same way as a painting is
not the person it portrays, everything in that file was only a kind
of illusion, a guess at the real her. The facts, in fact, were not the
answer; the data were a dead end; the empirical approach was no
approach at all. To solve the problem of her mysterious responses I
would have to go well beyond the reach of conventional science.

In short, I was going to have to find some different way of getting to know her. But how?

---

[3] The drawbacks of face-to-face interviews as a basis for assessing sexual history in the
case of female subjects have been noted by several commentators. In one study, men and
women were asked about their sexual behavior under several different testing conditions, including administration of a questionnaire in which the participants believed,
falsely, that they were anonymous; the results were then compared to those given in a
face-to-face interview, with markedly different results. "Women are sensitive to social
expectations for their sexual behavior and may be less than totally honest when asked
about their behavior in some survey conditions," said a co-author of the study, published in *The Journal of Sex Research*.

12.1

Massive row with Simon. I tell him I'm going to give up English litera-ture to become a scientist. Simon—who is many things but no fool—immediately wants to know "who put *that* ridiculous idea into your head."

"That is so typical of you," I retort. "You assume that any idea in my head must have been put there by someone else."

His eyes narrow. "It's the pointy-head, isn't it? Fisher. The one who lent you that book."

"Of course it isn't," I say, unconvincingly.

At which Simon accuses me of collecting clever men like other women collect stamps.

I say that there are actually very few female philatelists, the urge to collect and classify being a male attribute linked to the hunter-gatherer instinct. (See *Enzymes and Influences*, page 112.)

He asserts that I'm now trying to change the subject.

I suggest that it's him who's changing the subject, not me, and that all I was doing was correcting his lazy metaphor.

He retorts that it was an analogy, not a metaphor, and notes that I have still not denied being attracted to Fisher.

I point out that (a) he didn't actually ask me if I was attracted to Dr. Fisher; (b) it's impossible to prove a negative; (c) the whole idea is completely ludicrous; (d) not everything comes down to sex, for Christ's sake; and (e) even if I did fancy Steven Fisher, which I don't, my feel-ings would have nothing to do with wanting to change to science. In fact, if I *were* attracted to him—which is, as I said, a ridiculous notion—it would make a change to science less likely, not more, given the theoretical restrictions on shagging your supervisor.

Simon shouts that I am now trying to blackmail him.

I respond that this is ridiculous. I have made no reference to blackmail, only to the fact that sleeping with one's students is frowned on.

Simon begins to cry.

He tells me that I'm the best thing that has ever happened to him, that he loves me, that I'm his golden beacon of innocence and youth, and that if he sometimes gets angry, it's only because of his frustration at not being able to satisfy me sexually.

(Satisfy me—what an odd phrase. It makes me sound like a raging nymphomaniac, when the truth is nearer the opposite. I'm perfectly satisfied *not* being satisfied, thank you.)

But you can't go on being cross with a man who's crying, can you? So I say I love him too. And then of course he wants me to go to bed with him.

I even fake it, just a little.

What a mess.

UrlGirl67 ☺

"When the only tool you have is a hammer,
you tend to treat every problem as if it's a nail."

Was Simon right? *Do* I collect clever men?

It's true I've always been attracted to intelligence. Men who know things—smart men—make me want to get to know them. Partly because I want to know what they know, partly because I feel they'd be good at getting to know me. (Not that it worked in Simon's case.)

On the other hand, my perfect man is still Chewbacca.

Five Things That Make Chewie Sexy

5. Hairy. Well, obviously. But it's such nice hair.

4. Loyal. Han Solo once saved his life, so according to the Wookiee code of honor he has to spend the rest of his life making sure Han never comes to any harm.

3. Superbright. Wookiees don't speak much, not having the facial structure for it, but they have a genius for all things mechanical. Chewie can always rebuild C-3PO from scrap, which is a pretty neat thing to be able to do for your friends.

2. Big. Strong. Dependable.

1. His name is based on the Russian word for dog, and his face on a dog George Lucas had as a boy, who died in tragic circumstances. Bless!

UrlGirl67 ☺

*"When the only tool you have is a hammer,
you tend to treat every problem as if it's a nail."*

Something else about this whole KXC79 malarkey. I keep getting this sudden, vivid, uh, *thing*. What I can only call a fantasy.

Us, together. Me and Steven Fisher.

And what's disturbing about this is that it's the real deal—a real sexual fantasy, I mean, the sort I never have. In full pornographic detail, right down to the bad lighting and the cheesy music. And the naked stud—the surprisingly hard-bodied geeky scientist stud—who's holding my ankles up by my shoulders while he bangs me like a—

HEY, STOP THAT.

I think I've had enough of being sexually normal. It just seems to make everything much, much more complicated.

So later I swap the KXC79 patch for one of the nicotine patches Simon bought when he was trying to quit smoking. No one will know—they look just the same. Maybe that will reduce the effects of the pills.

In the meantime, better try to think of some way of resolving this whole science/literature dilemma.

I think I mentioned that I am obliged to do a certain amount of teaching of undergraduates. These are generally rather tedious occasions, in which my attempts to impart a sense of the glories of the natural world are met with a row of heads bent over ring binders as thirty diligent but dull-minded students concentrate on getting down enough notes to pass their exams. That week, though, one attendee stood out from the rest. To my surprise, Miss G. was sitting at the end of the fourth row. Seeing me notice her, she gave a brief smile of greeting.[1]

My subject that afternoon was how Otto Loewi, the father of modern biochemistry, discovered neurotransmitters. Remarkably, the experiment came to him in a dream. He woke up, wrote it down, and immediately fell back into a deep sleep. Next morning he looked at what he had written, aware it was something momentous—only to discover that his writing was completely illegible, almost as if it were in some unknown language.

"Loewi spent the day in a state of extreme frustration," I told them. "To his amazement, though, the next night he had exactly

---

[1] Smiles are usually grouped into two categories: Duchenne and Pan American. The Duchenne smile, named after researcher Guillaume Duchenne, involves movement of the major zygomaticus muscle, around the mouth, and the orbicularis oculi, around the eyes. It is believed this smile can only be produced as a result of genuine emotion, making it involuntary. By contrast, the Pan American smile involves voluntary use of the zygomaticus muscle and can thus be used to show politeness or conceal emotion. Miss G.'s smile, though brief, was most definitely a Duchenne, and it lit up her whole face.

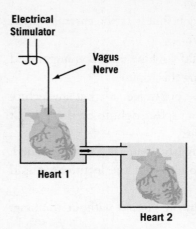

Electrical
Stimulator

Vagus
Nerve

Heart 1

Heart 2

Figure 14: This experiment came to Loewi in a dream.

the same dream again. This time he took no chances. Rushing to his lab in his pajamas, he immediately set up the experiment he had dreamt about. Taking a beating frog's heart, with its vagus nerve attached—luckily he happened to have some beating frogs' hearts to hand, or history might have been very different— he suspended it in a jar of saline solution, into which he introduced a second beating heart." I sketched the experiment on the board. "When the first heart was made to slow down, he observed that, after an interval, *the second followed suit,* thus proving beyond all doubt the existence of a chemical messenger between the two." (See figure 14.)

Miss G. listened to all this with an expression of intense concentration, occasionally jotting down a note. (What had Susan called her in her notes—dreamy? There was certainly nothing dreamy about her that afternoon. In fact, she was one of the few people in the audience giving me their full attention, and one of only two to laugh out loud at my joke about Loewi having some beating frog's hearts to hand—and the other was Helen Chang, who laughs at everything.)

When I had finished my introduction, I organized the students into small groups to replicate the experiment. This soon led to the usual undergraduate chaos—escaping frogs leaping all over the place, some trailing their half-removed hearts; iron-deficient and hungover students fainting when they put the knife in; and so on. I went over to see how Miss G. was getting on. I was pleased to note that she displayed no trace of squeamishness as she carefully pried an amphibious heart from its owner.

"I hope you don't mind," she said, looking up. "You mentioned the other day that you were covering this topic."

It is in fact a point of principle at our university that any lecture is open to any student, so she had a perfect right to be there. I just expressed surprise that she had time.

"I've given up going to my English seminars," she explained. "They're so unbelievably dull. Nothing but the lecturer's stupid opinions."

"You should have been a scientist," I said without thinking. "We only deal in facts."

There was a brief pause, during which it seemed to me that Miss G. was looking at me in a rather strange way.

"Do you really think I could be?"

"What?"

"A scientist."

"You mean . . . switch subjects?" I asked, surprised. "It's— Well, it's a big decision. Are you sure?"

Miss G. bent her head back over her frog. "It's because of you," she said abruptly.

"Me!"

"You and Susan. The way you talk about things. You even make sex interesting."

The student next to her paused, his scalpel in midair.

"Yes," I said. "Well, sex *is* interesting. In an academic sense, of course. What does your supervisor say?"

"He *definitely* thinks sex is interesting," she said with just a hint of bitterness.

"I meant about switching."

Miss G. speared the frog viciously with her scalpel. "I haven't talked to him yet."

"You should really discuss it with him before you do anything else," I said. "Science isn't something to be undertaken lightly."

13.2

After the lecture was over, Miss G. and I found that we were the last two people in the lecture room. After she had helped me tidy up the bits of dead frog we left the faculty building together, talking about Loewi and the whole problem of neurotransmitters and their identification, and moving on from that to the odd/even rule of *Star Trek* movies.

Without my even noticing it, we had cut through Wadham to the corner of Broad Street, opposite the Bodleian. It was one of those beautiful Oxford spring evenings, the sunset washing the sandy stone of the medieval buildings with golden light until, like the petals of a buttercup, they seemed to glow with the sun's reflection. Still talking, we were now standing outside the King's Arms, where our paths would take us in different directions. Miss G. shivered.

"I'm sorry. I'm going on as usual," I said.

"No, it's fascinating. I'm just a bit—"

"Would you like to—?"

"Why not?"

13.3

We sat in a quiet corner, two pints of beer in front of us.

"It was just one of those random things," I explained. "My real interest was in hiccups."

"Why hiccups?"

"Well, they're fascinating too, in their way. And relatively

unstudied. As a scientist, that's what you're always on the look-
out for—areas of interesting ignorance. "Do Hamsters Get Hiccups?"—that was the title of one of my early papers. It turned out
they didn't. I hardly need tell you the implications of *that*."

"That some animals don't get hiccups?"

"Exactly. And therefore—the question we must always ask ourselves—what are hiccups *for*? People used to assume it was something to do with the swallowing reflex, hence all the old wives' tales
about drinking a glass of water upside down. But then I observed
that bonobo apes had a particular way of stopping their hiccups."

"Which was . . . ?"

"Having sex."

"Really? And that goes for humans too? If you have hiccups,
sex can stop them?"

I nodded.[2] "It was due to one of the neurotransmitters being
released during orgasm—oxytocin, was my guess. The bonobos
had worked it out, and we hadn't. That's why it's so important to
keep studying species like theirs: they know so much more than we
do. Anyway, I was talking it over with Richard one day—I'd happened to bump into him on the stairs—when he stopped and said,
'There's your next project, Steven. Why don't you see if humans

---

[2] In order to avoid boring Miss G., my nod rather oversimplified the current state of research on sex and hiccups. See, for example, the pioneering paper by husband-and-wife
researchers Roni and Aya Peleg, "Sexual Intercourse as Potential Treatment for Intractable Hiccups," *Canadian Family Physician* 46 (2000): 1631–1632. "On the fourth day
of continuous hiccupping, the patient had sexual intercourse with his wife. The hiccups
continued throughout the sexual interlude up until the moment of ejaculation when they
suddenly and completely ceased . . ." The authors conclude, "It is unclear whether orgasm in women leads to a similar resolution, an issue that could be investigated further."
Indeed. Several commentators have noted that singultus (the medical term for hiccupping) is more frequent in men than in women; some women report that they have never
had a hiccup, others that they have never had an orgasm. Are they the same women? Is
there an overlap? So much remains to be done.

can get some of what those monkeys are getting?' And of course it turned out to be an area of research that had access to vast amounts of funding." I glanced at her. "What about you? Why did you choose English literature?"

She shrugged. "I'd always preferred science, actually. But at my school the girls were steered towards the arts. Like drama, God, how I loathed drama!" she said with feeling. "What was the point of giving a performance when you had to come back and give it all over again? Literature too—I can see the point of reading a book. But why sit around and *talk* about it?"

"But you must have been good at those subjects."

She nodded. "Six straight A stars. Well, it was hardly difficult."

That explained something which had been puzzling me. The fact was, Miss G. was so unusually clever that she had even been able to excel in subjects she didn't particularly like.

"And now you're thinking of doing some science again?"

"If I can," she said. "If you don't think it's completely unfeasible." Her attention was fixed on the table between us, where she was turning a blob of spilt beer into an irregular dodecahedron with her finger. Her long hair fringed her face. Falling almost to the tabletop, the hair was only slightly lighter in color than the polished surface. I felt a surge of tenderness, mingled with what I can only describe as a ferocious and involuntary vasodilation. In short, I was having an RAE. Luckily the table was between us, and the moment passed without Miss G.'s noticing.

I coughed. "How are you getting on with *Enzymes*?"

"Oh." She looked up, her eyes alight. "I'm on the last chapter. It's so interesting. Did you know there's a mud snail called *Potamopyrgus antipodarum* which switches between sexual and asexual reproduction to ward off parasite attacks? So Professor Collins hypothesizes that all of sexual reproduction may have evolved from nothing more than a parasite infestation."

"That would make sense," I said thoughtfully. "Reproduction lets us shuffle our genes more rapidly."

"But there's more. He argues that if sex evolved in response to a parasite, it would quite naturally have taken on parasite-like properties itself."

"That's brilliant!" I said. Once again the sheer audacity of Richard's insights took my breath away. "It means that rather than human beings using sex to reproduce—"

"*Sex* is a parasite which uses *humans* to reproduce. Exactly. And that makes you look at the whole problem of sexual dysfunction in a different way, doesn't it? Because instead of developing a treatment to make women with low libido *more* interested in sex, you could solve the problem from the other end—you could start developing a treatment to make everyone else *less* interested. In fact, it would be much more logical."

"But that's remarkable, Annie!" I said. "That's a doctoral thesis, right there. In fact, it's more than a thesis; it's a theory. It could open up a whole new area for research—"

"I know." She sighed. "Unfortunately, for the moment I'm stuck with Victorian semicolons."

"What you need," I said with conviction, "is a mentor. Someone who can teach you the basics, but also steer you in the right direction with reading lists and so on."

"Yes," she said. "That is *exactly* what I need."

As she looked at me and nodded, I wondered how I could ever have described her features as unremarkable.

"A good postgraduate or research fellow could teach you all you need to know in a couple of terms," I said.

She nodded again, even more enthusiastically. There was a long pause. She seemed to be waiting for me to say something else.

"I'd do it myself," I added reluctantly, "if only I weren't so busy. With the FSD study."

"Oh. Yes, I can imagine." Her face was once again hidden by her hair as she added some antennae to her dodecahedron.

"We've got a big conference coming up. There's no way I'd have time to teach chemistry to a beginner."

"It was just a thought." It seemed to me that she sounded a little wistful. "Perhaps I'd better stick to being on your study instead. That is, if I'm still useful."

"You're extremely useful," I said. "In fact, you're more than useful: you're almost an area of interesting ignorance. There are several aspects of your sexual responses I'd certainly like to investigate further."

13.4

Not long after that, Miss G. had to go. As she walked away, though, on an impulse I called her name.

"Annie . . . ?"

She turned, one hand on the door.

"There was something else I wanted to ask you, actually. Something quite important."

Once again a Duchenne reaction lit up her face.

"Last time, in the lab," I continued. "Did you have an orgasm?"

Her smile faded, and she shook her head. It was not clear, however, whether she was replying to my question in the negative or simply reacting with disbelief to the fact that I had asked it at all.

"Men," she said, almost to herself. "You're all the bloody same."

As she pulled open the door she paused again. "To answer your question, I've had more enjoyable afternoons at the dentist having a root canal drilled."

Then she was gone.

Which was, I'm sure you'll agree, a curious response to a perfectly reasonable inquiry on my part.

Although of course it is possible that Miss G. just has an unusually attractive dentist.

So, still undecided about whether or not I am actually attracted to Steven Fisher, or if I should be trying to change to science, or both, I went along to one of his lectures to see if I understood it. And I did, mostly. Actually, it was pretty amazing. Did you know that two hearts can send chemical messages to each other, so that whatever one heart does, the other heart does too? OK, put like that it starts to sound like a metaphor from some stupid Victorian novel. But at the time it was just a fascinating bit of science. (And it's so nice, incidentally, to talk to people for whom things really are just what they appear to be and not some complicated symbol for something else entirely.) Then afterwards we walked out of the seminar building together, talking. Talking about—everything. How he got into orgasms in the first place, and what he really wants to do, which is find a cure for hiccups, and—

And it's a beautiful Oxford sunset. He looks up and says matter-of-factly, "Ah, look at that remarkable refraction. It's because the earth's atmosphere is filtering out the longer wavelengths of light, of course."

And in that moment I realize that, whatever my feelings are for Dr. Steven Fisher, they are (a) definitely not just physical, and (b) not just to do with KXC79.

Damn.

Then we're in the pub. Where I do a little fishing to try and find out what he thinks about *me*.

At which point he makes it pretty evident that I'm just an interesting source of sexual data.

So that's that. Not that I was seriously thinking about any other possibility, but it's good to have things absolutely clear. So that we both
know exactly where we stand.

All the same, I feel remarkably depressed.

UrlGirl67 ☺
"When the only tool you have is a hammer,
you tend to treat every problem as if it's a nail."

On the following Tuesday Miss G. came in for her fourth session. On this occasion my colleague Dr. Minstock administered the series of standardized stimulation programs known as the Duchowski sequence, involving visual, neurostimulatory, and transcutaneous cues presented in a steadily escalating progression.

Miss G. again reported that she felt no arousal or sexual response of any kind. In this session, however, the instruments seemed to confirm, rather than contradict, her statement. Even the GSA, to my surprise, showed absolutely nothing—what we call a flatliner.

Miss G. seemed to me to be unusually quiet during this visit. She made very few remarks, even in response to a direct question on my part about the final section of *Enzymes and Influences*. I can recall only one unprompted comment she volunteered that day, in fact; when the tests were finished and she was departing, she muttered something under her breath that sounded like, "There. Happy now?"

15.2

Later, upon examining the data more closely, I noticed that after seven minutes a series of jiggles appeared in the response line (figure 15). "Look—there is *something* here," I said to my colleague.

Susan shook her head. "Ghosting from the stimulators. I had everything right up to the max."

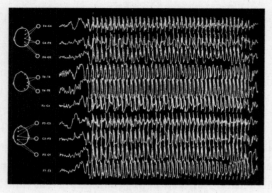

Figure 15: Secondary vibration from the stimulators.

"And we're sure she felt nothing?"

"Of course she *felt* it—it would have been like standing next to someone digging up the road with a jackhammer. It just didn't *do* anything for her. Face it, Steve. It's a big fat zilch."

I brought up the other data. Temperature—nothing. Galvanicity—Miss G. had broken a sweat, but not in the steadily escalating pattern that indicates arousal. On every measurement, she had shown minimal response.

"Maybe you should look at the formulation again," Susan suggested.

"Maybe," I said doubtfully.

To recap: In her first session, Miss G. had received the treatment and it hadn't worked. In her second and third, she had received the treatment and denied that it worked, even though the machines clearly showed that it had. In the fourth, she had received the same treatment, said it hadn't worked, and it hadn't.

This was getting more, not less, confusing.

15.3

Once again I e-mailed Richard Collins explaining my predicament, and once again I received no reply. Checking his Web site, I saw that he was currently engaged in a five-continent PR tour to promote *Enzymes and Influences*. So, somewhat reluctantly, I turned to Wulf instead.

"Wulf," I said as we left the faculty building together that evening, "that girl who said she wasn't having orgasms is now not having orgasms."

He considered. "Then you have, surely, no problem."

"But I still don't know why she was saying she wasn't having orgasms when she was," I pointed out. "And I certainly don't know why she isn't having them now. As for not having a problem, at the very least her current result means KXC79 isn't doing what it's meant to."

"On one level, that may not be such a bad thing. It simply proves the existence of a profound submolecular chaos—"

"Unfortunately," I retorted, somewhat tersely, "I have to give a paper at a major international conference in just over two weeks' time. At which I do not want there to be a single submolecule of doubt that KXC79 does exactly what we are claiming it does."

"Ah."

"Ah, indeed."

"In the case of Rhona's orgasms, I was able to prove their existence by means of a simple experiment," he said thoughtfully.

"What!"

He nodded. "I was worried by what you said—you know, about the possibility she was faking her climax. So I borrowed a few basic testing devices from the lab and checked."

"But that's unethical!"

He looked a little shamefaced. "Perhaps. But I needed to know."

"How did you carry out the measurements without her realizing?" I asked, interested despite myself.

He shrugged. "Air temperature, electrical charge, pheromone density. I doubt it's as accurate as lab readings, but it was good enough for my purposes."

"And what was the result? Did you get the answer you wanted?"

He looked even more crestfallen. "Not exactly. It seems sometimes she is lying, and sometimes she is telling the truth."

"Well, that's not too bad. Think of Schrödinger's cat. On average, Rhona's moderately aroused by you."

"Yes," he said doubtfully. "On a submolecular level, Rhona's pussy does tend to confirm Schrödinger's cat."

We were silent for a while, each contemplating his differing problems.

"So what you're suggesting," I said at last, "is that I need not only to establish the facts about Annie, but to carry out some experiments to see if they hold true under different testing conditions."

" 'Theory guides, but experiment decides,' " he said, quoting one of Professor Collins's favorite sayings. "Remove the guesswork, Steven, and what's left is science."

15.4

The key to research is to keep an open mind. Not many people know, for example, that Viagra was originally devised as a treatment for angina—it was only because an alert researcher followed up some reports of unexpected side effects that its potential as a treatment for male sexual dysfunction was spotted. Sometimes, what appears to be a problem turns out to be a solution in disguise.

However, this sort of discovery can happen only if you are accurately testing what your treatment is doing. This usually requires two separate groups, one of which receives a placebo instead of the treatment.

On a more basic level, you can use the same test subject but swap the treatment back and forth between the real thing and a placebo, to see what difference that makes.

15.5

The following Tuesday, I was at the lab at the appointed time. In a paper cup I had some of the dummy pills I had made up previously.

However, on this occasion another important variable was missing—Miss G. herself.

Twenty minutes went by. "Looks like she isn't coming," Susan said, glancing at the clock.

After half an hour I had to admit that Susan was right. "Give it ten more minutes, just in case."

When ten minutes were up, Susan disconnected the neurostimulators and the session was terminated.

16.1

Simon's away at some conference in Philadelphia. Thank God. We could both do with a break from each other. I go into the College for Swamps and Sorcerers night. Don't have to think about Simon or Steven or Susan all evening.

But I do. In fact, after we've rid the Malevolent Marsh of hydrochloric imps I go for coffee with Beth, who's the Swampmaster, and talk about it endlessly.

"Look," she says when I've finished, "what you're basically saying is that you've finally realized Simon's a creep, right?"

I nod doubtfully.

"And as part of all that, you've developed a slightly unlikely infatuation for this scientist person."

I nod again.

"The thing is, none of that's remotely surprising. It's like fancying your shrink—a classic case of transference. All it means is that you're suffering from low self-esteem because of your defective sexuality."

"Ye-es," I say. Beth's subject, as you may have gathered, is psychology. And while I can't fault her logic, something about this interpretation of events doesn't ring quite true to me.

"So it's pretty obvious what you've got to do," she concludes. "Finish the treatment, dump Simon, and start dating."

"Dating!" I groan.

"No pain, no gain. Look, why don't you use an online dating site? They have these neat little questionnaires which match you with compatible psychological types."

"I can hardly do that while I'm still with Simon, though, can I?"

"Why not? You don't have to actually make your profile live. You could just have a look to see what you're missing."

So later I go online and do a search for internet dating sites. And something rather odd happens.

As I start typing in the words, they appear, as if by magic, in the search box, already formed.

How does it know what I'm going to write?

Then a more likely explanation occurs to me.

I pull down the list of recently visited Web sites and I see that the last one visited—just before Simon left for the airport—was offering: "No-strings fun in Philly. XXX escorts unlimited."

The fucking, fucking *bastard*.

UrlGirl67 ☺

*"When the only tool you have is a hammer,
you tend to treat every problem as if it's a nail."*

I call him in America to tell him he's a cheating slimeball and a pathetic excuse for a human being. I tell him he's spineless, amoral, and a pathological liar. By now I've even been to his in-box and read his e-mails—though I notice that it's only the ones promising "dirty flirty adventures" or "commitment-free naughtiness" he's replied to.

And then I get all my things together and move them out of his house.

Best to do it now, you see, before I start crying.

UrlGirl67 ☺

*"When the only tool you have is a hammer,
you tend to treat every problem as if it's a nail."*

The following day there was still no communication from Miss G. On Thursday morning, the time for her test session came and went with no sign of her.

It was not the first time such a thing had happened, of course. In the nosebleed phase of our research, even the Ukrainian prostitutes seemed to turn up only when it was raining. But Miss G. was different, I was sure of it. Something had to be wrong.

To: urlgirl67@hotmail.com
From: Fisher.s@nb.ac.uk

Dear Miss G.,

I could not help but notice that you have missed your last two appointments. That is all very well, but you still have my copy of *Enzymes and Influences: How Biochemistry Built Our Brains*, by R. A. Collins. I shall be in your vicinity this afternoon, so I will drop by and pick it up.

Kind regards,
Steven Fisher

17.2

Miss G. lived off the Iffley Road, in a shared Victorian house. "Oh, it's you," she said tersely as she opened the front door.

She looked tired. Her hair, which was unwashed, was pulled back and fastened with an elastic band, and she was wearing a scruffy old tracksuit. Even her skin seemed more pallid than usual. Although—to my great relief—I could see no signs of acne, there was a small pimple high up on her forehead.

"May I come in?" I asked.

"Well, I suppose you're here now," she said grudgingly, standing back.

It was a typical Oxford graduate house. There were bicycles in the hallway, and piles of junk mail addressed to long-departed residents on the stairs. Her flat, though, was a surprise. I had been expecting, well, cosy Victoriana, I suppose: dainty teacups, teddy bears, clothes drying everywhere, the usual female clutter. But it was nothing like that.

In her kitchen was a life-sized cardboard figure of Chewbacca, the hairy hominid from the *Star Wars* films. He was wearing a necklace of computer cables. More cables were festooned around the furniture, and there were bits of what looked like computer hard drive on the kitchen table. Even more incongruously, next to the fridge was a flip pad on an easel. The top page was covered in what appeared to be wiring diagrams.

"Sorry about the mess," she said abruptly. "I'm networking my peripherals." She hung another LAN lead around Chewbacca's neck.

"Looks like a big job," I commented.

"It's keeping me busy." There was a brief pause. "I'm sorry I haven't been in touch, Dr. Fisher. But you're here now, so I can tell you face-to-face. I won't be coming back to your study."

"Was it something we did?"

"Let's just say it's no longer relevant." Suddenly her eyes were brimming with tears. "It's the way I was made. It's like he said. I'm a . . . a defective frigid *failure*."

A tear spilled over her lower eyelid and made its way down the soft skin of her cheek, as slowly and deliberately as a snail. With a gulp she turned away from me. A desperate choking sob escaped her throat.

She put her hand over her eyes, as if she could not bear to have me see her crying—like a child who thinks that because it cannot see, it cannot in turn be seen—and that gesture, so futile and yet so vulnerable, touched me almost as much as the tears themselves. I took a step towards her. How I longed to take her in my arms and hold her, to encase her in the protective strength of my embrace until those sobs were over!

But I did not.

Instead I said, "I see that you are crying, Miss G. There have been some very interesting studies about crying—or lacrymation, to give it its proper name. Tears, it has been shown, contain the chemicals lysozyme, lipocalin, and lactoferrin, as well as concentrations of the hormones produced by the body when stressed. So crying really does make you feel better. You are literally flushing the emotions out of your system."

She took a deep, shuddering breath, but otherwise made no sound as she wept.

"And yet humans are the only mammals which cry," I continued. "Why? There may be a clue in the fact that saltwater crocodiles lacrymate, while freshwater ones do not: crying may be a relic of a distant episode in our evolutionary history, when we lived in the sea like dolphins."

Both her cheeks were now lacquered with tears. I took another step towards her, helpless to comfort her, my hands twitching awkwardly by my sides. "Whales, elephants, and even pigs do it," I gabbled, "but chimpanzees and apes do not. When Bob Dylan wrote "It Takes a Lot to Laugh, It Takes a Train to Cry," he was in fact revealing his ignorance, not only of locomotive engineering, but also of basic biochemistry."

"Please shut up," she said in a strangled voice. And then, almost as if she were doing it without thinking—almost as if she were ignorant of what a momentous step it was—she had buried her face in my chest, and the dampness of her cheeks was on my neck. As if of their own accord my arms wrapped themselves around her, and the top of her head nestled against my chin.

I hardly dared to breathe. Images flipped through my mind. I was falling through space and time. I was in the shallow waters of a green lagoon, warmed by the tropical sun. But somehow I was, not just under water, but *of* the water—an aquatic porpoiselike creature, like nothing I had ever seen before. And there, nosing towards me in the warm sea, was another of the same species. As our sleek bodies touched, everything exploded into pieces, and then . . .

It seemed to me that her tears had subsided, a little.

"Miss G.," I said to the top of her head. "I came here today to ask a favor."

"What?" she said without lifting her head.

"You are of course at liberty to withdraw from the study at any time. But the truth is . . ." I hesitated. "The truth is that if you do so now, I will have to cancel the launch of my treatment. And if the launch is canceled now, I suspect the moment will be lost and my backers will turn their enthusiasm to some other approach. As things stand, you are my only hope."

As I was saying these words, she raised her head to look at me wonderingly.

"I cannot tell you how important this is to me. Miss G., I am placing myself in your hands. All I ask is that you think about it—and that if you withdraw, you do so knowing that science may be the poorer for it."

She took a step back. Tearing off a paper towel from the kitchen roll, she blew her nose.

"Please, hear me out," I went on desperately. "I also believe that whatever is wrong with you—whatever problems you have been having—I can solve them. You can make the KXC79 project work, and KXC79 can make *you* work."

"But what you don't seem to have grasped," she said flatly, "is that my boyfriend and I have split up. So there's precious little point in going on, as far as I'm concerned. Personally I don't care if I'm cured or not. In fact, I think I'm happier as I am." She threw the paper towel in the bin. "Look, I'll think about it, all right? But right now I'd like you to go, please."

18.1

The following days are pretty miserable ones. It's like a bad dream (even the bit—can it really have happened?—when Dr. Fisher comes round and tells me that I can't come off his study because he needs to write me up for some stupid paper).

And then, gradually, I start to realize something.

I'm not actually as upset as I ought to be.

It's like when you cut yourself—sometimes, it just doesn't hurt as much you think it's going to. I'd been dreading the breakup with Simon for so long that now that it's actually happened it really isn't as bad as I'd expected.

And I think Simon too—once the inevitable drunken phone calls and the tears and the rambling, groveling e-mails are out of the way—is only going through the motions. If anything, he seems almost relieved.

And I find myself thinking about Steven Fisher again.

Not in that way, you understand. Because one thing I'm very clear about is that I don't intend to get into another mess like the one I did with Simon, sleeping with my supervisor.

Ah, I hear you say. But didn't Dr. Fisher also make it quite clear that he wasn't interested in being your supervisor?

True.

But I've had this germ of an idea. Which, the more I think about it, seems less and less like a germ and more and more like a way to change my life completely.

UrlGirl67 ☺

*"When the only tool you have is a hammer,
you tend to treat every problem as if it's a nail."*

19.1

Would she come back? I didn't know. A day stretched into two.

With a heavy heart, I started work on what Kes Riley had called paper B, the paper I would deliver if the mystery of Miss G. was never solved and we had to cancel the launch. It was full of platitudes and waffle and gently encouraging "maybe's." It was the epitaph of KXC79, and of my career.

In the evenings I went home to the copy of *Lady Chatterley's Lover* I was working my way through. It had been some time since I'd read a book that was not about science, actually, and I was finding it hard going. Also—somewhat to my surprise—so far as I could tell it was not in the least bit erotic. I had reached chapter 9, and the two main characters had not even kissed.

19.2

Then, three days after I had visited Miss G., there was an e-mail—a very brief, two-line e-mail—waiting in my in-box.

An e-mail, as it later turned out, that was to have profound repercussions for the KXC79 project, and indeed for my career.

20.1

To: Fisher.s@nb.ac.uk
From: urlgirl67@hotmail.com
Subject: **Study**

Dear Dr. Fisher,

Can you meet me in the Museum of Natural History at six
o'clock? There's something we need to discuss.

Annie

She was waiting for me under the skeleton of *Tyrannosaurus rex.* She seemed different, somehow. More purposeful. More *determined.*

"Miss G.," I said, "what is it? Why are we meeting here?"

She didn't answer me directly, but turned and gazed around her. "This was where it happened, wasn't it?" she said. "The debate which launched the theory of evolution. Right here, in this room."

"Indeed." I have imagined that scene so many times—the dinosaurs and stuffed birds watching over the heads of the audience; the great crowd of men with mutton-chop whiskers and black frock coats held spellbound by the principals as they argued back and forth, speaking the words that would revolutionize the way men thought about science, about God, about life itself. Sometimes I have dared to dream that the launch of KXC79 too might be an occasion of such historic significance.

"To present your paper, you need me on your study," she said matter-of-factly.

I nodded.

"And I'll do it," she continued. "I will help you. But I have a condition. And it's not negotiable."

"Name it," I said, vastly relieved.

"I want a job in your lab. As one of your assistants. I want to help you write the KXC79 paper."

Openmouthed, I stared at her.

"I've been writing Simon's for years," she went on calmly. "I can do the citations, look up references, format the footnotes.[1] And I'm a far better stylist than you are—the syntax in that last paper you published was almost ungraspable."

"But . . . why?"

"If KXC79 is going to be as big as you say it is, once my name's on that paper I'll be able to walk into any university in the country and get a place to read science. I'm changing disciplines. I've decided."

"Miss G.," I said, as politely as I could, "this is all very well, and naturally I wish you good luck in your endeavor to become a scientist, but what you seem to have overlooked is that the assistants who work for me are accomplished biochemists in their own right. You, as I understand it, are not."

"Of course," she went on as if I hadn't spoken, "you'll have to teach me a certain amount of basic science as well. It shouldn't be too onerous. After all, I've got an IQ of a hundred and sixty-two. Even if I *have* been wasting it on Victorian poetry for the last five years."

"I'll think about it," I said, slightly annoyed.

"There's nothing to think about. If you don't agree, KXC79 is history. Like that iguanodon." She folded her arms. "Well? What's it to be?"

It was becoming apparent to me that Miss G. had planned this meeting thoroughly, and that, moreover, she was not going to be

---

[1] Formatting footnotes, as Miss G. observed, is a tedious business. Every time you add or subtract a paragraph or two, anywhere in the paper, all the footnotes shift position, and it can be the very devil trying to get the footnote back onto the same page as the sentence it relates to. For example, this footnote I am typing now has been on six different pages during the process of tonight's redrafting. I am not trying to justify the fact that I succumbed to Miss G.'s insane proposal, but having someone take care of all the typographical details does save a lot of time. As I write this now, I could sorely do with Miss G.'s assistance. In fact, I could sorely do with her presence in many, many ways.

swayed from her intention. If I wanted her back on the study, I would have to give her a job.

Fatally, I hesitated. "I suppose it's not completely unprecedented. Take Virginia Johnson—she started off as William Master's secretary, but eventually she became a respected researcher in her own right."[2]

"There's one other thing," she interrupted.

"What's that?" I was still turning her proposal over in my mind, looking for flaws. Rather to my surprise, I couldn't find any.

"This is going to be complicated enough without any personal feelings getting in the way. *This* is all about the science. And nothing but the science."

"Of course."

"I just want to make that absolutely clear."

"I'm glad you did. If you hadn't raised it, I would have done so myself."

"Then that's settled," she said. "Now, Dr. Fisher, you'd better give me a reading list. I've obviously got a lot to catch up on."

I realized that I had just been outmaneuvered—and by an arts graduate, of all people. But, somewhat to my surprise, I found that I did not mind at all.

Apart from anything else, I told myself, it would give me an opportunity to study her much more closely.

---

[2] Sex researchers Masters and Johnson married in 1971 and divorced in 1993, citing pressure of work as a factor in their marital breakup. Incidentally, Americans still refer to penises as "Johnsons"—immortality of a sort. I am not, however, aware of any women who call their pudenda "Masters."

The others were somewhat puzzled at first to learn that someone with none of the usual qualifications would be joining us in the lab. But when I explained the unusual circumstances they soon rallied round. It helped, of course, that they already knew and liked Miss G. Rhona found her a white coat and a spare pair of goggles, and the team members divided up among them the teaching she would need.

"It's not like we're busy," Rhona pointed out. "And I've still got all my old course books."

"It'll be fun going through energetics again," Heather added. "There's so much about enthalpic reactions I've almost completely forgotten."

A timetable was drawn up—biology, differentials, organic chemistry, kinetics, compounds, analytical chemistry, interspersed with sessions to test Miss G.'s sexual responsiveness.

"And we're going to be having regular breaks for pelvic-floor exercises, too," Susan warned, to a chorus of groans from the others. "In fact, we should get rid of these chairs—if we replace them with exercise balls, we can flex our PC muscles while we're studying."

"What about you, Dr. Fisher?" Rhona called.

"Am I going to replace my chair with an exercise ball?"

"No, what will you teach Annie?"

"What's left?"

Rhona looked down the timetable. "We don't have anyone taking care of chemical bonding yet."

I bowed. "In that case, bonding it is. I shall brush up on my noble gases forthwith."

22.2

While they got to work I went on the internet, trying to find out more about Miss G.'s unusual combination of symptoms.

Few people now remember that the internet was actually invented by scientists who wanted a way to access one another's data.[1] And it was a scientist—Tim Berners-Lee—who, by refusing to patent his invention of hypertext software, passed up a certain fortune but ensured that the World Wide Web became the democratic, free-to-use network that it is today. The legacy of this academic parentage still quietly survives, almost unnoticed amidst the pornography and the chat forums. Research papers, for example: once stored in a dozen far-flung libraries, they are now archived online as soon as they are published. Scientists can access almost all of human knowledge within moments.[2]

[1] The first "live" image to be transmitted on the internet—the term World Wide Web was originally intended ironically—was of a coffeepot at Cambridge University. According to Quentin Stafford-Fraser, "Being poor, impoverished academics, we only had one coffee filter machine between us, which lived in the corridor just outside the Trojan Room. . . . Some members of the 'coffee club' lived in other parts of the building and had to navigate several flights of stairs to get to the coffeepot, a trip which often proved fruitless if the all-night hackers of the Trojan Room had got there first." You can see the coffeepot's home page at http://www.cl.cam.ac.uk/coffee/coffee

[2] For example, I have just used the internet to double-check that the etymology of "Johnson," meaning penis, really does come from Virginia Johnson, sex researcher. To my surprise, this derivation is by no means universally accepted. Amongst Australians, it is widely believed that it derives from the name of Dick Johnson, a well-known—and apparently somewhat priapic—racing driver. Some Americans believe it refers to a town called Dick Johnson in Indiana; others, that it refers to R. G Johnson, a baseball

I typed in "orgasms" and "can't feel them" and then added "peer-reviewed."

There was some very interesting literature. In fact, the more I read, the more intrigued I became. It seemed that Miss G.'s arrival on the study, despite all the problems it precipitated, had actually saved me from making a fundamental error in the formulation of KXC79.

"What's up?"

It was Miss G. herself, coming over to see what I was doing. She was sipping from a bottle of water, her face flushed from Susan's Kegels.

"Nothing much. How are you?"

"Somewhat overwhelmed. I've just done three terms' worth of A-level modules in one morning. *And* flexed my pubococcygeus muscles for the first time."

"This isn't going to be easy," I warned. "If it gets too much . . ."

"No, I'm enjoying it. But it'll be good to take a break."

"Oh. Of course." It was almost noon: time for Miss G.'s test session. "I'll be right with you. I just need to print out these papers."

"Dr. Fisher?"

"Steven, please. We're colleagues now."

"Steven . . . Before we do the tests . . . there's something I probably ought to tell you."

---

bat manufacturer, who burned his name into the side of his bats. Here in the UK, it is thought by some to be a corruption of "John Thomas," first used to describe the male organ in 1887, while the *OED* ascribes the neologism to a Canadian explorer called W. B. Cheadle, writing in his *Jrnl. Trip across Canada* (1863), who related how his "neck, face and jnsn" were all frozen by the inclement weather. Another suggestion is that it refers to President Lydon B. Johnson, who apparently had a penchant for displaying his organ in public. There seems to be no way, now, of proving which hypothesis is correct.

"Yes?" The printer gave a sudden mechanical death rattle. "Oh—damn. No paper."

Miss G. was looking a little embarrassed. "Those earlier results of mine . . . They may not be quite what they seem."

"I know. That's what I've just been researching, actually. What is it *now*?" The printer was flashing an error light at me.

"American source material, perhaps? You may need to set it to US Letter instead of A4," she suggested helpfully.

"Of course. Thank you. Where were we? Oh, yes. Take a look at this: "Muffled Orgasm Syndrome. A condition in which the sufferer experiences orgasm without gaining sensation or satisfaction from it."[3] You see, Annie, what's been puzzling me is that, according to all our readouts, you *appeared* to be orgasmic."

"Oh," she said slowly. "So the machines told you that?"

I nodded. "At first I thought it must be because of some problem with the KXC79. But actually it's good news."

"Why?"

"Because KXC79 is all to do with the pathways between the brain and the genitals," I explained. "If *any* treatment is going to work on muffled orgasms, it's this one. Basically, it's a whole boxful of nails in the coffin of rival, testosterone-based approaches."

"So my results . . . They've actually been useful?"

"Very much so. If I'm right, we're going to unmuffle your orgasms and prove KXC79's worth across a whole new subset of

[3] "There were extended discussions amongst panelists about the introduction of a new diagnostic category of sexual satisfaction disorder. It was proposed that this diagnosis be applied when a woman is unable to achieve subjective sexual satisfaction, despite adequate desire, arousal, and orgasm. It was noted by several panelists that this diagnosis applied to a significant number of women who sought help for sexual dysfunction. . . . Further research on this topic is strongly encouraged." R. Basson et al., "Report of the International Consensus Development Conference on Female Sexual Dysfunction: Definitions and Classifications," *Journal of Urology* 163, no. 3 (2000): 888-893.

sexual disorders. The science is somewhat comple—complicated, but in laymen's terms, we're going to vastly increase your dose. That should deal with the muffled orgasm and restore normal function."

"And what would that mean," she said hesitantly, "for someone who already had normal function? Hypothetically, of course?"

"Well, you'd never give KXC79 in those circumstances; but hypothetically, I think it's fair to assume you'd be scraping them off the ceiling. If not the ceiling of the room above that."

"I see," she said, in a rather small voice.

"I wonder if we should start with an 'attack' dose—quadruple it, say," I mused. "We might even blast open a whole new pathway to the genitalia." I suddenly remembered how this conversation had begun. "Didn't you have a question? Or did I answer that?"

"You answered it."

"Good. Shall we get to work?"

22.3

In her sixth session Miss G. performed a standard set of tests, with my colleague Dr. Minstock running through a basic three-stage stimulation program.

At four minutes forty seconds, Miss G. began to shake. The shaking was recorded by the monitor as being at a steady 14 Hz. By five minutes this had increased to 18 Hz, and was of a markedly pronounced amplitude. Skin galvanicity of $\pm$ 9.5 μV indicated that Miss G. was now perspiring freely across her chest and neck.

At six minutes two seconds, as the alternating mild-and-forceful-stimulation phase commenced, Miss G. uttered what my colleague Dr. Minstock described—accurately, in my opinion—as "a strangled groan through gritted teeth."

At six minutes thirty-five, the first of twenty-eight internal muscular contractions began. These were at exactly 0.8-second intervals.

When the contractions finally ceased, Dr. Minstock ended the stimulation program. Her voice is audible on the tape at eight minutes five seconds, asking, "Anything that time, Annie?"

Miss G. does not answer.

At eight minutes twelve seconds Dr. Minstock repeats the question.

At eight minutes eighteen seconds—i.e., a full six seconds later—Miss G. replies, "I definitely. Something. That time. Yes. Little bit."

On the recording, you hear what sounds like Miss G. panting. Then you hear Dr. Minstock's voice again.

"Good! We seem to be making progress. I bet those Kegels are helping too."

22.4

"The mole," I explained, "is a convenient way of measuring molecules. It's similar to the way a cashier counts the number of coins in a bag by weighing it. Or when you buy a pack of paper—"

"Ream," Miss G. said.

I raised my eyebrows interrogatively.

"A pack of paper is called a ream," she explained. "If it's five hundred sheets."

"Yes. Good. Well, a mole is six hundred and two sextillion molecules."

"Why?"

"Why what?"

"Why are there that many molecules in a mole?"

"No reason. Well, it's because that's Avogadro's constant, which is based on the number of atoms in one gram of hydrogen.[4] The point is, it's an arbitrary amount."

"Like fourteen lines to a sonnet," she said, making a note. "So two moles is—"

"Actually, the plural of mole is 'mol,'" I corrected. "No *e*. And we don't say 'is.' We say 'equals.'"[5]

"Got it," she said, writing it all down.

22.5

"Basically, you've got chemical reactions which take place in one direction—that is, they're irreversible," Rhona's voice was saying. "Then you've got others where the products combine and reform the reactants. Those will eventually reach a state of equilibrium in which—"

"Both reactants and products are present?"

"Good. Well done."

I tiptoed to the open door of Rhona's cubicle. The two women were sitting on those ridiculous silver exercise balls, leaning forward over the desk, on which was an open Nuffield course book. Two sets of hair fringed its pages.

"So," Rhona was saying, "ready to do homogenous reactions?"

"Bring it on."

I must have made a sound, because one set of hair turned. Miss

[4] According to the latest studies, Avogadro may have miscounted. Some people have therefore suggested basing Avogadro's constant on the mass of carbon 12, this having the advantage of being rather more constant than the present constant.

[5] Also, quantum biologists like Wulf prefer to say "implies" rather than "equals," as in "two plus two implies four," given that nothing is certain any longer. My points to Miss G. were intended as a general introduction to a complicated subject and should not be taken as definitive.

G. looked up, flashed me a radiant smile, and turned back to the book.

"Let's start with the Haber-Bosch process," Rhona said. "Now, this is particularly used in industrial laboratories. . . ."

22.6

"Good night, Dr. Fisher."

"Good night, Heather."

"Night, Dr. F."

"Good night, Rhona. Wulf, I'll call you."

Wulf waved as the two of them left.

"I'll see you tomorrow morning, Steve," Susan said, putting on her coat.

"Yes. And, Susan, thank you for all your help today."

"No problem. Annie and I covered a lot of ground, actually. She's a smart girl."

"She's certainly that. What's she doing at the moment?"

"I've left her a reading pile. I think she has homework from Rhona too."

"Okay. I'll see how she's getting on."

When Susan had left, the lab was silent. I have always loved the stillness of a deserted laboratory, actually. Sometimes it feels to me as if this is the one place in the world where I am completely and utterly at home—like a fish in water, or a meercat in sand. This is my element, almost as if I had somehow been designed for it. I often stay late at the lab after the others have gone, just to enjoy the sense of quiet, peaceful solitude.

But tonight there was no solitude. Despite the silence, Miss G. was there, in Rhona's little cubbyhole, working her way through her reading list.

And somehow it felt even more peaceful—even more right—than it did when I was alone.

I tiptoed over to Rhona's door. Miss G. was there, but she wasn't working. Her head was resting on a pile of open books amidst a swirl of conker-brown hair. Her eyes were closed.

I picked up her ring binder.

"What?" she said, starting upright.

"These are pretty good," I said, flicking through her notes. "You've mixed up sodium chloride and sodium carbonate. But that's an easy mistake to make."

She groaned. "My head's spinning." She glanced at the clock. "Is it time for sex?" She blinked. "Damn, that didn't come out how I meant it."

"Don't worry, I know what you meant. Why not take the night off? We'll run the tests again tomorrow. Go home and get some sleep."

"Nope." She yawned. "Gotta finish reacting calculations. I'm on a schedule."

For a moment I looked at her. "You're pretty determined to do this, aren't you?" I said quietly. "An A-level syllabus in a week, a degree in a fortnight, your first graduate paper in less than a month . . ."

She nodded. "Think anyone's managed anything like it before?"

"Actually, I know they have. Nine years ago. A schoolboy—the youngest person ever to get a science degree at Oxford."

She looked at me. She was suddenly thoughtful, completely alert. I could see her brain—that giant brain of hers—working away.

"So, Dr. Fisher," she said at last. "Any chance I can beat your record?"

"No. But you'll be the first person who's come close."

As I walked away I called, "Turn the lights off when you leave, won't you?"

22.7

When I think back to those days—that heady, brief period in which we taught Miss G. the rudiments of the scientific method—I find that my own scientific method deserts me, and I am no longer capable of thinking objectively. For they were undoubtedly amongst the happiest days of my life—as happy as the days in which, as a junior postgraduate, I made the connection between singultus and oxytocin, or that summer evening when I finally made the breakthrough from KXC78 to KXC79.

There is an old saying that the teacher learns as much as the pupil. When you have a pupil as bright and inquiring as Miss G., it is certainly so. As I explained things to her, I found that I myself began to look at them with fresh eyes—bluey-grey-brown eyes. Certain long-held assumptions suddenly seemed questionable or curious, and more than one topic was mentally marked for further investigation and possible research at a later date. There was no time for that now, of course; there was no time for anything except the project. But despite our workload, I sometimes found myself daydreaming, my attention wandering as I thought back to some especially insightful comment she had made in our last tutorial, or her look of delight as yet another facet of the natural world, previously shrouded in mystery, became comprehensible to her.

I even bought flowers for the lab—great armfuls of daffodils and tulips, the fresh, vibrant colors of spring. If the others thought this was odd or out of character, they made no comment—we were all caught up in it, in the excitement of working together on the approaching launch.

And yet, all the time, we were sleepwalking to disaster. And that too is part of the bittersweet taste of my memories of those days: the knowledge that, for all our expertise, we were completely ignorant of the dark times that were to come.

But all that, of course, was much later. I must be careful not get ahead of myself.

22.8

The next time I checked my in-box I found that I had been sent a Wink by a female scientist at Birmingham University. She worked in a field similar to mine—her specific area of research was the phosphorylation of fructose-6 on the glycolitic pathway—and she wrote a sweet note explaining that she'd realized she was spending too much time in the lab and not enough meeting new people. Hence she had joined the same dating site I had.

> So, basically, if you fancy meeting up for a drink, or even just going to one of the Royal Society lectures together, let me know.

> Best, Ruth Cowper.

> PS: I'm attaching a photo.

It had been so long since I'd joined the dating site that I had almost forgotten about it. I looked at the photograph. Ruth Cowper looked nice—beautiful, even. I knew I should reply in the affirmative. After all, why else had I joined the site, if not to meet people like her? But the truth was that I had no desire whatsoever to make a date with her. I sent a reply, hopefully polite, pleading pressure of work.

Rapid as Miss G.'s progress was, I could not afford to wait for her to cover the ground she really needed to before we started on the paper. And so, in addition to all her other lessons, I began to explain to her the inner workings of the KXC79 treatment. This was hard for her: the science was not just advanced but deeply theoretical, and a less intelligent student would quickly have got frustrated.

"I think I understand the K and the X now," she said after a particularly daunting session of equations. "But what does the C stand for?"

I sighed. "I don't think you're quite ready for the full explanation—it'll just fry your brain. Basically, any chemical reaction requires three things—"

"Reactants, energy, a rearrangement of atoms—"

"—and it's a fundamental principle of chemistry that every equation must eventually balance out—that the two sides have to be equal. But for KXC79 to balance out, we need to postulate the existence of some other factor—what we would call a constant, except that it doesn't actually seem to be that constant. I mean, *really* not constant: not like Avogadro's constant, which is just a little bit fuzzy—"

"Dr. Fisher," she said, frowning, "are you saying you don't actually know yourself how KXC79 works?"

"In a manner of speaking. That is, I can describe *how* it works; I just can't explain exactly *why* it works. Or at least not without going into a very long and theoretical digression about submolecular chaos theory and quantum biology."

"So it's like I said before—women are complex?"

I shook my head. "No, they're chaotic. Which I'm pretty sure is a slightly different thing."

23.2

That afternoon, a very large and fragile piece of equipment was delivered to the Department.

"What is it?" Heather asked, as the team of engineers who had traveled with it from Cologne began to assemble it in a corner of the laboratory.

"It's a brain mapper," I said.

Rhona whistled.

"A what?" Susan said.

"A brain mapper," Heather explained, "is a very powerful scanner that allows you to see the neural network of a living brain in real time. All the billions of connections show up as a kind of three-dimensional electronic hairnet. They cost a fortune."

I nodded. "And we've got this one for as long as we want it, courtesy of Trock."

"What's it actually for?" Susan asked.

"Well, we know it isn't Annie's body that's stopping her from experiencing orgasms," I said. "So it must something to do with her brain. I'm hoping this machine will help us delve inside her hypothalamus. If we can see where the neural blockage is, we may be able to fix it."

Next to me, Miss G. was looking somewhat anxious.

"Don't worry," I said, patting her on the shoulder. "It's basically just a glorified photocopier. There's nothing to be worried about."

23.3

The results of the next set of tests were fascinating. We turned on the mapper, and Miss G.'s brain—her beautiful, vast, Rolls-Royce of a brain—was revealed in all its glory (figure 16). On the 3-D monitors, it pulsed and glowed like a jellyfish in the deepest, darkest oceans. When stimulation was applied, you could actually see her hypothalamus becoming incandescent, like the coil of a lightbulb. When stimulation was alternated in intensity between mild and forceful, her cerebral cortex flashed as if in response. And when her body was gripped by a cascade of muscular spasms, each one exactly 0.8 seconds apart, hundreds of brilliant connections flickered back and forth across the parietal lobes, like flashbulbs going off in a crowd.

Yet she still reported that, for her, the sensation was nonexistent.

I sighed. There was no obvious blockage anywhere. I was still no closer to solving the puzzle.

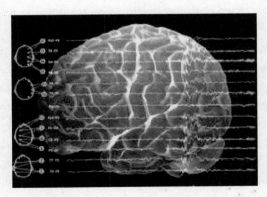

Figure 16: Miss G.'s brain. Note the unusually well-developed frontal lobes.

23.4

I made my way down to the basement. When Lucy saw me she bared her teeth and pointedly turned her back.

"I know, I know," I said. "Far too long. But something came up. Fancy an outing? I could do with some fresh air."

She danced to the bars of her cage, shaking them enthusiastically with all four hands and shrieking her agreement.

I drive a low-emission G-Wiz—fine for the two of us, although it can be an unsettling experience being overtaken on downhill stretches by energetic cyclists. Several times as we made our way out of the city I had to pull over to let the queue of lorries that had built up behind us go past, which they did in deafening clouds of foul-smelling diesel. Once they were gone, though, it was just us and the near-silence of the electric motor, until we came to the pretty country park where the university keeps its arboretum.

I pulled into the parking area. Lucy was by this time enthusiastically signing "tree," but had to contain her impatience until we had bought our tickets. I had barely got my seat belt off before she had her door open and was leaping straight into the low-hanging branches of a chestnut.

The parking attendant strolled over to watch as Lucy effortlessly hoisted herself arm over arm to the very top of the tree, before flinging herself with casual grace into the one next to it. Then, catching sight of a Labrador and its owner coming towards us, she stopped and started to display.

"What's your chimp doing now?" the attendant asked.

"She's not a chimp. She's a bonobo," I reminded him. "And the reason she's doing that is—" I stopped. Better not to say that Lucy was rubbing her genitals in order to signal to any other bonobo in the vicinity that she was ready to trade sex for whoever would take care of that damned dog. "Is because she's not very keen on dogs."

He grunted. "Don't blame her. Anyway, that one should be on a lead." And he strolled off again, to intercept the owner.

When the dog had gone, Lucy and I continued on our way through the arboretum. It was a perfect spring afternoon, cold and clear, the ground covered with a mass of daffodils and crocuses that stretched, like an endless Milky Way, around the deep black holes that were the tree trunks.

In front of me, two young people—students, from the look of them—were strolling hand in hand. They paused for a moment, then turned to kiss each other, oblivious to everything around them, and indeed the presence of Lucy and myself. Something snagged at my mind, something too fleeting and ethereal to be called an idea: a half-realized intimation, no sooner glimpsed than gone.[1] What had it been? Something about that pair of lovers, the way they laughed as they looked into each other's eyes . . .

Suddenly, Lucy gave a cry and hurled herself towards a large cedar. She too had seen something, but her eyesight was far sharper than mine and I couldn't at first make out what it was. Leaping up the trunk, she grabbed her genitals and enthusiastically displayed herself to what I now saw was a small, coated figure clambering into the branches.

"Mum!" a terrified voice shouted. "Mum! Help!"

It is hard to say who was the more frightened, Lucy or the child.

---

[1] It is a curious fact that many discoveries of science have come about in a quiet moment of intuition, rather than by logical deduction. Newton was struck by a falling apple. Archimedes was soaking in a bath. Watt invented the two-chamber steam engine during a Sunday walk. Einstein said that the formula for relativity came to him long before the proof. Loewi, as related elsewhere, discovered neurotransmitters in a dream. And when they started to pursue the structure of DNA, Watson and Crick decided they would recognize the correct answer when they saw it because, as they said, in nature the truth is always beautiful.

Unfortunately, Lucy showed her fear by baring her teeth, then rubbing her genitals some more, neither of which is calculated to go down very well with a small child who at that moment is hanging by one arm from a tree twelve feet above the ground, or indeed the small child's alarmed mother, standing just below holding her Labrador. There was a yell, followed by the words "I'm falling!" as the child bounced from branch to branch before hitting the ground with a sickening thud.

23.5

Twenty minutes later Lucy and I were in the car again, permanently barred from Harcourt Arboretum. "Sorry, Dr. Fisher," the park attendant said apologetically. "We could stretch a point before there were complaints, but health and safety . . . From now on that chimp of yours will have to be classed as a dog."

"Of course she's not a dog," I said wearily. "She's not a chimp either, for that matter."

"Whatever. The point is, she can't come in unless she's on a lead."

"How could she possibly climb trees on a lead?"

"Then you'll just have to take her somewhere else," he said, with the finality of one who believes his own logic to be irreproachable. "This isn't the African jungle, you know."

I did know. Of course, I had tried to explain what had happened—that Lucy had mistaken the small child, climbing with childish agility up the tree, for another bonobo, and that her genital display was simply her equivalent of a friendly handshake. But in my heart I knew we'd had a lucky escape. Bonobo society, as I said, is based on sexual interactions, and in a large colony each animal has indiscriminate intercourse as many as twenty times a day. If

Figure 17: A bonobo.

Lucy's overtures hadn't been curtailed by the child's fall, anything could have happened.

I glanced across at her as we drove back into Oxford. She seemed somewhat subdued. I could guess why. It wasn't because of the park attendant's shouting, or the small child's tears, distressing though both of those had been.

It was because she had thought, just for a moment, that she'd finally met another bonobo to have sex with.

"Never mind, Lucy," I said. "Not your fault. We'll find you a partner one day, I promise."

Then the idea I had half-glimpsed earlier slipped back into my mind, more clearly this time. "Of course!" I said aloud. "Those students! Lovers! A courting couple! Lucy, that's where we've been going wrong."

23.6

"My idea," I explained to Miss G. later, "is context."

"Context?" she repeated skeptically.

"The lab is a sterile environment. Not literally. I mean, it's unexciting."

"Is it? I rather like it here, actually," she said, looking around.

"Well, so do I, but that isn't the point. Women don't normally have sex in science labs. Usually it's when they've been out on a date. And even in those circumstances they have to be wooed, courted, seduced . . ."

She frowned. "You're saying I need to be *wooed*?"

"It's a possibility. And if it's a possibility, it needs to be tested."

"And who's going to do this . . . wooing?"

"It should be a man, I think, so it had better be me rather than Susan. Of course, I won't be doing it for real. There would be no actual physical contact; it would be a simulated wooing, just to make the context a little less artificial."

She gave me a strange look.

"Unless you have any objection," I added.

"No. No, being wooed sounds . . . fascinating and rather pleasant. When?"

"Shall we say eight o'clock? I think the simulation would have more verisimilitude if you were to come back after the others have gone home."

I spent considerable time, with Wulf's help, preparing for this session. When Miss G. arrived at eight o'clock, the lights had been turned off and the lab was illuminated only by the violet flames of half-a-dozen Bunsen burners.

"What's this?" she asked, looking around.

"Today's context," I told her, "is dinner."

I had laid a bench table for two in the center of the lab, improvising from what was available. The bench was spread with graph paper instead of a tablecloth, and the wine and water glasses were test tubes held upright in a tube rack. The wine—a Puligny-Montrachet—was chilling next to the table in a portable freezer, and in place of a candle the center of the table held a single Bunsen, its flame turned down low to make a smoky, drifting cuticle of yellow.

I pulled out a stool for her. "Do you do this for everyone on the study?" she asked as she sat down.

"Oh, no," I said, pouring her some wine. "You're a special case. But it's a perfectly valid hypothesis that social environment may affect sexual function, for example by relaxing you. All we're doing here is replicating the circumstances of a normal date—purely for scientific purposes."

"I see," she said, and it seemed to me that she did visibly relax as she slid her napkin from the myograph ring in which it was rolled. "So, is there a menu?"

I shook my head. "But here's the first course."

I put in front of her a plate on which there were three small pink pills. Her face clouded momentarily as she washed them down with some wine.

"And now," I said, "for the food." I placed a small box on the table and opened it. Smoke immediately began to pour out—but this was heavy smoke. It cascaded onto the table, surrounding the base of the test tubes and the burner in a thick mist, and from there slipped down towards the floor in long, sinuous scarves.

"Liquid nitrogen," I explained. "Or, in common parlance, dry ice." I plunged two spoons into the mixture inside the freezer. "And this is ice cream."

"We're starting with *ice cream*?"

"Not just any ice cream. Freeze-dried carrot and violet ice cream."

She made a face. "Sounds revolting."

"May I suggest, Annie, that if you really want to be a scientist you should refrain from jumping to conclusions," I said mildly. I passed her the spoon and watched as she put it into her mouth. Her eyes grew very round.

"Carrots and violets both contain a flavor molecule called an ionone," I explained. "Putting them together means each amplifies the taste of the other. How is it?"

"It's . . . it's the most amazing thing I've ever eaten," she said, astonished.

"Oh, I nearly forgot. Some music." I pointed a remote control at the CD player, and Stockhausen's *Telemusik* filled the air—shimmering, almost-there whispers of almost-music, like a computer dreaming in its sleep.

"Who made this?" she asked, licking the spoon.

"Did I not mention? Molecular gastronomy happens to be one of my hobbies. Here." I handed her a plate containing a tiny jelly on a bed of what looked like small pieces of liquorice.

"What's this?"

"Salad."

"What sort of salad?"

"Chocolate and caramelized cauliflower salad."

She almost made another face—then caught herself and took a first, experimental mouthful. Moments later, her face lit up. "That's *fantastic*. Even better than the ice cream."

"Of course. Everything I serve you this evening will be good, Annie. I can say that with confidence because it's all based on valid principles of science." I stood up. "And now, if you'll excuse me, I have to prepare the steak."

"Steak? I was starting to imagine something more adventurous."

"Believe me," I said, "this is steak cooked under laboratory conditions. I don't think you'll have tasted anything like it."

The steak, in fact, had been vacuum-packed and then cooked at a very low temperature for over two hours in a thermostatic basin; the meat was as soft as melting butter. All I had to do now was to take it out and brown it for a few seconds on both sides with a powerful Primus burner, thus producing the Maillard reactions which are such an important part of the taste of caramelized onions, vintage champagne, and roast beef. Meanwhile, I was using an ultrasonic bath to mix together eggs, vinegar, butter, and lemon for a perfect Hollandaise sauce. There was also mashed potato to provide a carbohydrate base, infused with a little yeast to bring out the methional compounds in the tubers. This was now being stirred very slowly to a perfect creaminess by a magnetic whisk set at exactly 15 rpm. Finally, peas were being cooked in a rotary evaporator, to ensure that all the flavor molecules which normally get boiled off were collected and returned to the dish. Each pea had previously been injected by Wulf and me, using a needle so fine it was capable of fertilizing a human egg, with a single droplet of vaporized ham stock.

None of this was groundbreaking. As I explained to Annie while we ate, molecular scientists and a few enlightened chefs had been using these techniques for years: I was simply following recipes (or rather, formulae) that were readily available in the scientific literature. But for someone used to the haphazard cuisine of commercial restaurants, every mouthful was a revelation.

"So," she said at last, wiping her plate clean, the flickering lilac flames of the Bunsens reflecting prettily in her eyes. "I have to tell you, Dr. Fisher, that your attempt to replicate a normal date has failed completely. This is way, way better than any date I have ever been on." She blushed and added quickly, "Food-wise, of course."

"Good." I took her empty plate and replaced it with a Parmesan and blood-orange sorbet made in the Pacojet and shaved into thin curls. "But if you think there's anything missing from the simulation—anything we could do to make it more realistic—will you let me know?"

"Well, in my experience, if this were a normal date you would probably be trying to get me drunk. Whereas . . ." She held up her empty test tube.

"Oh, I apologize. That's one condition we can easily replicate." I poured her some more Puligny-Montrachet.

"And if it were a normal date—that's fine, thanks—you'd probably be doing some cheesy flirting by now."

"I'll do my best," I said. "Although I should warn you, I'm rather better at cooking than I am at flirting."

"Maybe you just need the right person to practice on."

I glanced at her, surprised. Had she really just said that? Seeing my look, she lowered her eyes.

"Ah," I said. "I see what you did there. You were replicating the flirtatious banter of a real romantic encounter."

"Exactly."

"In the same spirit . . . if I were to waste my time exchanging trivial flirtatious chitchat with anyone, Annie, it could well be with you."

"Thank you. Speaking of which," she said thoughtfully, "I've been thinking about that theory of yours. You know . . . that kissing is a way of exchanging chemical messengers."

"That overly sentimental, unproven theory," I said, getting up to fetch the fruit salad—a single piece of banana wrapped in parsley, on the one hand, and a single strawberry, halved and layered with coriander leaves, on the other: another example of matching and contrasting volatiles.

"Yes, but—" She gasped as she bit into the strawberry. "Oh, my God, that's good, by the way—I was wondering how one knows what the messengers have decided."

"You'd have to trust your instincts, I suppose. Although, now I think of it, some kind of blood test could prevent an awful lot of unsatisfactory relationships." The music stopped. "Would you like to choose what we listen to next? I'll get the last course."

I went to get the final dish: a tiny sliver of concentrated chocolate, flavored with pink peppercorns, smoked eel, caraway seeds, and merlot vinegar, combined without heat using a vacuum aspirator. As I turned back from the bench she was standing by the CD player, changing the music.

Our paths crossed, and as she stepped out of the way I inadvertently found myself moving in the same direction.

"Oops," she said.

Our eyes met.

Just as in the bookshop, I had the curious sensation that the distance between our heads was somehow shrinking. It was like the optical illusion you get when you look up at a skyscraper and it appears to be falling on you, even though it isn't.

I swallowed. I was acutely conscious that I had promised Miss G. that there would be no physical contact.

"Of course," she said slowly, "there is a possibility that kissing might . . . That is to say, if what we're trying to do here is replicate the conditions of a normal date, then to specifically *exclude* physical contact is hardly useful. Or accurate."

"There is also a theory," I said, "that because a man's saliva contains traces of the male hormone testosterone, kissing may actually help to trigger a woman's arousal."

"Well, then. There you are."

"Naturally, it would ever only be . . . that is, strictly and exclusively . . . controlled experiments . . . laboratory conditions . . ."

"Quite," she breathed.

We leaned together. I took her lower lip gently between mine and tasted the sweetness of her breath.

Ohhhh . . .

And then something extraordinary happened, something so strange that I hesitate to write it here, for fear that some of you will think that my own perceptions were in some way influenced by the agreeable context Wulf and I had created for the evening's experiments. But science is nothing if it is not the truth, so I will set down my reactions to that kiss honestly and precisely, no matter what mockery they may expose me to amongst my peers.

As our lips met, I felt what I can only describe as a sense of temporal fluctuation. It was quite pronounced. The fabric of space-time seemed to loop around on itself, encasing us in one endless, frozen moment. And in that moment, something clicked. It felt like tumblers in a combination lock slotting into place. It felt like two modems whistling and beeping as they connected across a network. Like a million bytes of data, downloading and uploading in a flash . . .

I have no idea how long that kiss actually lasted. Possibly it was less than a minute. But—and once again I find myself at the limits of what scientific language can convey—it seemed as if in that brief space of time our bodies had begun a conversation of their own, a conversation that they would now continue of their own accord, without any more agency on the part of their owners.

"If this were a date," I said at last, breathlessly pulling away, "would you be—that is, am I right in thinking—is this the point at which your companion would be trying to persuade you to have sex with him?"

She nodded.

"I'd say no, of course," she added, a little reluctantly. "On a first date. I'd almost certainly say no."

"Then let's say it's a second date we're replicating. Or even better, a third."

"Well, in that case . . ."

This time it was she who kissed me. Once again time seemed to solidify. Past, present, and future were one and the same, an infinite Möbius continuum. . . .

"Sex. Would. Definitely. Be. A. Possibility," she murmured.

"Good," I said. I released her. "We'd better start the tests."

"Tests?"

"I've got everything set up next door. I know Susan isn't here, but I think you're familiar enough with the equipment not to need—" I stopped. Miss G. was staring at me, her expression what I can only describe as "aghast."

"Dr. Fisher," she said slowly, "I don't quite know how to say this. I've changed my mind. Sorry. I just don't feel like . . . like doing those tests right now. I thought I did, but I don't. For some reason I just feel completely asexual."

"Don't you mean anerotic? 'Asexual' would mean that you reproduce like a mud snail."

"Oh. Yes. Anerotic, then."

"Ah," I said, somewhat nonplussed by this unexpected turn of events. "Well, of course, that's perfectly all right. There is never any obligation to complete a session. It is completely up to you."

"Thank you."

"Was it something I said?"

She shook her head.

"My kissing?"

"No."

"Some error in the date-replication scenario?"

"I don't think so."

"Well, another time, perhaps."

"Yes, another time."

We looked at each other.

"Good night, then, Annie."

"Good night, Steven."

We kissed each other awkwardly on the cheek.

"Would you like me to walk you home?"

She shook her head. "Best not."

"Oh."

"But thank you anyway."

Then she was gone.

I was left with a feeling that, in some way I couldn't quite fathom, I had not handled the evening particularly well.

24.2

What could I conclude from the latest experiment?

First, that a romantic meal, no matter how well cooked, was no guarantee of sexual arousal.

Second, that kissing her, whilst very pleasant, did not seem to make much difference either.

Third, that context—wooing—did not appear to be the missing factor.

So far so good, although it was a shame she had declined to take part in the tests. While I could assume from her reaction that they would once again have been unsuccessful, it would have been useful to have the data to confirm it.

I've been way too busy to write this blog for—what, must be over two weeks now. Too busy and, I suppose, too happy.

I was busy because after Simon dumped me I persuaded Steven to take me on as his student, his assistant, and his co-writer. Result!

Simon dumped me; I dumped Tennyson. I reckon I definitely got the better deal. Science is fantastic: everything I expected, and more. It's hard work—I'm trying to cover about four years' worth of syllabus in a couple of months—but I actually like a challenge as crazy as that.

I felt bad, of course, that Steven had no choice about this. And I felt doubly bad that I still wasn't being completely straight with him. In fact, I'd decided that I'd stop—stop not being straight, that is. Once I was on the team and getting what I wanted, I reasoned, I'd just announce that now I was having orgasms and everyone would be happy.

But of course it wasn't quite that simple. Because by then Steven had worked out that I *was* having orgasms—he just assumed, being a scientist, that I was telling the truth and somehow wasn't feeling them. And that took him off into a whole new area to research. That's when he started giving me these extra-massive doses of KXC79, thinking he was compensating for muffled orgasms or whatever they're called. It's a wonder I can concentrate on my A-level chemistry modules at all.

(Actually, I can't—not always, and particularly not if Steven's the one teaching me. When he talks about noble gases, which are really easy, I sometimes drift off into this lovely, lovely fantasy in which I'm a sixteen-year-old schoolgirl and he's my geeky-but-fanciable science teacher giving me extra tutorials, and I'm still in my games kit after netball, and little by little my PE skirt starts to ride up my—)

HEY, STOP THAT.

Noble gases are interesting too, of course.

Then Steven gets me doing this whole date-replication thing. And that's nice in a completely different way. In fact, I get so caught up in our pseudo-dinner that I completely forget it's an experiment. And I've just got to the point where I'm practically begging him to rip my clothes off when I realize it isn't actual sex this is leading up to, it's his tests.

Suddenly everything—the whole perfect-date fantasy he's conjured up—goes pop and vanishes. I find myself standing in a lab lit by Bunsen burners instead of candles, with some kind of horrible sex drug coursing through my body, and Steven looking at me like I'm a lab rat he's especially fond of.

I do a runner. Which I feel bad about, but it's got to be better than the alternative. Quite apart from anything else, I'd have lit up his machines like a set of Christmas tree lights.

(Or would I? Even with KXC79, there's a point where neurostimulators are not enough. What I really want is to be kissed all over, tenderly, and to dance naked in the rain, and have forget-me-nots threaded through my pubic hair like Mellors does for Lady Chatterley, and then to be laid down on a bed of soft moss and opened up slowly and sensually like a blossoming flower—)

WHOA! NOT AGAIN!

Bloody, bloody KXC79.

I'd better find some work to distract myself with, or this is going to get messy.

And, yes, it is definitely time to stop faking my unresponsiveness. Tomorrow, maybe? Apart from anything else, my teeth are getting worn down from the effort of keeping quiet during the tests.

26.1

The next morning I arrived at the Department in a slightly frazzled mood. Nor was my temper improved when I discovered that the space where I usually parked my G-Wiz, next to Julian Noble's Renault Laguna, no longer existed. Instead, two boxes had been painted on the ground. One read RESERVED FOR DIRECTOR. The other read VISITORS ONLY. Of Julian's Laguna there was no sign.

Annoyed, I reversed onto the road and slipped the G-Wiz in between two motorbikes. (It is a useful feature of these vehicles that, as they are no longer than a motorbike, they can easily be left in motorcycle parking bays.) As I strode towards the Department building, however, I was amazed to see a brand-new Porsche with the number plate JUL 1 roar into one of the new white-painted parking spaces. To my even greater astonishment, Julian Noble stepped out of it.

As he swung the door shut he paused for a moment to admire the car's gleaming bodywork.

26.2

"What on earth is going on?" I asked Susan as I went into the lab. "Julian Noble appears to be driving a Porsche."

"Didn't you read the press release?" She handed me a sheet of paper that was sitting on the desk.

" 'With immediate effect,' " I read, " 'the Department of Molecular Biology, Oxford University, will be renamed the Trock Institute of Submolecular Medicine. This recognizes new sponsorship arrangements put in place to secure the long-term future of the Institute and to establish it as a leading supplier of effective, evidence-based research to the pharmaceutical industry. Professor Julian Noble, named as the Institute's first Director, confirmed that a number of projects are already being developed, including a genetically modified earthworm that may have important applications in agriculture.'"

"Take a look at the photo."

I turned the press release over. The piece was illustrated with a black-and-white portrait of Julian, beaming proudly at the camera.

"He's wearing a tie," I said.

"More than that." She pointed. "Unless I'm very much mistaken, that's a toupee."

" 'Welcoming the announcement, Trock's International Director of Marketing Kes Riley said, "This partnership between the world's number one pharmaceutical company and the world's number one center of research excellence is good news for all involved." ' "

"Is it?" Susan asked.

"Is it what?"

"Good news."

I sighed. "Frankly, I don't think it means anything at all."

"But Julian gets a Porsche."

"I suppose so."

"I hope you don't mind my asking, Steve, but what are you getting out of this?"

"This?" I pointed to the press release. "Oh. I didn't even know it was happening. It's just marketing, Susan. It's of no concern to us."

26.3

"I've taken a look at the paper," Miss G. said briskly, handing me a sheaf of pages. "My suggestions are in blue."

"Thank you. But when on earth did you find time?"

"Last night. Well, this morning." She shrugged. "Couldn't sleep."

When she'd gone I looked through what she'd done. Even I could tell that it was much better. She had not only improved the style immeasurably, but had brought in references from other peer-reviewed papers to make it clear that KXC79 was both based on, and a radical development of, a number of previous attempts by other scientists. It was a very good job, and I immediately went and told her so.

"Anyone can polish a document," she said modestly.

"Nevertheless, I appreciate it."

As I turned to go she said, "Steven, what will happen . . . that is, assuming I *do* become orgasmic. Will that be the end of my involvement with the project?"

"Well, it could be." I guessed that she was referring to the episode the night before, and her reluctance to take part in the tests. "Annie, of course we'll completely understand if you decide at some point you've had enough. My hope, though, is that you'll stay with the program while we're refining the treatment. That way we'll be able to double-check each development against your responses, to make sure we're still on the right track. You'd be a kind of ongoing control." I added, "But we're leaping ahead of ourselves here. We still don't know for sure that KXC79 is going to work."

"I think it will," she said slowly.

"Oh? Why's that?"

"Each time I do the tests . . . Something's starting to happen. I'm sure of it."

"Well, fingers crossed. But whether KXC79 is successful or not, I'd want to keep you on the team now. You've proved your worth here. As far as I'm concerned, you're just as much a scientist as any of us."

I saw her shoulders lift as she took a deep breath. It seemed to me that she was struggling with some emotion so large it was preventing her from speaking.

Then she nodded, and I nodded too, and we both got back to work.

26.4

She spent the morning polishing off AS-level energetics. At twelve o'clock, it was time for her tests.

While Susan took her into the testing room I put on a CD—Enigma's *Principles* if my memory serves me right. The swooping mixture of electro-melodies and Gregorian chant mingled with the beeps of computers booting up as I prepared the GSA.

"Someone's happy today," Susan commented as she came back into the testing room.

"She certainly seems to be in a good mood."

"Who?"

"Annie."

Susan pressed some buttons, and the music was joined by the tenor-and-bass choral hum of multiple stimulation devices whirring into life. "Actually, I meant you."

"Me?"

"You were whistling."

"Was I?"

"And I see Annie's bought herself some new knickers. It's a good sign, don't you think?"

"In what way?"

"Well, it might suggest she's becoming more sexual. Ready for me to start?"

I nodded. Susan fitted her headphones and turned on the mikes. "Okay, Annie. You know the drill. Nice and relaxed, please."

"I'll try," Miss G.'s voice said.

"Good girl." Susan twisted a knob. "Here we go."

We waited.

"Dr. Fisher?" Miss G.'s voice said in my ears.

"Yes?"

"I finished *Enzymes* last night as well. I can give it back to you now."

I had almost forgotten that she still had Richard's book. "There's no hurry, really."

"But I can't wait to talk to you about the last chapter. Did you know that when men are aroused, the part of their brain that lights up is the caudate nucleus—what Richard Collins calls the reptilian part? But when women have sex, it's the cortex and limbic system?"

"Interesting," I said. I was looking at Miss G.'s cortex at that very moment, as it happened. It was glowing a deep, almost ultraviolet, purple. "That certainly supports Richard's assertion that lust is not so much an emotion as a reward system."

"We're good to go to four," Susan said. "You two should probably stop chatting." She turned a dial to its next setting.

"Dr. Fisher?"

"Yes?"

"When I read the KXC79 paper . . . there was just one thing I still didn't understand."

"What's that?"

"What was the breakthrough? In the paper you said you were walking by the river one evening, when you had this insight. But what exactly was it?"

"Oh. Well, I was thinking about sexual function in bonobo apes, actually, when it occurred to me that really thinking is the key to it all. You see, up to that point no one had investigated the role of the brain."

"Annie, I'm going to play some video clips on your monitor," Susan said sharply. "Try to concentrate on them." She typed a command into her laptop.

"Because, you see, most people had been looking at sex as a purely physiological phenomenon," I went on. "But if that's the case, *why is merely thinking about someone enough to cause arousal?* Clearly there's a mechanism somewhere, deep in our brains, that converts thoughts into physical response . . . a kind of neurochemical network interface. It occurred to me to look for a way of hacking into that system."

"So KXC79 isn't really a drug at all?"

"Exactly. It's a chemical messenger—in essence, it's a *thought,* just as all thoughts are ultimately chemical messengers, flashing from synapse to synapse within the brain."

Beside me, Susan was furiously typing more commands on her keyboard.

"Did I tell you," I said, "that amongst females of other species, it's only the intelligent animals, the higher primates and dolphins, which have orgasms? The logic's inescapable, really: it's all in the mind." Was it my imagination, or had a low sigh just escaped Miss G.'s lips? "Well, the rest was straightforward. After binding to cytoplasmic receptors in your brain cells, the receptor-hormone complex translocates to the cell nucleus. The result, obviously, is release of new proteins with the same information into the cytosol, where the physiologic response is triggered."

I distinctly heard her gasp. "But the peptide action . . ."

"Is simply a correlation of brain function."

"I hate to interrupt," Susan interrupted, looking at her screen, "but I think the moment is right to go to five."

I waved her on. "Once you know that every thought in your mind is only a chemical, the question is: What thought, what chemical, shall we place there? Everything else is just molecular fine-tuning."

Miss G. drew in her breath. On the thermograph a warm flush suffused her chest, rising up her neck in a brilliant sunrise of yellows and oranges.

"Something's happening," Susan said.

"What?"

"Put it this way," Susan said, pressing buttons rapidly. "Unless I'm very much mistaken, she's not going to be thinking about peptides for a while."

Miss G. moaned. She has, as I have probably remarked, a pleasant voice, dry and husky. But that moan was something more—it was like the sweetest, richest song that lips had ever uttered.

My colleague was undoubtedly right. Something was happening.

"Come on," Susan muttered. "Come on, Annie. Come on."

Miss G. gasped.

"Yes!" Susan said with satisfaction.

"YAARGH," Miss G. said.

"Houston to Shuttle: We have launch in zero minus ten," Susan said happily.

"BORIS YELTSIN," Miss G. yelled. Quite why she was shouting the name of a former president of the USSR I do not know.

"Nine . . . eight . . . seven . . . six . . ."

"Is this what I think it is?" Heather said, sticking her head round the door.

"It certainly looks that way," Susan agreed.

"Rhona! Annie's having an orgasm," Heather called. After a moment Rhona too pushed into our tiny control booth.

" . . . three . . . two . . ."

"Whoa!" shouted Miss G. Her heartbeat was at the very top of the graph. Temperature was off the chart, and skin moisture was going crazy.

"Lift-off," Susan said.

For a long, agonizing moment nothing more happened. Then, abruptly, the EMG erupted into an arpeggio of peaks—a volley of uncontrollable spasms, each successive contraction-and-release larger and more splendid than the one before (figures 18a–d).

"Oh!" Miss G. cried in a strangled voice. "No! Yes! Gorbachev! Putin! Fuck! OH!"

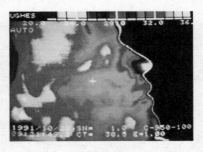

Figure 18a: Thermograph view of Miss G. at T07.43.

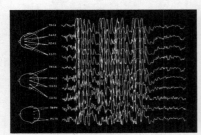

Figure 18b: Another view, T07.50–T08.21.

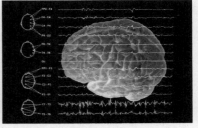

Figure 18c: Brain-mapper output, T07.50–T08.27.

Figure 18d: Subjective impression of To8.18. The American government code-named this 61-kiloton XX39 atomic bomb "Climax."

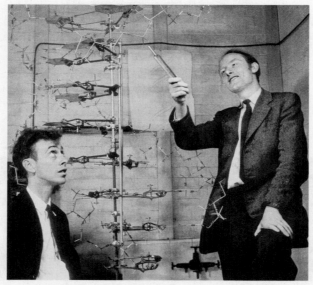

Figure 18e: Francis Crick and James Watson with their DNA model. "It's beautiful . . . so beautiful," Watson was later heard to remark.

We watched the spikes on the graph gradually fade away. There was a long silence, broken only by the amplified sounds of Miss G.'s panting. Susån leaned forward to her microphone.

"Annie?"

"Uh?"

"How was that?"

"Fucking amazing," Miss G. said in a strangled voice.

We scientists are not given to overdemonstrative shows of emotion. It is said, for example, that when Watson and Crick completed the first helical model of the structure of DNA and saw, as the last molecule slipped into place, that it was beautiful and it was right (figure 18e), Crick offered Watson his hand and the other man shook it. In our own lab, I am glad to say, there was nothing unseemly. No one gave anyone else a high five. But we exchanged handshakes—that is to say, I offered Susan my hand, and she, completely missing the quiet symbolism of the gesture, ignored it and hugged me. Then everyone was laughing and hugging everyone else, and Susan started crying, and Rhona did a rather extraordinary little war dance in the middle of the lab, and all the while Miss G. lay there in the testing room, panting, the aftershocks of her orgasm bouncing along the floor of the EMG printout, like a dying cascade of echoes.

26.5

That lunchtime, to celebrate, they went off to play Swamps and Sorcerers with Annie's fantasy society.

"I'm going to be an Orc! I'm going to be an Orc!" Susan said blissfully.

"Are you coming, Dr. Fisher?" Rhona called.

"I'd love to, but I can't. There's some work I've got to do."

"What about you, Heather?"

"Sorry, I'm meeting someone."

"Ooh—anyone exciting?" Susan asked.

"It's just lunch in a pub. I'll be back by two."

When the lab was empty I exhaled a long, quiet breath. Then I went back to Miss G.'s test results and ran through the data again.

There was no doubt about it—she'd had an orgasm, and one of impressive amplitude at that. But then, I reflected, all her orgasms had been substantial—according to the machines.

Which left me with a puzzle.

Why had Miss G.'s orgasm today been different—why had this been the first one she had actually *felt*?

You see, it wasn't the KXC79.

I knew it wasn't the KXC79 because she hadn't been given any.

On this occasion, the pills I had administered to Miss G. fifteen minutes before the start of the tests had been dummies. I had given her a placebo.

26.6

I went through the tests. Then I went through them again. Backwards, forward . . .

Nothing made sense.

The only thing I could spot was a faint glow on the brain-mapper output in a part of the brain I hadn't expected to be working at all—the anterior cingulate. According to the literature, that part isn't associated with sexual response at all. According to the latest studies, it's associated with conflict resolution, strategic planning, and deception.

26.7

Oh, and something else rather curious happened that lunchtime. Towards two-thirty I heard a roaring engine pull up below my window. I looked down, annoyed: it was Julian Noble, parking his ridiculous German sports car. As soon as he got out, he hurried round to open the other door for the young woman who was swinging her rather shapely legs out of the passenger seat.

Somewhat to my surprise, it was Heather Jackson.

26.8

"You know, we should probably make sure those results are replicable," Miss G. said to me that afternoon. "After all, one success might just be a fluke."

I nodded. "The same thing had occurred to me. You're already thinking like a scientist, Annie."

She flushed with pleasure.

That evening, before she left, we carried out an identical set of tests. Once again, without her knowledge, I gave her a placebo instead of the real KXC79.

Once again she reported that the treatment was 100 percent effective.

26.9

The following day, I switched the placebo back to KXC79.

The results were identical in every respect to the placebo sessions. Once again, the machines showed that Annie was experiencing climax; once again, Annie reported that this was indeed the case.

And, once again, there was a faint, flickering luminescence in the depths of her anterior cingulate.

26.10

"What are you doing, Dr. Fisher?"

It was Miss G., leaving for the night. She was carrying a large bag full of science books that knocked against her legs. Rhona and Heather were, if anything, stepping up the academic pressure.

"I'm just incorporating these latest findings into the paper."

"What happens after that?"

"Well, I'll send it to Trock—they may want to change a few references, if there's anything commercially sensitive. But other than that, it's done. There's plenty more for us to do in the meantime, of course: variables we should adjust for, different conditions we should test under, just to make absolutely sure the results are as robust as we'd like."

She nodded. She seemed, I thought, to be waiting for me to say something else.

"Good night, Annie," I said at last.

She nodded. "Good night."

When she had gone I e-mailed the paper to Kes Riley. Then, on an impulse, I created a new message.

To: RCollins@collins.com
From: Steven Fisher
Subject: **KXC79**

Dear Richard,

Attached is the paper I'm going to be delivering at SexDys. The thing is . . .

I paused. What was the thing?

The thing is, the most recent volunteer is showing some rather odd results (see data). Should I be alarmed? Does it mean something—or nothing? What should I do?

I pressed Send, and the paper flew off into cyberspace.

26.11

"What should I do, Wulf?"

"The only thing you *can* do—hypothesize some possible explanations, and devise an experiment to test each one. Don't try to prejudge the results. Keep an open mind."

"Sometimes," I said moodily into my beer, "I think an open mind may actually be a disadvantage."

"Oh? How?"

"Perhaps there's some totally obvious conclusion that we're failing to see, because we're so intent on considering all the possibilities. You know, like that tomato effect you talked about."

Wulf nudged me. "This will cheer you up." He took something from his bag—or rather, two things: a small white box with an aerial attached, and a strange, bulbous, corkscrewlike object.

"What is it?"

"Can't you tell?" He pressed a switch on the box, and some lights along the base of the bulbous object flickered into life.

"No," I said, still mystified.

He pressed another button, and the top part of the thing began to rotate, like some kind of burrowing machine.

"It's a stimulator," he said proudly. "The Evans-Sederholm Submolecular Stimulator, to be precise. It's only a prototype, but it's fully functional."

Intrigued, I picked the thing up. It was soft to the touch, like silicone, and it was vibrating, very quietly and smoothly, at quite a low amplitude. But, as I held it, I felt the vibrations move up a gear—then another—and another. I glanced at the white box, although so far as I could tell Wulf hadn't touched it. "What is that—some kind of remote control?"

He shook his head. "Biofeedback."

"Biofeedback!"

I loosened my grasp, and the vibrations settled to a steady but pulsing rhythm—almost, I thought, as if the thing had a heartbeat. When I opened my palm the end section spun round once or twice, as if trying to blindly peer about.

"I got the idea from talking to Rhona," he explained. "It responds to temperature, galvanicity, muscular activity, vasodilation—that LED there is the photoplethysmograph diode. Basically, the stalk contains a tiny Bluetooth transmitter that sends information to the box, where a simple piece of software processes it and sends back instructions." He pointed. "There are dedicated stimulators for each of the major erogenous zones—even the AFE. And this ledge here at the base contains a stimulator and a logic gate—"

"Wulf," I said. "Wulf—"

"Wait, there's more," he said happily. "I wanted to find some way of incorporating my own work on undecidability. There's a secondary software program which completely randomizes the experience, depending on an algorithm with a whole range of variables: date, time, weather, frequency since last use—"

"Wulf," I said incredulously, "this vibrator has *moods?*"

He nodded. "But—and here's the kicker—they aren't immutable. For example, it reacts to the user's level of arousal. Depending on the other variables, it can then decide to make more of an effort, or not to bother—it can just switch itself off, if it wants to, completely without warning. It's utterly unpredictable. If my theories are correct, it'll make for a much more realistic sexual experience. What do you think?"

I looked at the stimulator. It seemed to have gone to sleep—bored, doubtless, by our conversation. But as I looked it wriggled briefly, and a purring sound issued from somewhere deep inside.

"I think you should probably destroy it. Now. Take it outside and drown it." As I spoke, the stimulator buzzed and hummed briefly, like an angry chain saw.

"Rhona thinks it's great," he said.

"I bet she does. Wulf, don't you see? All you need is an artificial inseminator attachment and you and I are completely redundant."

He laughed. "It's just a bit of fun."

On the table, the ESSS shook briefly in response. For a brief moment, it almost looked as if it were chuckling too.

Whatever I thought of Wulf's invention, his reminder that I should stick to basic science in tackling the problem of Miss G. was timely.

Researchers have long been aware of something called the placebo effect. In a nutshell, it has been proven that if you give someone a pill and say it will have a certain effect, in many cases it will have that effect *even when it is actually a dummy pill.* This is because we are all of us deeply suggestible, irrational beings whose brains do not function as logically as we would like to think. For example, studies show that a placebo is far more effective than any real treatment for back pain, leading to calls amongst some scientists for dummy pills to be prescribed by doctors just like medicines.[1]

This could be what was happening to Miss G. It was not that the KXC79 wasn't working, but rather that, *having read my paper,* she had convinced herself so thoroughly of its effectiveness that any pill which she believed to be KXC79 would have the same result, irrespective of what it contained. This might also explain why the anterior cingulate was becoming luminescent during these tests: I was watching the brain literally fooling itself into producing the placebo effect.

---

[1] Obviously, they couldn't be called "dummy pills," as that might limit their acceptability. Some name, such as "Placibrium," would have to be thought of which conveyed that this was a tested, effective treatment. Something similar already happens in the labeling of food ingredients, where water can perfectly legally be called "acqua."

In future, therefore, if I was to rely on the evidence I gathered, I would have to gather it in a situation where Miss G. *did not think she had been given KXC79*. Since the reverse placebo effect would also apply—i.e., she would be equally suspicious not to receive any treatment, and would simply tell her brain that she was no longer orgasmic—I would have to proceed under a different set of conditions altogether.

In short, I was going to have to take my experiment out of the laboratory and into the real world—or, as we scientists call it, the field.

For inspiration, I turned to the book Miss G. had recommended: *Lady Chatterley's Lover* (Lawrence, D. H., 1928). I had by now reached chapter 15, and the protagonists had at last started having sex—or rather, having long conversations about the feebleness of modern postindustrial society, interspersed with sex.

As I read on, I became increasingly incensed. It was not so much the sex that was the problem—although the way the author described it made it almost impossible to work out what was going on: What on earth were "glimpsey" thighs or "meaningful" breasts? It was the way that the book's real hero, a brilliant wheelchair-bound academic who single-handedly sets about saving the local mining industry by introducing more progressive engineering practices, is completely overlooked by the author and his female creation Connie in favor of a surly, bad-tempered, oversexed gamekeeper. As for the lovemaking, once again I could make neither head nor tail of Lawrence's physiology:

> And this time his being within her was all soft and iridescent, purely soft and iridescent, such as no consciousness could seize. Her whole self quivered unconscious and alive, like plasm.

"Plasm." I knew that word, of course. But Lawrence appeared to have completely misunderstood its meaning. According to the Oxford *Dictionary of Biology,* "plasm"—which should be used only as a suffix—refers to the proteins and other contents of a cell.

Hence "protoplasm" (the cellular nutrients) or "cytoplasm" (the part surrounding the nucleus). Despite being a published author, D. H. Lawrence had failed even to consult a reference book before using an unfamiliar word!

> The billows of her rolled away to some shore, uncovering her, and closer and closer plunged the palpable unknown, and further and further rolled the waves of herself away from herself leaving her, till suddenly, in a soft, shuddering convulsion, the quick of all her plasm was touched—

There it was again—that bloody "plasm." It seemed to me that Lawrence was probably thinking of oxytocin, or possibly the pituitary hormones serotonin and dopamine, but he was so imprecise about the context that it was hard to be sure. And what in heaven's name was a "palpable unknown"?

I was certain it could not be these passages that Miss G. had found stimulating. And I hoped it was not the dialogue between the two lovers:

> "Tha'rt not one o' them button-arsed lasses as should be lads, are ter! Tha's got a real soft sloping bottom on thee, as a man loves in 'is guts. It's a bottom as could hold the world up, it is!"

Frankly, I couldn't imagine Annie and me having a conversation about whether her bottom could hold up the world. However, if it was gamekeeping she wanted, then gamekeeping I could provide. Like most Oxford colleges, mine owned vast swaths of the Cotswold countryside, and there were huge wooded estates not far from Oxford where Fellows who were so inclined could still blast innocent birds pointlessly out of the sky. A twenty-pound note slipped to the burly Foreman of Works, and I was in temporary possession of the key that unlocked the gates of Stowood Farm, five miles beyond the Oxford ring road.

28.2

I intercepted Miss G. by the stairs before lunch.

"I thought perhaps we wouldn't stay in the lab today. After all, it's a lovely afternoon."

"Yes, but . . ." She looked puzzled. "What about the tests?"

"We can do those another time. I'm much more interested in replicating the conditions in which you might experience desire."

"You mean, another date experiment?"

"Sort of. I thought we'd go for a picnic." And despite her questions, I refused to tell her any more until we were in my car and driving out of the city center.

28.3

"This car's so quiet."

"It's electric. Climate change is a scientific fact now—the evidence is incontrovertible. Driving a vehicle like this is the only logical choice." I pumped the accelerator as we struggled up the hill towards Headington. "Unfortunately it's not very powerful."

"And you obviously eat a lot of fruit," she said doubtfully.

The floor around the passenger seat was strewn with orange peel. "Oh, that's Lucy. She likes oranges."

"Oh." We took a right at the Marston roundabout and headed over the ring road. Miss G. pulled a banana skin out from the seat crease and said—in a rather small voice, I thought—"And how long have you and . . . Lucy . . . been together?"

"About three years now. She wanted to come along today, actually." Lucy, whom I had been neglecting even more than usual of late, had not reacted well to being told she couldn't come on the picnic, and had ended up by biting me. I very rarely discipline her, but when all my positive-reinforcement programs had failed to stop her behaving badly I had been forced to give her a small smack. I do not believe in physical punishment except as an absolute last resort, and Lucy had been so surprised she had gone into a sulk. "I think she was a bit jealous."

"And has Lucy been involved in your . . . research?"

"Oh, yes. I'd never come across any female with her extraordinary ability to have orgasms. Three, four, even six at a time sometimes. I started to wonder what it was that made her so special . . . and that became an important part of the theory."

We had by now reached the pretty plateau above Elsfield, where the G-Wiz once again managed to achieve a respectable speed. Miss G. turned to look out of the window. I glanced across at her, and to my surprise saw in the reflection of the glass that she appeared to be scowling.

"Incidentally," I said, "if you reach into that bag at your feet, you'll find something I'd like you to wear."

Wordlessly she reached into my rucksack and pulled out the device I had rigged up especially for this afternoon's outing. It looked like an ordinary baseball cap, with the insignia of Oxford University embroidered on the front—I had got it from the University Merchandise shop on the High.[1] But its appearance was deceptive: it was actually a remarkable work of miniaturization, rigged up by Wulf and me, incorporating sensors cannibalized from the brain mapper as well as Wulf's biofeedback software (figure 19). On the

---

[1] Now I think about it, it is perhaps odd that they stock them, since baseball is a sport Oxonians rarely play.

outside, positioned where the wearer could not see them, colored LEDs—blue, amber, green, and red—ran up the seam towards the crown. These were driven by a tiny processor which in turn channeled data from electrodes on the inside of the cap. Apart from a few wires sticking out here and there, the electronics were unobtrusive. I had got some of the lab assistants to road test it for me, and they reported that there was indeed a rough correlation between the lights and the wearer's physioemotional state: blue meant no or negative response, amber meant receptive, and so on.

"You want me to put this on?" she muttered.

"Yes, please. You just need to turn the power on—here."

I reached across and showed her where the switch was. The lights flashed once to show that the device was operational.

She jammed the cap down on her head, pushed her hands under her arms, and leaned into the corner of the seat, as far away from me as possible. The lights on the cap were resolutely blue. I was struck, suddenly, by how much she reminded me of Lucy, and I could not help smiling.

"What?" she said sourly.

"You look just like Lucy when she's sulking."

"She sulks a lot, does she?"

"Sometimes, yes. This morning I had to spank her."

Miss G. turned her head to stare at me. "Er . . . Dr. Fisher. Please. Too much information."

"I've never really understood that expression," I mused. "I mean, how can one possibly have too much information? That would be like having too much truth, or too much oxygen."

"I can't speak for other people," Miss G. said shortly. "But what *I* meant was that I really don't want to hear what you and your girlfriend do in bed."

"Ah! I think we've been talking at cross-purposes. Lucy isn't my girlfriend."

 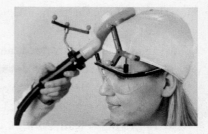

Figure 19: Specially adapted baseball cap (left) incorporating battery-powered sensors from the laboratory brain mapper (right).

"Oh. Who is she, then?"

"She's a primate I rescued from the lab."

"So when you talked about spanking her, you actually meant"—she frowned—"disciplining your monkey."

"Exactly!"

"Oh," Miss G. said again. The blue light flickered, briefly, to amber and back. "Do you in fact *have* a girlfriend?"

"No, no. Much too busy."

The light went to amber, and even briefly flickered green. Miss G. was looking out of the window thoughtfully, but she was no longer scowling.

28.4

As I drove I explained the ground rules of the experiment I was about to conduct.

"I'll be guiding you through a range of activities that I think may trigger certain responses. I'll be with you, but I want you to forget I'm here. I'm an observer, not part of the experiment. Just pretend I'm invisible."

"How will that work, if you've got to tell me what to do?"

"Well, semivisible, then. Think of me as a ghostly voice inside your head."

We parked in the farmyard, and I consulted an Ordnance Survey map before leading her down a track into some woods. The bluebells were out, carpeting everything in a shimmering mist of bright blue.

"If I'm right," I said, "it'll be round here somewhere. . . . Yes, over there."

In the middle of a clearing stood a small hut with a corrugated-iron roof, a bit like a cricket pavilion. To one side, an enclosure about forty feet long had been fashioned out of chicken wire.

I pushed open the door. Inside, it smelt of moist earth and beechnuts and old sacking. But along one wall there was a bench, which held a row of wooden boxes, and above the boxes glowed a row of infrared heat lamps.

I beckoned Miss G. over to the bench. Reaching into the first box, I closed my fist gently round one of the faintly peeping pheasant chicks and softly drew it out.

"There!" I said, holding out my hand to her. She took the little brown bedraggled thing between her hands, and there it stood, on its impossible little leg-stalks, trembling on its weightless feet. Despite its fear, it lifted its little head, looked sharply around, and gave a tiny peep.

"Oh!" she said. "It's adorable!" Then she looked at me. "You read it, didn't you—you read *Lady Chatterley*."

" 'Tha's got a real soft sloping bottom on thee, as a man loves in 'is guts,' " I said proudly. Then I stopped. Had I really said that? But Miss G. seemed not to mind. In fact, the lights on her cap flickered rapidly, right up and down the scale.

The chick peeped again, more anxiously, and Miss G. returned it carefully to the box. "This is the hut, isn't it?" she said, looking around. "The gamekeeper's hut in the woods where they make love."

"It's very similar," I agreed. I was watching the lights. Green. Then, as she looked at the floor, amber. Then she looked at me. Green again.

"Are we going to do kissing today?" she asked. "Or isn't that part of this experiment?"

"Hmm." I thought about it. "Well, strictly speaking, we shouldn't, I suppose. As I'm not here."

"Unless you were imaginary rather than invisible," she suggested. "You know, like a fantasy."

I considered. "Yes, that should work. After all, in a sense I am a stand-in for the character of Mellors, who is little more than a fantasy figure in the book himself."

"Exactly," she agreed, raising her chin and waiting to be kissed. I stepped forward, took her in my arms, and kissed her.

Or rather, I tried to. Presumably it is possible to kiss someone wearing a baseball cap, but it must take considerable ingenuity.

"Are you all right?" she asked anxiously.

"Yes, I was just—" I rubbed the spot on my forehead where the hard brim of the cap had struck me.

"Here," she said, and twisted the cap sideways.

I kissed her again, properly this time. I kissed her slowly and hungrily, as Mellors and Lady Chatterley would have kissed, without shame. I put my hands around her head and held it against mine. It was so fragile in my rough male fingers, like a delicate porcelain bowl, a bowl from which I drank deep and long.

And, once again, it happened: that bizarre sense of time coming to a standstill. It was like the two sides of a long, complicated equation suddenly canceling out, so that x really did only $= y$. It was like ice-cream sellers all over Oxford simultaneously bursting into song. It was like pheasant eggs hatching, and bluebells blossoming. It was soft and iridescent and throaty and caressive. It was like current flowing through a brand-new circuit, and applause, and rain drumming on a corrugated roof. . . .

Reluctantly, I pulled back. As I did so I realized that the noise I had heard *was* rain—a sudden downpour, almost deafening us.

"And that's the clearing where they danced naked in the rain," she breathed, looking outside. "Their wet feet trampling the bluebells, like two pagan gods, at one with nature and the tumultuous passions of the earth."

"I believe it is," I said anxiously. Much as I liked Miss G., I was not sure that my plans for that afternoon had included dancing in the rain.

She went to the door. Outside, it was bucketing down—raindrops the size of golf balls tearing great chunks of earth out of the ground. It had also gone rather chilly. The cap lights, I noticed, were now flickering hesitantly between amber and blue.

"Shall we?" she said.

"If you would like to dance naked in the rain," I said, "please, go ahead. Don't mind me. I am simply a figment of your imagination."

Miss G. took a deep breath and ran out a few paces. Immediately, she was drenched. I saw the lights die completely—the cyber cap hadn't been designed to take that sort of punishment. She lifted her streaming face to the rain.

"Do you have the book?" she asked, turning back to me. "Just to—you know—double-check how it goes."

"As it happens, yes," I said. I pulled my copy of *Lady Chatterley's Lover* out of my rucksack.

"Chapter fifteen, I think."

I turned to the relevant chapter and found the section she was referring to.

28.5

She opened the door and looked at the straight heavy rain, like a steel curtain, and had a sudden desire to rush out into it, to rush away. She got up, and began swiftly pulling off her stockings, then her dress and underclothing, and he held his breath. Her pointed keen animal breasts tipped and stirred as she moved. She was ivory-coloured in the greenish light. She slipped on her rubber shoes again and ran out with a wild little laugh, holding up her breasts to the heavy rain and spreading her arms, and running blurred in the rain with the eurhythmic dance movements she had learned so long ago in Dresden. It was a strange pallid figure lifting and falling, bending so the rain beat and glistened on the full haunches, swaying up again and coming belly-forward through the rain, then stooping again so that only the full loins and buttocks were offered in a kind of homage towards him, repeating a wild obeisance. . . .

She was nearly at the wide riding when he came up and flung his naked arm round her soft, naked-wet middle. She gave a shriek and straightened herself and the heap of her soft, chill flesh came up against his body. He pressed it all up against him, madly, the heap of soft, chilled female flesh that became quickly warm as flame, in contact. The rain streamed on them till they smoked. He gathered her lovely, heavy posteriors one in each hand and pressed them in towards him in a frenzy, quivering motionless in the rain. Then suddenly he tipped her up and fell with her on the path, in the roaring silence of the rain, and short and sharp, he took her, short and sharp and finished, like an animal.

"What I don't understand," I said, "is why Mellors speaks to Connie in that ridiculous accent, when to everyone else he talks absolutely normally. After all, we were told at the beginning he used to be an officer. Presumably he didn't spout dialect in the officer's mess."

"It's his way of reminding her of the social difference between them. He's goading her, because she's an aristocrat and he's a self-made man."

We were sitting together on some sacks by the doorway, sharing the picnic I had brought. After we'd reread the passage, Miss G. had decided to see if the rain would ease off a little before dancing in it. Since the cap was no longer working, there was in any case no urgency in continuing with the experiment, and we had retired to the hut to wait.

"That makes him a rather unpleasant person, surely?" I said, passing her a roll.

"Oh, he's a bastard. That's part of Lawrence's intention—she calls him a brute, and he calls her a bitch, and most of the time they don't even like each other very much. But they're drawn together by something that's bigger than either of them, something beyond their conscious control. She doesn't love him, but she can't help being attracted to him."

"So Lawrence was almost writing an anti-love story—"

"Exactly! That's what no one ever understands. He's saying that passion is something quite different from love—it's something brutal, something to be feared, but it's also something we can't ignore. Clifford's in a wheelchair because he's literally emasculated—"

"Hang on. I thought he'd had an accident in the war."

"Well, yes. In the story he had an accident, but the *reason* he had that accident was because Lawrence needed a symbol of the postwar exhaustion of European culture."

"But that's terrible. That's . . . doing horrible things to your characters just so they'll fit your own purposes."

"That's what writers do, Steven. They're not so very different from scientists—they perform nasty experiments on their characters to see what happens."

"But then they make up the results. Not to mention words like 'plasm.'"

She laughed. "I'll never make you like D. H. Lawrence, will I?"

"Actually," I said, "now that you've explained this book, I do quite like it. Or at least I understand it, which is almost the same thing. But that's only because you explained it so well."

We were silent for a moment. It was a curious thing, but when I was talking to Annie the silences were almost as pleasant as the conversations. It was rather extraordinary, to know that even though neither of you was talking out loud, your thoughts were continuing to run along similar lines, so that when after a few minutes she said, "Perhaps he just meant cellular nutrients," I knew that she had returned, as I had, to Lawrence's misunderstanding of the word "plasm."

Outside, the rain was easing. The sun came out, and the two—rain and brilliant sunshine—overlapped briefly, so that it was almost impossible to say which was going to prevail. Suddenly, a spectacular shimmer of colors burst like a firework above the trees, the colors glittering with a soft iridescence against the raindrops.

"Look!" she said. "A refraction spectrum! What a beauty!"

Somehow I thought it completely unsurprising that Miss G. knew the proper term for a rainbow.

"Do you know how to remember the order of colors?" I asked.

"Easy. 'Roy G. Biv.' That's red, orange, yellow—"

"—green, blue, indigo, violet," we finished together.

"Which Pink Floyd got wrong when they designed the cover for *Dark Side of the Moon,*" she added.

"I thought it was only me who'd noticed that!"

She shook her head. "It wasn't an accident, though."

She had taken off the defunct cyber cap so that her hair would dry. Now, as she told me some of the theories circulating on the internet relating to my favorite prog-rock album, she idly put it back on. I was pleased to see that, the circuits having dried out, it was working again—and even more pleased, as well as a little intrigued, to note that it was registering amber, or "receptive," even though we were doing nothing more than chatting.

There was another, longer silence. A rainbow of colors shimmered on her head, the lights flickering from amber up to green and even touching orange before they went back to blue again.

"Penny for your thoughts," I said.

She smiled—a strange wry smile. "Sorry. Secret." She started to get to her feet. Our legs had become entangled, and there was a sudden warm smell of freshly dried denim from her jeans as we unpeeled from each other. "But I've enjoyed this," she said. "It's been one of the nicest afternoons I've had in ages."

"Actually, that isn't quite true. According to the cyber cap, you've definitely had more exciting experiences in the lab."

"Now *that,*" she said, slipping her arm through mine as we walked back through the woods, "is because you are still thinking like D. H. Lawrence."

"How so?"

"Do you ever find yourself wondering . . . if sex doesn't get in the way sometimes?" she said, not answering me directly.

"Frequently. But that book was your suggestion, not mine."

She laughed. "Just because I find the story erotic doesn't mean I want to be like that myself. Anyway, I still think orgasms are a bit overrated."

"Hmm," I said. "Well, given that they're my life's work, I hope not."

I had been right—there was *definitely* a placebo effect. During our picnic Miss G., without realizing it, had been given KXC79, ground up and mixed into a ciabatta roll containing pheasant pâté and crunchy cornichons, and yet she had barely reacted to the stimulation provided by reenacting what was, by her own admission, a favorite work of erotica. And although the crudity of the testing rig meant that I couldn't be sure exactly *how* unaroused she was, I could certainly say that she had been less aroused by D. H. Lawrence's copulating gamekeeper than she had been by a discussion about an incorrect sequence of colors on the cover of a rock album.

So what was the answer? What should I do next?

For the moment, at least, I was stumped.

30.2

Back at the lab, an e-mail was waiting.

To: Steven Fisher
From:RCollins@collins.com
Subject: **Re: KXC79**

Steven,

Congratulations—you've cracked it. I just got off the phone
with Kes: Trock is set to make KXC79 the star of SexDys and of
course I'll do all I can to help.

The paper reads well—I've got a few suggestions if you'd
like them, but the science looks good: remarkable, even. As
for your anomaly, I don't think you need to worry about her
too much. Let's talk about that when we meet—I can swing
through Oxford next week en route for Dublin. What about
dinner—you, me, and your people—a real celebration for the
KXC79 "team"! I'll have my PA set something up.

Best,
Richard

Then there was another e-mail, this time from Kes Riley.

To: Steven Fisher
From: Kes Riley
Subject: **Project Oxford**

Steven,

What's this Richard Collins tells me about a possible problem?

Call me.

K.

30.3

"Kes," I said for the eighteenth time, "she has no acne."

"What about depression?"

From where I was speaking I could see Miss G. going through a complicated set of diagrams with Rhona. "She has one of the most cheerful dispositions of any woman I've ever met."

His voice came back on the line, and I was struck once again by how shrewd Trock's marketing director was.

"Listen, Steve. You tell me she's fine, so of course I'll take your word for it. But you're bothered by something, I can tell. And if you're bothered, I'm bothered. This isn't about the launch. This is about you and me—being open with each other so we can agree between ourselves the best way to play it for Vitalia."

"'Vitalia'?"

"Oh. It turns out Desiree is the name of a potato. Steve, stick to the point—is everything all right for the conference, or isn't it?"

I hesitated. Once again I had the feeling that I was putting everything—my career, my reputation—on the line.

But this time, I also had a sense that I was gambling with something else as well: the feelings, and the future, and, yes, the admiration of a very special young woman.

"Really, it's all fine," I said.

30.4

I had barely put the phone down when Julian Noble strode into the lab. He did not seem very happy.

"Fisher!" he hissed.

"Here I am."

"What in God's name are you playing at?" Behind him, Heather also came into the lab. It seemed to me that she was trying to give the impression that she had nothing to do with this. "Animals!" he snapped.

I looked around. The lab was quiet. Rhona and Annie were hard at work, Susan was oiling the Sybian, and Wulf was using some of our tools to tinker with his stimulator.

"Scientists," I retorted.

"Not here. There!" His bony finger stabbed at the floor. "You have an animal in this building. Of a species banned from scientific research."

With a sinking heart I realized he meant Lucy. "Technically, yes. But—"

"An animal, moreover, which has just urinated on my girlfriend and myself."

I stared at him. "Did you just say—"

"Yes. Urinated," he said firmly.

"—'*girlfriend*'?"

Behind him, Heather was taking a close interest in *Canadian Family Physician*.

"My girlfriend and I"—his smug gesture took in Heather— "were in the basement, when we became aware that there was a *creature* down there. A creature, I might add, doing something of a particularly revolting nature."

"She's a bonobo, Julian. That's what they do. They're like teenage boys. Only with rather less sense of personal decorum." A thought occurred to me. "What were you doing down there?"

"That is absolutely no concern of yours." He looked shifty. "We were seeing where the new labs might go. For some possible new projects."

I glanced at Heather, who was by now immersed in a scholarly article about moose bites.

"It's just that if Lucy thought you were having sex, she would look for a way of joining in," I explained. "It's a kind of parallel play."

He flushed. "I want that animal out of here by nightfall. You will take it to the Department of Veterinary Services immediately and have it humanely put down."

"I will do no such thing."

"Oh, yes, you will."

"I have just got off the phone to Kes Riley," I pointed out. "Shall I call him back and tell him that I am wasting time I haven't got arguing over a monkey?"

I realized that the whole lab team was now watching us, agog. Julian realized it too. With a snarl he turned and walked away.

I called after him, "By the way, Julian, that definitely wasn't urine. I can send you the reference, if you're interested."

30.5

When he had gone, there was a long silence. Heather put *Canadian Family Physician* down.

"I'm not his girlfriend."

Nobody said anything.

"He's taken me out a few times, that's all. He wants to give me a research project of my own."

Wulf, over in the corner, snorted.

"What?" she demanded. But then Susan was laughing too, and Rhona, and even Annie, and then—I couldn't help it—I was joining in as well.

"Oh, shut up, the lot of you," Heather said, marching over to her computer.

31.1

"So this is Lucy."

"It is," I agreed.

"What will you do with her?" Annie offered her a banana through the bars. Lucy took it shyly. She was on her best behavior now, aware that she was in trouble.

"She's safe enough here during the day. But I suppose I'd better take her home with me at night, or Julian might find a way to sneak her away when I'm not around." I sighed. "The trouble is, she gets so bored. I used to take her for walks, but since we brought the KXC79 launch forward I simply haven't had the time."

"Why don't I do it?"

"Really? You wouldn't mind?"

"Of course not—I'm a lab assistant, it's all part of the job. I can take her out every lunchtime, if you like."

31.2

And so walking with Lucy became another of the ways in which Miss G. became a part of our life. Often I accompanied her. The fresh air helped to clear my head, as I continued to puzzle over the last few amendments and additions to the KXC79 paper.

If the truth be told, I was still of two minds about what to do about that. From his e-mail, Richard Collins seemed to think I was worrying too much, and perhaps I was. But, equally, I could not

bear to launch my discovery to the world only to have some glitch
or anomaly gleefully exposed in the academic journals.

It was in the park that I told Miss G. about the forthcoming
dinner with Richard.

"You mean he's read the paper?" she said, clearly excited.

"Oh, yes. And likes it. In fact, he described it as 'remarkable.'"

"Really? Did he comment on the way I brought in that Syrian
golden hamster reference?"[1]

"Not specifically. Though I believe he's got a number of suggestions. I haven't looked at them yet. Why don't you ask him about
it yourself?"

"I could do that? I could actually talk to Richard Collins about
science?"

"Of course. You're one of us now, Annie—a scientist. I'm sure
Richard would be delighted to discuss issues of biochemistry with
you."

31.3

On another occasion, as we sat on the bank of the River Cherwell
watching the tourists attempt to master the art of punting, she said,
"Do you know how to punt, Steven?"

"Oh, yes. That is, I've never actually done it, but from my observations I can see how it's done."

"Come on, then. Let's hire one." She was on her feet before I
could object.

---

[1] K. C. Bradley and R. L. Meisel, "Sexual Behavior Induction of c-Fos in the Nucleus
Accumbens and Amphetamine-Stimulated Locomotor Activity Are Sensitized by Previous Sexual Experience in Female Syrian Hamsters," *Journal of Neuroscience* 21, no. 6,
(2001): 2123–2130.

Five minutes later I found myself stepping into a narrow canoe-like craft, carrying on my shoulder a long and surprisingly heavy steel pole not unlike a piece of scaffolding, while Miss G. untied the rope securing us to the pontoon. Lucy squatted in the bow looking at the water doubtfully.

"The mistake I have noticed many people make," I informed them, "is to fail to allow for the fact that the pole has to be placed to one side of the boat. To go forward in a straight line, one must therefore employ some basic trigonometry."

I pushed off. Unfortunately, the punt had been tied up at a slight angle to the river current, and my initial attempt to propel us into the middle of the stream thus overshot. The boat performed a semicircle, returning us almost to the bank from which we had set off.

"Of course, one must be in the right position to begin with," I conceded. "I'll just straighten us up, and then we'll be on our way."

I pushed off again. The river bottom at that point was rather muddy, and in freeing the pole from the sticky mud I was required to employ a certain amount of force. This, in turn, meant that when the pole suddenly came free our punt moved rather abruptly, sending us crashing into the foliage on the opposite bank.

"Don't be alarmed. I can push off again with my foot, like so—"

"Steven! Quick!"

In the heat of the moment I had somehow made the beginner's gaffe of leaving one foot on shore and another in the boat. At some point, as our craft moved with surprising rapidity back into the center of the river, I had to make a decision as to which I wished to be committed to. Given that I was holding the pole, I realized just in time that it had better be the boat.

"There," I said. "I think you'll find that we are now under way. What is it?"

Miss G. and Lucy had adopted similar postures. But whereas I knew that, in Lucy's case, lying in the floor of the boat, baring her teeth, and pressing her hands under her armpits whilst gasping for breath was a sign of terror, in my other passenger it seemed to indicate mirth.

"I will try to make it a slightly smoother ride from now on," I said stiffly. I judged the angles, dug the pole into the riverbed, and pushed firmly.

The punt described a perfect about-turn and grounded itself on the bank. Miss G. hooted with laughter.

"I see this is amusing you." I was by now going somewhat red in the face. "It's a shame you can't punt yourself."

"But I can," she managed to say. "Rather well, actually."

"Why didn't you say so? In that case, perhaps you would like to take over."

"Certainly not. Watching you is much more fun."

I pushed again, more gently, with the pole, which again stuck in the mud. Determined not to let go of it, I hung on for dear life, becoming for a moment a sort of human halyard—I believe that is the correct nautical term—attaching pole to boat. The obvious disadvantage to this arrangement was that the human body is incapable of elasticating any farther than four or five feet. Only prompt intervention from Miss G., paddling us backwards with one of the seat cushions, prevented me from ending up attached to neither.

"All right. I'll show you the basics," she said, getting to her feet. The punt, which had seemed unsteady enough with just one person standing up in it, wobbled alarmingly. "I'll go behind you— don't worry, you won't fall in—and put your hands in the right place—here and here, that's it. Now relax. Gently raise the pole up—easy—and place it forward, so."

It was rather pleasant to have Miss G. directing my movements like this. Was this, I wondered, why punting existed in Oxford at all—so that young men and women could flirt with each other? It was not an explanation that had occurred to me before.

"Use the pole as a rudder to straighten yourself out. Wait, not so fast. You don't want to be in such a hurry: you've got to use the current, not fight it."

We were now achieving a respectable and satisfying mutual rhythm. At this point, however, the river suddenly became very deep, and in order to keep hold of the pole Miss G. and I had to squat together in unison as we sank it right down into the water. Pressed against each other as we were, her entire body—from soft breasts to firm thighs—was folded against my own, as if we were two Zs. I could not see her, of course, but I could feel her; I smelt her fragrance and her hair was silky against my cheek. I experienced a sudden moment of breathlessness, brought on no doubt by the exertions of my punting.

"I think you've got it now," she said, standing back.

She sat down again on the cushions, and I found to my great satisfaction that I had indeed "got it." In fact, I became so confident that I was soon able to turn my thoughts to how the general technique of punting could be improved. I realized that the whole process of raising the pole hand over hand was wasteful of both time and effort, and that it would be far more efficient simply to alternate different ends of the pole in the water, flipping it over like a giant javelin. After a short while I became so proficient with this revolutionary technique—which I named the Fisher Maneuver— that I was able to perform it one-handed. It was, I have to confess, with a certain degree of satisfaction that I proceeded back down the river towards the boathouse in a swift, straight line, speeding past struggling tourists and undergraduates alike. Unfortunately I had forgotten that this area was crowded with trees, and my pole became entangled in the branches overhead. This caused more merriment for Miss G., but, as I pointed out to her on the way back to the lab, it was not a fault of the Fisher Maneuver per se, only of the environment in which it was applied.

31.4

And then there was the time a couple of days later when, as we sat eating our sandwiches, she pulled something from her bag and said shyly, "Here. This is for you."

It was an old book, a hardback, almost falling apart. I looked at the title. *Collected Poems of W. B Yeats.*

"I don't think I've ever owned a book of poetry," I said, turning it over in my hands.

"It's to say thank you."

I started to leaf through it. There is something about poetry, if I am honest—something about the way it is laid out on the page—that I find rather daunting.

"This one," she said gently. She reached across me and pointed. A curtain of brown hair obscured the text for a moment. "Read it aloud—it'll make more sense that way."

A little reluctantly, I read:

> "When you are old and grey and full of sleep,
> And nodding by the fire, take down this book,
> And slowly read, and dream of the soft look
> Your eyes had once, and of their shadows deep—"

"You don't have to make a face while you're reading it," she commented. "It's poetry, not cough mixture."

"I was trying to look poetic."

"Well, don't. Just speak it like you mean it."

> "How many loved your moments of glad grace,
> And loved your beauty with love false or true,
> But one man loved the pilgrim soul in you,
> And loved the sorrows of your changing face—"

"There," she said. "*Now* you've got it."

"Be quiet, will you? I'm trying to read it, and you keep interrupting.

> "And bending down beside the glowing bars,
> Murmur, a little sadly, how Love fled
> And paced upon the mountains overhead
> And hid his face amid a crowd of stars."

There was a silence. "What does it mean?" I said at last.

"A poem doesn't have to mean anything."

"But it does. You can tell it does—you can *hear* it."

She nodded. "When he wrote that, Yeats had just met the woman he was going to love for the rest of his life. He knew it, but he also knew that she was never going to love him in return. He was a shy, studious poet; she was a revolutionary, a firebrand and freethinker."

"It reads like a dedication."

"Yes. But what he's dedicating to her isn't just a poem, or even a book; it's his life."

"'But one man loved the pilgrim soul in you. . . .' What's a 'pilgrim soul'?"

She shrugged. "No one really knows. No one except him, and possibly her, and perhaps not even them. That's why it's so beautiful. When you hear it, you *think* you know. . . . It makes sense, you can tell it does. But you can't define it. You can't explain it. The words just kind of . . . strike off each other."

"Like a chemical reaction."

She nodded again. "You can analyze everything there is to analyze about that poem—the rhythm, the rhyme scheme, the language. You can compare it with the much older French poem it's based on. You can know every fact of Yeats's own life. But you will never be able to define exactly why those two words—her 'pilgrim soul,' and his recognition of it—are the very essence of his love."

For a long moment I looked the words on the page, and I saw—I *felt*—the truth of it.

But one man loved the pilgrim soul in you.

"Thank you, Annie," I said, closing the book. "Thank you for giving me that."

31.5

Even now, as I sit here, writing these words in the quiet of this big, anonymous hotel—even now I can still feel their force.

But one man loved the pilgrim soul in you.

And I think I do understand now what Yeats meant by that phrase. I think he meant that she was brave, and quick, and a seeker after truth: that her soul was pure, like a pilgrim's, but restless and passionate too, and that her pilgrimage, her search, would take her farther and farther away from him.

I think he meant that to be with her was like being lit up from within.

And I think the sadness, the regret that fills the last two lines, is not the sadness of a love unrequited, or a passion unfulfilled. I think it is the sadness of a man who realizes that, ultimately, his passion is not as pure or as unswerving as the pilgrim's—that being human, his love, unnourished by affection, will eventually wither and die.

Murmur, a little sadly, how love fled.

I know the chemical composition of tears.

But I cannot begin to understand the extraordinary alchemy by which a man can put two simple words together, and make the tears start in another person's eyes, even now.

Even now.

32.1

And I give him a Collected Yeats, and get him to read "When You Are Old" aloud. . .

Did I mention that Steven has the most amazing voice? Dry and sardonic and clever.

When he gets to the words "And loved your beauty with love false or true," he gives me a sideways look that just melts—I was about to write "my heart," but actually it melts something else as well, a little lower down.

But one man loved the pilgrim soul in you.

Or maybe it's just that my heart and my other organs are starting to become one and the same thing.

Something has changed, since I've been at the lab. Something huge.

Because the Steven Fisher who once told me "You're more than useful: you're almost an area of interesting ignorance" is now spending every lunchtime with me, walking Lucy in the park and talking about— oh, everything from the different erogenous zones (he knows the precise location of something called the anterior fornix, which has only just been discovered, whereas Simon didn't even know where my clitoris was) to poetry. Not to mention climate change, Richard Collins's early books, bell ringing, molecular gastronomy, and *Watership Down*.

And although I still can't work out exactly how or why this has happened, or why it's him rather than someone else it's happened with, I'm starting to realize that something rather unprecedented is occurring— viz., I actually seem to fancy someone who I also quite like. And who also, unless I'm very much mistaken, seems—finally!—to quite like me as well.

Which is all so unlikely, and so wonderful, that I decide I don't want to mess it up it by doing anything too quickly.

Or do I?

When it's this wonderful, why wait?

33.1

It wasn't only Annie who was excited about the dinner with Richard Collins. As I shaved beforehand, I glanced at the piece of paper pinned over my mirror.

For every human action, there is a chemical reaction.

For so long, that line—so brilliant and witty and provocative—had seemed like a rallying cry for a revolution. A revolution that was already taking place in universities and research institutions all over the world, led by provocative, brilliant men like Richard.

And now, at last, I was going to play my own part in that. For—finally—I was starting to let myself believe that it was no longer a question of whether KXC79 would happen, but when.

All the same, excited as I was, I could not help comparing that great aphorism of Richard's with the words of Yeats.

But one man loved the pilgrim soul in you.

33.2

Richard had booked a private room in Oxford's best restaurant. From the way the chef came out to greet him, he seemed to be well known there. But then, Richard is well known everywhere.

"Bertrand is a friend," he explained in his soft Irish accent. "We were on *Jonathan Ross* together. And, of course, he's a brilliant chef."

"Does he cook?" Susan asked.

Richard turned his gaze on her. "What?"

"This brilliant chef. I was just wondering whether he will actually be cooking tonight, or whether he will be leaving that to others."

Susan, it seemed to me, was the only one of us not particularly excited to be having dinner with the great man. But—typically—seeing that she was in a sour mood, Richard set himself to charm her.

"Bertrand creates," Richard said, with an easy smile. "He leads. He teaches. That is what brilliant men do: they spread their influence. There's probably a thesis in that somewhere: now that alpha males can no longer impregnate a whole community of women, we seek to scatter a different kind of seed instead. Now, then: let's get that Bollinger open. Tonight we are toasting your success." He looked around at the table. "Can I just say, Steven, I had no idea sex researchers were such a beautiful lot. How have you managed to assemble such a remarkable collection of genes in one place?"

I had to admit, the girls did collectively look rather good that night. They had all made an effort—although that effort had taken different forms: Susan had made an effort to bare as much cleavage as possible, while Rhona was demure in a simple black dress. Heather had gone for a sophisticated jacket-and-trousers combination that must have cost a fortune, while Annie was wearing a pale orange shirt that showed off her dark coloring. It was the first time I'd seen her like that, with earrings and a discreet dusting of makeup. The effect was rather astonishing.

Richard was an excellent host. He held us spellbound—even I, who have read all his books and devoured every word he has ever written. I swear there was barely a word or a thought he uttered that night that was not new to me, and I was as transfixed as any of them.

"For my next book," he said thoughtfully, "I'm looking at

what I call 'geekonomics'—the way that men and women's sexual strategies vary to maximize their chances of success. For example, young men in their teens and early twenties find it very hard to attract women, because the available women are mostly pursuing older, higher-status men. But in your late twenties and early thirties the position is reversed: the same women are not only having to compete for men their own age with a new generation of younger women, they're also increasingly driven to find the person they're going to have children with. Suddenly, men who haven't been able to get a sexual partner for a decade start to look quite attractive."

"That's very clever," Susan said. There was a general murmur of agreement. "So, if that's right, sooner or later even Dr. Fisher should be able to get a shag."

There was an awkward silence. Then Richard Collins politely changed the subject, and the conversation moved on.

33.3

Later on, he and I found ourselves in the men's toilet at the same time.

"Once again, Steven, I have to say congratulations," he said, washing his hands.

"Thank you," I said modestly. "I could never have done it without you."

"Oh, I doubt that. I suspect it's your bevy of beautiful research assistants you should thank." He winked at me in the mirror. "Although that can't be without its problems either, I imagine."

"How do you mean?"

"Oh, come on, man. They're almost fighting over you. That Susan—"

"Oh." I hastened to correct him. "No, she's always like that."

He raised his eyebrows. "Well, she certainly had me fooled." He hit the dryer button. "What are you going to do about your volunteer, by the way? The one who gave you those anomalous results?"

"What do you suggest?"

"Have you looked at the possible formation of enzyme-substrate complexes?"

"Yes. I've eliminated all I could think of."

"Irreversible inhibitors?"

"Not that I can see."

"In that case," he said, clapping me on the shoulder, "it's probably just some random reaction. You know, like a shellfish allergy. The main thing is, she was anorgasmic when she joined the study, and she's orgasmic now. Or, to use the technical term, cured." He shook his head. "I have to tell you, Steven, I envy you. What you've achieved here is quite remarkable."

33.4

"What about love?" someone asked, just as the meal was drawing to a close.

"Love! Now that's a very interesting question. What about love, indeed?" Richard rolled the brandy around in his glass.

"Compared with sex, love is a relatively recent evolutionary phenomenon," he said thoughtfully. "After all, sexual reproduction predates the entire animal kingdom, let alone that tiny offshoot of it which consists of the mammals, or the even smaller twig which we call humanity. We can assume it only came about at all because of our unusual, not to say highly inefficient, method of perpetuating our species: that is, singly, the mother needing to devote several years to each offspring until it is ready to fend for itself in the wild. No other species invests so much time and personal vulnerability in the individual embryo. No other species, therefore, invests so much in each act of sex. No wonder we have allowed ourselves to buy into the comforting—and in evolutionary terms entirely bogus—notion that each human being is in some way sacred."

There was a murmur of agreement around the table.

"Seen from that perspective," the great man went on, "it is clear that love is simply a compensatory strategy—in the case of mother-child love, a way of inducing the female to stick around for as long as the offspring needs her care, and in the case of love between mates, a way of inducing the male to assist her.

"But—and this is surely the more interesting aspect of all this— *it is no longer necessary.* There are no longer saber-toothed tigers prowling around outside the cave, waiting for us to turn our backs for an instant so they can devour our young. We can assume that like the human tail, then, which gradually shrank, once it was no longer needed, into a vestigial remnant of itself; or the appendix; or the wing feathers of the ostrich, love, being no longer an evolution-ary advantage, slowly, slowly is on the decline."

He took a sip from his glass. "It is no longer the embryo whose parents have pair-bonded who survives; therefore, generation by generation, the ability—the *necessity*—for pair-bonding will be bred out of us, and in a million years or so people will look back on our brief obsession with it and marvel, just as we marvel at the furry bodies of the Neanderthals or the diminutive stature of the Cro-Magnons. Sex, of course, will suffer no such decline, sexual re-production being, one imagines, the sole prerequisite for evolution to take place at all."

Richard raised his glass. "To the triumph of evolution, and the death of love. Or should I say, the death of pair-bonding."

We all echoed his toast.

"Isn't it possible, though," somebody asked, "that love will survive as an anomaly—like goose bumps, or male nipples, or blushing?"

"Hmm," Richard said. "Well, I suppose it's possible. But we must always be wary of sentiment in our approach to science. We leave that to the physicists, hmm?"—an aperçu which, of course, caused us all much merriment.

34.1

After the dinner Annie and I walked through the medieval quads of the Bodleian, up the High, and thence to Magdalen Bridge, talking. Richard's words were still ringing in my ears. *What you've achieved here is quite remarkable.* From a scientist of his stature that was high praise indeed.

"I'm taking you out of your way," Annie said at one point.

I shook my head. "Frankly, I doubt I'll be able to sleep. Besides, I want to know whether you picked up on his refutation of Bohr. . . ."

We were so deep in discussion that we had reached the Iffley Road almost before we realized it. Now at last we fell silent, our shoulders bumping companionably as we walked.

"Steven?" she said hesitantly.

"Yes?"

"I'm cured now, aren't I?"

"The tests certainly show that you're fully orgasmic, yes."

"But that's just in the lab. I'm wondering . . . That is, I won't know if everything's *really* working all right until I've had sex again, will I? With an actual person, I mean."

I glanced at her as we passed under a streetlight, and even in the sodium-yellow glow she seemed to me to have turned a little pink.[1]

---

[1] Technically, I suppose, she had turned orange, since the pink of her cheeks would have combined with the yellow glow of the streetlights. So-called sodium lights—actually a mixture of sodium, neon, and argon gases, held under vacuum in borosilicate

"It's like riding a horse, isn't it," she added. "Got to get back in the saddle."

"So they say."

"And when it happens . . . I want to make sure it's with someone I really like."

"Of course."

There was a pause.

"I don't do this," she said with a strange little laugh. "I just don't ever do this. I still can't quite believe I'm doing it now."

"Doing what?"

We had reached the corner of her street by now. We stopped. She seemed to be struggling to say something.

"What would you say, Steven, if—oh, God—if, purely theoretically, I were to ask you to go to bed with me?"

"I'd say you mean hypothetically, not theoretically," I said automatically.

"Sorry—hypothetically. Except that it isn't. Hypothetical, I mean." She swallowed. "Steven. This person I sleep with. I want it to be you."

34.2

"I was thinking of asking you in for coffee," she said with a nervous laugh. "And then I thought, He'll think I actually mean a bitter-tasting hot beverage served with milk. So I decided—just ask him. That's science, isn't it—speak the truth."

"Annie," I said wonderingly. "*You* want to have sex with *me*?"

"God, yes. Please?"

---

pipes—have a very narrow color spectrum which makes almost anything viewed by their light seem monochromatic, even Miss G.'s cheeks.

34.3

I could hardly believe it. Annie. The most beautiful, brilliant, de-lightful person whose company I had ever shared. She wanted to have sex with me.

"But . . . ," I said. "Don't you see? It's completely out of the question."

The light seemed to drain from her eyes.

34.4

"You're a research subject," I said gently. "Don't you know what that means?"

She shook her head.

"Sexual relationships with research subjects—in any area of science it's frowned on, but in this field in particular it's completely unthinkable. It would undermine the whole KXC79 project. And not just the project: I'd never be allowed to work in this field again. I would probably be banned from research forever."

"Oh," she said slowly. "I hadn't realized."

"It's not quite as bad as fiddling your results, but it comes a pretty close second. No one would believe in the integrity of a single claim I had made."

It seemed to me that she flinched. "But why would anyone have to know?"

"*We* would know. And sooner or later someone would find out. It would be a time bomb waiting to go off under the project. I'm sorry, Annie. It's just impossible."

"I thought . . . I thought . . ." Even in the borosilicate light her face looked ashen. "I thought you liked me."

For a moment I too hesitated. But my duty now was very clear.

I shook my head firmly. "If on occasion I have tried to establish a friendly rapport with you, it was only ever for professional reasons. My own feelings had nothing to do with it."

34.5

"Now I'm really embarrassed."

"Don't be. You weren't aware of our ethics—"

"Your *what*?"

"I mean, you weren't aware of how we scientists operate—"

"Oh, it's *we* scientists now, is it? Because obviously I'm too much of an arts slut to be one of those." She stared at me. "I can't believe I just humiliated myself like that. What was I *thinking*?"

"Annie, wait!"

She turned and ran up the steps to her door. As she fumbled with her key I thought I caught a sob.

34.6

I so nearly went after her.

As Richard Collins never tires of pointing out, every one of us alive on the planet today is the product of a million successful copulations. We are the lucky ones, the few who have made it despite the odds, and in our genes the urge to repeat our ancestors' successes pulses continually, like a second beating heart.

For a long moment I stared at her house. She hadn't turned any lights on. I guessed she was still sitting in the hall, in the dark, crying.

I took a step towards the door.

But in my head I could hear the snide footnotes of future authors, couched in the diplomatic language of science but devastating nevertheless: *"Fisher, whose project was terminated after accusations of inappropriate relationships with test subjects, was a proponent of the now-obsolete submolecular approach. . . ." "A failed attempt to synthesize oxytocin from an enzyme called KCX79 ended in allegations, subsequently upheld, of sexual misconduct. . . ." "Fisher's theories, which are generally considered to be on the fringe of scientific thinking, were thoroughly discredited after the KXC79 scandal. . . ."* And it would not just be me: all those I most admired would be caught in the crossfire: *"Richard Collins suffered a major dent to his reputation after being drawn into the KXC79 debacle. . . ."*

It was completely impossible.

I turned and walked away.

34.7

When I got home I discovered that Lucy, bored and lonely on her own, had wrecked my flat. She had tossed coffee mugs through a window, smashing it; ripped the stuffing out of the sofa; smashed the legs off the dining chairs, and thrown food on the kitchen floor. Then she had squeezed herself out of the broken window and escaped. There was blood on the broken glass, like the smear of red on a slide, where she'd cut herself doing it.

Oh, dear.

How am I going to write this bit?

Everything seems to have got messed up.

So I finally decided to sleep with Steven.

It was kicked off by something Susan said. I don't think Steven real-izes that whenever he leaves the lab someone puts a kettle on and all us girls get together over peppermint tea to talk about boys. Rhona's having a thing with Wulf—How's that going? We get the blow-by-blow account. (Synopsis: It's going pretty well but she's not sure he's quite grown-up enough for a serious, long-term relationship. Also, he tends to be a bit quick in bed.) Heather—beautiful, poised, clever Heather—is being courted by Julian Noble, the Professor. It's been a big secret—seems everyone was worried about Steven finding out. (I'm picking up a little radar-bleep that maybe Heather and Steven once almost had something . . . Interesting.) Heather doesn't exactly reciprocate Julian's feelings, but, equally, it's clear she's very ambitious.

"The thing is," she says to me, "science is still an incredibly sex-ist field. You've no idea how difficult it is to get your foot on that first rung."

And then there's Susan. One time, when we're alone, I ask her if she's seeing anyone.

"I haven't got a boyfriend, if that's what you mean," she says.

"Boyfriend, partner . . . ," I say casually.

"Ah." She nods. "I was wondering if you'd realized."

We look over at where Heather is working on her computer. Beautiful, sphinxlike Heather.

"I know pretty much everything there is to know about female sexuality," Susan says softly. "And at the end of the day it doesn't matter a hoot. All that matters is whether the person you want to go to bed with wants to go to bed with you." She sighs. "What about you, Annie? Found yourself a new man yet?"

I shake my head. "No time."

"Take my advice. Don't hang around here. Get out there and find the real thing. Or before you know where you are you'll have become crazy and bitter. Like us."

"You're not crazy."

"Believe me," she says, "you don't know the half of it. You really, really don't know the half of it." And she gazes over at Heather again.

Hmm.

So, anyway, that remark of Susan's gets me wondering who I *do* want to sleep with.

And I think, Well, why not?

And that, in a nutshell, is the sum total of my logic. Oh, I dress it up with all sorts of fancy justifications and postrationalizations (like: I did fib to him about my results, before, so if I sleep with him we'll be quits) but, basically, once I let myself think about the actual possibility of going to bed with Steven Fisher, I just feel this enormous surging excitement and I know for sure it's absolutely the right thing to do.

And, no, for once I don't think the KXC79 has anything to do with it.

So, if I was going to make a pass at Steven, how exactly did I end up sleeping with Richard Collins instead?

You may well ask.

•   •   •

Dinner with Richard was amazing. I mean, the man is brilliant, and he speaks beautifully, with a delicious soft Irish accent. Even when he's talking to an audience of just six people, it's like he's constructing these perfect, podium-quality paragraphs in his head. This is the only man I've had dinner with whose conversation contains *semicolons*. And even if he doesn't appear to have picked up on the sheer brilliance of the golden hamster reference I added to the KXC79 paper, he's full of praise for the project and for Steven, and we're all floating on air.

Apart from Susan, that is, who's in some kind of grump. In fact, I've noticed recently that the better the KXC79 launch goes, the grumpier she gets. Odd.

Anyway, after dinner I let Steven walk me home, and then I make my play. Subtly, naturally.

And then, when he doesn't respond, rather less subtly.

Eventually I just come right out with it. And he looks puzzled—he actually looks confused.

"You mean you want to sleep with me?"

"YES, PLEASE," I almost shout at him.

"But it's completely out of the question," he announces, as if this point were so obvious that only a fluffy moron like me wouldn't have spotted it.

You see, it turns out that scientists have principles about this kind of thing. Ethics, even. Which makes me feel even more humiliated.

I run inside and for a long time I just sit on the stairs in a crumpled heap.

According to Steven, the chemical composition of tears means they rid your body of toxins and stress hormones. In other words, crying really does make you feel better.

Doesn't work this time.

I then spend a pretty-much-sleepless night. During which I come to two conclusions:

    a. At least it was Steven I asked. Somehow I know he isn't going
       to go shouting this around.
    b. This is a test.

By which I mean, a test of whether I'm really a scientist. Am I going to
let my emotions get in the way, or am I going to get on with my job?
    So I grit my teeth and turn up at the lab as usual.
    To my surprise, Steven doesn't. Not like him at all. But then some-
one says he's had to take Lucy to a vet.
    So I start work and it's tough. It's really tough. Without Steven there
and with this whole thing hanging over me, it just feels all black and
depressing. To make matters worse, everyone else is in a bad mood too.
I don't know what's up with Heather—something to do with Julian, I
suppose. Last I heard he'd discovered Viagra, which can only be bad
news. Rhona and Wulf have had some kind of row, so they aren't speaking either. And Susan's just constantly in a bad mood.
    What with one thing and another it's a huge relief when it's lunch-
time and I can get out of there. I grab some reading matter and hurry
down the stairs with my head down, which means I don't see Richard
Collins until I've literally bumped into him.
    "Hello," he says, picking my books up off the floor for me. "Good
Lord—*A-Level Crystallography*. Haven't seen that for a while."
    I mumble something about giving myself a refresher course.
    "Don't bother," he says lightly. "Come and have some lunch with
me instead. I reread the KXC79 paper last night and there are a few
things we need to talk about. I was impressed by the way you brought
in that Syrian golden hamster reference—that *was* you, wasn't it?—but
there are a couple of other places where it could use the same sort of
sharpening up."
    Well, I'm hardly going to say no, am I?
    Outside, his car's waiting to whisk us back to the Randolph.

Normally I would get a bit irate about someone using a car to drive less than half a mile, but today is different. For one thing I just have to accept that this is his world and it's different from mine, and for another I'm so beautifully cocooned in the back there that for the first time all day I manage to relax.

At the hotel there's a Japanese TV crew waiting to catch a quick interview with him about his new book. He talks about *Geekanomics* briefly, with the Japanese presenter translating his remarks for the viewers, and then we go for lunch.

"Hope you don't mind," he says. "I've ordered it upstairs—the dining room's so public, we wouldn't be able to talk without being bothered by people wanting me to sign stuff."

"Sounds perfect," I say.

"Upstairs," of course, being the Presidential Suite, where he's staying. It's like being inside a very padded church, with High Gothic windows and deep bloodred carpets. The food arrives on a series of covered silver trolleys, wheeled by white-jacketed flunkys. Lobster, caviar, monkfish skewers, scallops, freshly made mayonnaise . . . Silver finger bowls full of cool water and slices of lemon, to rinse our fingers in. A stack of white linen towels to dry them with. Richard's voice—his brilliant, soft, hypnotic voice . . . He asks me about the project, and how I came to be involved, and I end up telling him rather more than I meant to. Heavily edited, naturally, but still.

When I get to the bit about not actually having a science degree he frowns. "But that's fantastic."

"It is?" I say doubtfully. "I assumed it might be a bit of a drawback."

He shakes his head impatiently. "No—I mean, you're just the sort of person we've been looking for."

It turns out he's on a committee that finds people with interdisciplinary skills and sends them to Harvard on a scholarship to study . . . well, whatever they like, really, so long as it's science-based.

"We're not talking scholarships in the piddling English sense here," he adds. "These are worth fifty thousand dollars a year."

Oh, my God.

"The only drawback, I'm afraid, is that you'd be under my personal supervision," he says with a disarming smile. "It's a competitive application, but with your background you'd be a shoo-in. Bristol, Oxford, coauthorship of the KXC79 paper—they'd be mad to turn you down." His smile broadens. "Well, when I say they, I mean we. In fact, I probably mean I. Since the endowment is technically known as the Richard Collins Scholarship, I hope I have *some* influence. Tell me about the golden hamster thing again?"

And I am not so naive that I don't know how this is going to play out. We're in the sitting room of his suite, but the double doors are open to the other room and the whole time we're having lunch I can see, over his shoulder, a big double bed, spread with crisp white linen like an altar. At some point, either directly or indirectly, Richard Collins is going to make a pass at me. Probably—since he is a charming and cultured man—in a polite, humorous way that makes it clear his regard for me will be entirely undiminished if I say no.

Which, of course, I am absolutely going to. In a polite, humorous way which makes it clear that I am flattered rather than offended to have been asked.

In other words, all very grown-up.

It's difficult, though. Because Richard Collins is not only charming and cultured, he is also the second most brilliant man I have ever met. And deep inside my cells a million years' worth of evolutionary imperatives are waking up in their cosy little burrows and shouting *Good sperm, Annie! Good sperm!* in voices that sound exactly like my mother's.

And then there's another little voice somewhere inside my head muttering: *Oh, just get on with it. You're pretty sure you're cured now, so let's just prove it and move on. That way, when you do meet someone you care about, it won't be an issue.*

And, as Simon so sweetly put it, I *do* collect clever men.

But even all that might not have been enough to persuade me, except that Richard Collins starts talking about Steven.

"God, that man is clever," he says, shaking his head. "The best postgrad I ever had. There are so few people I can have a conversation with as an equal. Steven's one of them. When he was working on hiccups—some of the discussions we used to have! Brilliant, brilliant stuff!"

He goes on, but I'm not listening by then. I'm thinking about Steven, and last night, and how it all went wrong. And I feel another stab of that complete, bewildering misery.

"Are you all right?" he says, glancing at me.

"Oh—fine."

And I think: If it can't be Steven I sleep with, who *is* it going to be?

So that when Richard eventually looks at me in a way that means the time has come, and says quietly, "Brandy? Unless, of course, you've got to rush back," I shrug and say, "Why not?"

Most small-animal vets refuse to stitch primates—it's beyond their usual expertise. So when I eventually found Lucy, bleeding and bedraggled, sitting in a tree, I had to spend hours on the phone finding someone who'd take a look at her. What with one thing and another, it was a day and a half before I got back to the lab.

What I found there perplexed me. Everybody seemed to be in the foulest of tempers. I couldn't understand it. We were now only a week away from SexDys '08, the moment when our little team would be taking center stage to lap up the applause of the whole scientific community, yet we were all at each other's throat.

Wulf and Rhona weren't talking. At least in that instance, I was able to find out what the problem was.

"It's the usual thing," Wulf said gloomily. "Evolution."

"You're arguing with Rhona about *evolution*?"

"Not *about* evolution, *because of* evolution. Women in our distant past invested more risk in sex than men did, having to look after babies and so on, so obviously evolution favored women who were picky about their partners. Being selective is literally second nature to them. But, equally, once they've found a partner they're happy with, they want to settle down. Or, as Rhona puts it, 'take this relationship to the next level.'"

"Whereas you want to . . . not settle down?"

He shrugged. "Men are different. Once we've found a partner we're happy with, we start looking for the next one. Job done: next job. Look, don't get me wrong. I adore Rhona. I'm just not sure I love her. Not like that, anyway. Women want commitment; men want freedom. It's hardwired into our biology. The difference is good for the species, but that doesn't help when your girlfriend's refusing to have sex with you because she's sulking."

Heather was upset because she was having to dodge Julian Noble. It was rather pathetic, actually—little cards and notes kept turning up in the internal mail, and a big bunch of flowers even arrived by courier. She threw them straight in the bin.

Susan was miserable because . . . Actually, I couldn't work out why Susan was miserable. Uncharacteristically, she seemed to be fretting about KXC79.

"Are you completely sure you're ready to launch this treatment?" she asked me several times. "Why not postpone for a year or so?"

"Susan, relax," I said at last. "Everyone is happy with the paper. Trock likes it. Richard Collins likes it. It's already being peer-reviewed for the *BMJ*."

There was a long silence. Then she said viciously, "I'm surprised Richard Collins has even read it. Given that he spent most of his time in Oxford screwing Annie."

36.2

For a moment I think I can't have heard her right. "What do you mean?"

"Oh, didn't you know?" she says grumpily. "I thought you knew everything." And with that she stomps off.

36.3

I can't believe it at first. Annie and Richard? It's impossible.

But then I look over at Annie. She's been avoiding me since the dinner, but now she glances up from her computer and I catch her eye.

In that moment I see that it's true. And something inside me—something that's been waiting there patiently, quiet but alive, for, oh, at least the last two million years—turns its head up to the sky and howls.

36.4

Eventually she goes into the testing room to set up the VPP and I follow her. I pretend to be rerouting the cabling for the biothesiometer, but I'm not.

"How was Richard?" I say curtly.

"What do you mean?"

"I gather you saw him again before he left."

"Oh. He was well, yes."

"What did you talk about?"

"He"—she hesitates—"he's suggested I might go to Harvard."

"Harvard!"

"Yes."

"'Ha-ha Harvard.'"

"Apparently there's some sort of scholarship."

"Well, you certainly qualify."

"What's that supposed to mean?"

"Didn't you know? Every single one of the Richard Collins

Scholarships is held by an attractive young woman. I believe over there they're known as Dick's Chicks."

"That's ridiculous."

"So it's not true you slept with him?"

There is a long, angry silence. "That is absolutely no concern of yours."

"Evidently not." I toss the biothesiometer leads into a corner. "But you did."

She turns on me then, her expression suddenly furious. "And why shouldn't I sleep with him, Steven? Isn't that meant to be what this is all about?" Her gesture takes in the testing room, the lab, and most of the rest of Oxford as well. "That's what you do here, isn't it? You take women who are completely happy not having sex and you stuff us full of your little pills and pronounce us cured. By which you mean, ready to go out and fulfill our biological function—or at least our function as far as men are concerned. You call yourself a scientist, but actually you're just doing nature's dirty work." By now she's shouting. "What have you ever created to make the world a better place? Nothing. You're just . . . You're just evolution's *pimp*."

For a long minute we stare at each other—me, stunned; Annie, defiant.

"You are quite correct," I say stiffly. "The question was inappropriate, and the answer none of my business. Please accept my apologies."

36.5

That afternoon, Miss G. was scheduled to perform a standard series of tests. Under the circumstances I deemed it inappropriate to
attend.

According to the notes I pulled up later, she reported a satisfactory orgasm and the stimulation program was terminated after
twelve minutes.

She was indeed, as Richard Collins had put it, cured.

37.1

I am a scientist.

Sometimes it is easier to be detached and rational than it is at other times.

Sometimes, in fact, it is very hard indeed.

37.2

There was still a lot to be done before SexDys. I threw myself into it. For the next few days I worked eighteen, twenty hours at a stretch. I slept in the lab. I blotted out my misery with the sedative of functional activity.

Did lack of sleep warp my judgment? Was the pressure of work a factor in what happened next?

Or was it something else entirely—something for which science has no name?

37.3

The myth that women are less promiscuous than men is, I need hardly say, just that—a myth. Over the last thousand years or so there have been periods when, for cultural reasons, men have tried to deny this truth. But biochemistry, as ever, soon supplies the proof. For example, there is the fact that the last portion of a man's seminal fluid actually contains a spermicide: it kills a certain proportion of the man's own sperm, but given the abundance of sperm produced, this is a price well worth paying for the opportunity to kill the most motile, active sperm of the man who comes immediately after you. Mechanisms like this one attest to the fact that while in our evolutionary past women may have been more choosy than men, having chosen a high-status man, they happily fall into bed with him at a drop of a hat, or indeed any more intimate item of apparel.

Even so, I was somewhat surprised that Miss G. had progressed so quickly and apparently with so little compunction from inviting one man—that is to say, me—to share her bed, to having brutish, recreational sex with a different partner altogether.

Was it just a coincidence? Or could it be—somehow—something to do with KXC79?

37.4

I read through the test data again. And again. Something was nagging at me. Something I couldn't quite put my finger on.

I kept hearing Annie snap, *"You're just evolution's pimp."*

I heard Susan saying, *"Maybe there's something you haven't thought of."*

I heard Annie's voice, as she and I walked back to her house after the dinner with Richard. *"I don't do this."* A strange little laugh. *"I just don't ever do this. I still can't quite believe I'm doing it now."*

And then: *"Why shouldn't I sleep with him?"*

Last of all, I heard Kes Riley's shrewd tones.

"No side effects? Are you sure?"

And I realized, with a dawning sense of horror, that there was something wrong—terribly, terrifyingly wrong—with the KXC79 project.

I grabbed my mobile.

"Wulf," I said, "we have a side effect."

I didn't have to tell him how bad this was.

"What is it?" he said at last. "Acne?"

"Worse. Much worse. It's *behavioral*. I think KXC79 is making women have sex with men they don't really want to have sex with."

He whistled. "But that means—"

"Exactly. An emotional response."

Emotional side effects are terrifying for us because they're so nebulous. If your headache pill causes acne, you can potentially do something about it. But if your acne cream causes depression—as it has been suggested, some acne creams do—then, given to the general population, it is going to be implicated in suicides, mental breakdowns, relationship problems, college drop-out rates . . . and, ultimately, huge and expensive class-action lawsuits.

Nobody wants a pill that makes women have sex indiscriminately. That is not what this project is about—far from it. We are trying to restore a normal function, not create an abnormal one. Imagine, for example, a treatment for FSD that became associated with rising rates of sexually transmitted diseases or divorce. No government would dream of licensing such a treatment. No pharmaceutical company would go near it.

"Are you sure?" Wulf said at last.

"Not yet. What should we do?"

"Stick to the science. Whatever happens, always stick to the science. Don't do anything hasty."

He was right. At this moment of all moments, I needed to think rationally.

I had my hypothesis. What I needed to do now was to test it. And the only way to do that—I immediately realized—was via the ultimate form of experiment: a randomized double-blind comparative trial.

39.1

That the placebo effect can distort a scientific study is well known, but what is less widely understood is that there are a number of other things that can also skew our results—what scientists call confounding factors.

For a start, there's "selection bias." In a proper study you need, as well as your treatment group, a control group who get a placebo instead. But it's been shown that if the researchers themselves decide which subjects receive the placebo and which the real treatment, they unconsciously steer the "best" patients into the treatment group. The only fair way to assign subjects is by flipping a coin—in other words, via a "randomized" selection process.

Then there's "observer bias." Even a scientist, when giving a treatment, may see improvements where in fact there aren't any. So the person running the test must be "blinded"—in other words, he mustn't know, himself, which subjects are receiving the placebo and which the real treatment. And to be completely sure of impartiality, he should continue to be blinded until after he has assessed the results as well.

If you follow these safeguards, you end up with what is known as a double-blind randomized trial. Such trials are routinely carried out before a drug is licensed, often with a large cross-section of the population, at a cost of millions of pounds.

I couldn't carry out a proper randomized double-blind trial of KXC79, but I could perform one on a smaller scale—a very small scale, in fact, with a sample of just two subjects.

I am referring, of course, to Miss G. and my colleague, Dr. Susan Minstock.

39.2

Believe me, I did not take this step lightly. There are serious ethical concerns in giving any drug to someone without his or her consent. But I reasoned that my co-workers, as scientists, would certainly have consented if I *had* asked them. The only reason I did not was that knowing they were test subjects could have affected the results.

The experiment I was embarking on was a little unorthodox, but it was completely scientific.

39.3

First I took care of my own observer bias by "blinding" myself.

I made up a set of dummy pills, by all appearances identical to the real thing. Then I took some real KXC79 pills from the locked fridge where they were kept. I spun the two sets of pills round and round in the rack until I had no idea which was which. One lot went into a pink pill bottle, the other into a blue one.

To find out which pills contained the active ingredient, even I would have to wait until I carried out a chemical analysis, after my experiments were complete.

40.1

I wasn't sure how Annie was going to be at her next testing session. Would there be any awkwardness between us after that argument?

But in fact she seemed almost determinedly cheerful. "Hello, Dr. Fisher," she said politely. "I haven't seen you for a few days."

"No, I have been somewhat busy." I said. "With my paper for the forthcoming Sexual Dysfunction conference, which is now only five days away. Unlike some others, I have had no time for socializing." I paused. "And how are you feeling today, Miss G.?"

"I feel *fine,* thank you."

"Excellent."

While Susan took her off to the testing room, I put on a CD—Jean Michel Jarre's *Equinoxe,* if my memory serves me right. Then I prepared the instruments to record.

Miss G. performed the standard and by now familiar series of tests. However, I couldn't help but notice that, although she reported her orgasm to be a good one—"Absolutely fantastic, thank you. I'm so glad I'm orgasmic. God, I could happily do that all day"—the machines told a different story. The VPP barely registered a blip, while muscular contractions were a puny $\pm 2\ \mu V$: hardly any more powerful than in a tightly clenched jaw.

40.2

When everyone else had gone home, I called Susan into the control room and asked her to look over the data with me.

"I'm really starting to wonder if there might be an issue of false reporting here," my colleague commented as we worked through the figures. "I could have sworn she was anorgasmic earlier."

"The data certainly suggest that she wasn't getting much out of it," I agreed. "But it's hard to say for sure. Perhaps there's an emotional problem we haven't accounted for?"

Susan frowned. "There was nothing in her Minnesota."

"The machines, then? Could we simply be reading too much into these numbers?"

"You mean, she might now be having orgasms but the machines aren't picking them up?" she said doubtfully.

"Exactly. Perhaps we calibrated the instruments wrongly in the first place."

"But the only way of double-checking—"

"Would be for you to go into the testing room and show us what an orgasm *actually* reads as. Yes, that had occurred to me, too."

Susan stared at me. "What?"

"Before we determine that Miss G. is lying, we need to be absolutely sure we know how a genuine orgasm presents," I explained. "With all these new instruments, an accurate recalibration is the only answer."

Susan was giving me a look that I found slightly unnerving. "And you think *I* should do it?"

"Well, it doesn't have to be you, of course. But it needs to be someone we can trust not to false-report. And it can hardly be me. Of course, if you're embarrassed . . ."

"I'm not embarrassed, Steve," she said slowly. "After all, it's nothing I haven't asked our subjects to do. I'm just wondering why you're asking me and not, say, Rhona."

"Rhona's not around." I busied myself with some charts.

"No, she isn't. We just happen to be having this conversation at quite a private moment." Susan pointed to the monitors. "Sure you can run all these without me?"

"Pretty sure. You might need to take it slowly."

"Don't worry. I won't rush you." There was a wry note in her voice I hadn't heard before.

"Right, then. If you'd just like to—"

"I think I know the drill, thank you."

She went over to the CD player and put on a disc.

> *"I want a man with a slow hand*
> *I want a lover with an easy touch*
> *I want somebody who will spend some time*
> *Not come and go in a heated rush. . . ."*

"Slow Hand," by the Pointer Sisters. Her favorite.

In the testing room a video monitor flickered into life. Susan typed a command on her keyboard, and a faint whirring sound cut through the music.

"I'll control those manually," she said. "Unless you'd rather do it from in here, of course."

Again there was that faint wry note in her voice. She sounded almost *mischievous*. I frowned. "Manual should be fine."

"Instruments ready?"

"GSA, Startle, biothesiometer, EMG. All ready to go."

40.3

Susan went into the testing room and I saw, on the thermograph, her head settle itself into position. On the Startle monitor the image of her eye, magnified a hundred times, filled the screen. Was it my imagination, or did the eyelid close over the pupil, slowly and deliberately, almost like a wink?

"The things we do for science, eh?" she murmured. The whirring noise intensified.

Susan grunted—a hard, guttural grunt, like a tennis player trying to pull off a particularly difficult backhand. A few seconds later, as if the ball had been unexpectedly returned by her opponent, she grunted again.

"Nngh. Nngh."

Her opponent must have sneaked the ball in behind her forehand, because she added a sudden howl of protest to the umpire: "Nnnnah!"

This pattern continued for several minutes. Backhand grunt, forehand grunt, backhand grunt, line call. After that, the tennis player was joined on court by a shot-putter.

"Nerrr," Susan groaned. "Nngh—nngh—nngh—NERRR."

On the music system, "Slow Hand" came to an end after only three minutes fifty-one seconds—ironically, it is one of the Pointer Sisters' briefest numbers—and was replaced by "He's So Shy." Evidently we were listening to one of my colleague's compilation discs. I checked the thermograph. A deep flush of heat had given Susan a bright yellow neck and the eyes of a panda.

"HOOOO!" she yelled. The stylus of the GSA recorder quivered, jiggled, hesitated—then drew a textbook orgasm pattern, a series of spires and steeples at intervals of exactly 0.8 seconds. It was, I thought, not unlike the skyline of Oxford—you could make

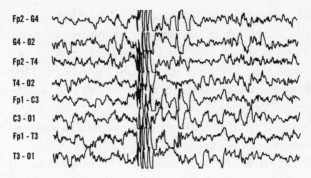

Figure 20: Instrument calibration test (excerpt).

out Tom Tower, and Carfax, and the steeple of St. Giles, and if you half-closed your eyes and squinted a bit, that final aftershock was quite like the Sheldonian Theatre (figure 20).

"Thank you, Susan," I said into the microphone. "That certainly seems satisfactory."

"Strike one," her voice muttered, oddly far away.

"Susan?"

I watched with a terrible fascination as the stylus fell back towards the bottom of the screen, bounced limply a few times, and began another arduous ascent.

"Nngh—nngh—nngh," grunted the tennis player.

"Nerr—nerr—nerr," strained the shot-putter.

There now seemed to be a third participant, making a high-pitched panting sound like someone who has just popped a very hot potato in her mouth. "Hor—hor—hor—"

"Susan?" I said again. No answer.

On the thermograph, vertical green streaks showed where sweat was trickling down her forehead. The stylus of the GSA flew up, stayed there for a long, paralyzed moment as if stuck, and then crashed back down to the baseline.

"Strike two," her voice gasped, still oddly distant.

Finally. I reached out to switch the monitors off "Record," but a loud buzzing sound, as if the lab had been invaded by a swarm of bees, told me that Susan, far from being done, had marshalled reinforcements. On the sound track, "He's So Shy" yielded to the 1977 classic "Vibetime."

I glanced at the clock. I had not imagined that this stage of the experiment would take quite so long.

On the camera, I finally saw why she wasn't answering: her headphones had slipped down and were now around her neck. I would just have to wait. I sighed, then reached for some pencils that needed sharpening.

After an encore of "I Want Fireworks," the Pointer Sisters had given up and gone home. In their place came "The Great Gig in the Sky," the final track of side one of Pink Floyd's *Dark Side of the Moon.* Susan had evidently misinterpreted the free-form vocals as being redolent of the sound of a female orgasm—a mistake that a lot of people make.[1][2][3][4][5] But at least I now had something interesting to listen to.

"Whoa-a, whoa-a, wah, whoa," sang Clare Torry. With a jerk of my head I realized that my attention had been wandering. But in fact, when I checked the readouts, nothing much had changed.

"Ng, ng, ng," panted Susan. "Oh-wo-wo-wo, whoa, whey," soothed the sound track. "ARRGH," sang Susan. "AAAARRGGH." At what point, I wondered, should I worry about hyperventilation?

On the GSA, sharp, jagged spikes of activity stabbed suddenly upwards. "Owww," Susan said. "Strike three!"

I looked at my watch. She had been in there for nearly twenty

---

[1] "The Great Gig in the Sky" is about death. In rehearsal, the song was known as "The Religion Song," and in live performances it was listed as "Mortality Sequence." As if this wasn't clear enough, the song also features two spoken sections. The first,

at 0:38—"And I am not frightened of dying. Any time will do"—was taken from an interview with Gerry O'Driscoll, the Irish doorman at Abbey Road Studios, where the song was recorded. The second, at 3:33—"I never said I was frightened of dying"—was a snippet of conversation with Clare Torry, a freelance session singer who was called out of the blue and asked if she could contribute some vocals to the track. For this she was paid £30—it was a Sunday, so she charged double her usual amount.

[2] One thing I have always found puzzling, though, is why the cover art for *Dark Side of the Moon* contains basic scientific errors. At first glance, it is a depiction of Isaac Newton's famous experiment which demonstrates that light is made up of many different wavelengths. But it actually contains a number of elementary errors—such as, on the back cover, showing the refracted colors of the rainbow recombining to make white light! In fact, that is simply not possible, as Newton himself demonstrated in 1670.

[3] Oh, and another thing—there is no "dark side of the moon." A "dark side" of any world is defined as a side that faces permanently away from the sun. One side of the moon does indeed face permanently away from the earth, but not from the sun, and every part of the moon gets both day and night in two-week alternations. The side of the moon that is turned away from the earth is the *far* side, not the dark side. So *DSOTM* should really have been called *FSOTM*.

[4] It occurs to me that I am probably now disregarding Kes Riley's advice to keep the footnotes in my papers to a minimum. Apparently there is some equation which correlates the number of footnotes inserted in the text to the number of readers who throw that text aside. And I believe it was Noël Coward who said, "Having to read a footnote resembles having to go downstairs to answer the door while in the midst of making love." But this is a very poor analogy. For one thing, you do not have to leave the room to read a footnote. Nor are you likely to be making love at the time. A far better analogy would be that made by the *New York Times* writer who said of a certain article that "reading it is a bit like playing a Bach toccata on the organ—you have to look not only at the keys but also at the pedals below."* Personally, I am rather a fan of the intriguing footnote, though not as great a fan as Edward Gibbon, who devoted one-quarter of *The Decline and Fall of the Roman Empire* to them.

*David Margolick, *New York Times*, August 5, 1990.

[5] Technically, when a footnote occupies the whole page like this, it is no longer a footnote but a bodynote. And when a footnote itself contains a footnote, like the one above, the latter is known as a toenote.

minutes now. And, incredibly, it was still not over. After just a
few moments, the tennis player was back on court. "Nngh," she
grunted. "Nngh—nngh—nngh—"

Then my colleague resettled her headphones, and I seized my
chance.

"Susan, we've got enough."

"Oh. In that case I'll just . . ." She unplugged the mike. I
reached out and killed *FSOTM* too. The only sound was the rattle
of the printer as it spewed out Susan's results. I took them from the
machine and slid them under a pile of other papers. Then I turned
off my laptop.

"So," Susan said, coming back into the control room. Apart
from a faint flush, she was no more out of breath than if she had
just run up the stairs. "How's it looking?"

"Good," I said. "The printer's just warming up. Can I make you
a cup of tea?"

"Tea? Yes, tea would be nice," she said, drumming her fingers
on the desk.

In the lab kitchen I tossed a coin. Heads. That meant blue.

I took the blue bottle from my pocket and slipped out a pill.
Grinding it up with the back of a teaspoon, I added it to Susan's
tea. "Here you are," I said, going back into the control room and
handing her the mug. I watched her closely as she drank from it.
Good.

Susan, meanwhile, was looking at the printer. "Did you say this
was warming up?"

"That's right."

"Nothing's come through."

"Let me check." I turned to my computer. "Oh, drat."

"What is it?"

"The system's crashed."

"What?"

"Completely frozen," I said, pressing buttons at random.

"What about the data?" she said, running her fingers through her hair.

"All gone, I'm afraid."

"You mean—"

"We'll just have to run those tests again. Sorry. I must have pressed the wrong button." I had done no such thing, of course. I had simply been establishing a baseline, *before* Susan drank the tea with the ground-up pills in it, so that I could compare the two sets of results and determine what difference, if any, the pills had made.

I glanced up. Susan was looking at me with the same wry expression she had been wearing earlier. "Let me get this straight. You want me to do that all over again?"

"Well, not immediately. Feel free to finish your tea."

"Steve?"

"Yes?"

Susan leaned back against a desk. "I think we both know what's really going on here."

"Do we?"

"It's hardly rocket science."[6] For one awful moment I thought she was trying to look coy. "Do you have a girlfriend, Steve?"

She *was* trying to look coy. "No, I'm currently—I'm between— that is, I'm thinking—"

"How long have we known each other?"

"Three years."

"In those three years, have you ever had a girlfriend?"

"As it happens, no."

---

[6] It is a common misconception that rocket science is in some way complicated. In fact, the physics of thrust, as explained by Tsiolovsky's rocket equation, is far more straightforward than, say, the biochemistry of female sexual function.

"While we've been working together—quite closely—in these unusually intimate conditions . . ."

"True, but—"

"And I know how tough it's been," she said. She slid along the desk towards me. "Tough for any man, but for a man with no emotional or physical outlets . . ." Her voice, I noticed, had taken on a husky quality I had previously heard only when she had a bad cold. "I've seen you looking at me. You think I haven't noticed, but I have."

"Noticed what?"

"Sometimes, when I look at you, Steve, I don't see a man. I see a beast. A hungry beast."

"If you're referring to the time I ate your Jaffa cakes," I said, "I apologized the moment I realized my mistake."

"I'm not talking about Jaffa cakes."

"Ah."

"You needn't feel guilty. You want to screw my brains out. It's only natural."

"I don't want to screw your brains out," I said. "On all sorts of levels, I really, really don't want that." My own voice, due to a sudden involuntary constriction of the throat, seemed to have become a little hoarse as well.

She sighed. "If you say so. Anyway, I'm going home now, where I intend to have a long soak in a hot bath with a large glass of cold wine. If you change your mind and decide to join me, you've got my number."

And with that, she was gone.

40.4

I created a new file in my laptop and made some notes.

KXC79—Double-blind trial—test 1

Subject 1—Dr. M.

Method

I established a baseline set of results without treatment. A first orgasm manifested after approximately six minutes forty seconds, with subsequent orgasms at 12.50 and 18.20.

I then administered 10 mg of KXC79/placebo (blue bottle) without the subject's knowledge and attempted to retest.

Results

Within a few minutes of the treatment being administered, the subject's behavior altered dramatically. I noticed fidgeting, drumming of fingers on table surfaces, facial flushing, self-caressing, self-grooming, and prolonged suggestive eye contact. Her conversation was unusually frank, even for her, and consisted of repeated invitations to have sex. This was accompanied by references to our past relationship which bore little resemblance to reality. Dr. M.'s mental state, in fact, seemed to me to be consistent with what psychiatrists call confabulation, self-deception of an extreme or psychotic nature.

When her advances were declined, Dr. M. abruptly left the building. I was deprived, therefore, of the opportunity to see if orgasms were (a) more frequent, (b) stronger, or (c) closer together than previously. However, on this first trial it certainly seems that the treatment had a marked and alarming effect on desire, arousal, and, indeed, behavior.

The first part of my experiment had been revealing, if hardly reassuring. Now I had to perform a similar test with Miss G.

I had already given her a placebo, of course, with inconclusive results. What I needed to do now, therefore, was to see how orgasmic she was without any treatment at all, not even a placebo, before carrying out an identical test with the pills, just as I had with Susan. It sounds a little complicated, put like that—although it became clearer once I had turned it into table form (figure 21).

	Subject 1	Subject 2
Blue bottle (subject unaware of treatment)	Done	
Blue bottle (subject aware of treatment)		
No pill (baseline)	Done	
Placebo (subject aware of treatment)		Done
Pink bottle (subject unaware of treatment)		
Pink bottle (subject aware of treatment)		

Figure 21: Double-blind schematic.

When I had written it all down, I stared at the chart for a very long time. I had just realized that there was absolutely no way I could carry out this test on Miss G. without sleeping with her.

41.2

Believe me, I resisted. I racked my brains for any other way—any way at all of doing this without compromising the project still further. But I had already established that Miss G. was susceptible to the placebo effect, and that her real-world results were very different from those we saw in the lab. For this test to be accurate, she had to be unaware that it was happening. There was simply no option.[1]

[1] I can imagine that at this juncture there may be some of you who are wondering how I reconciled this conclusion with my previous assertion to Miss G. that it would be inappropriate, not to say unethical, to have sex with her. The answer, which will surely become apparent after only a moment's reflection, is that I was now proposing to have sex with her not for personal gratification, but to serve the higher cause of science. There is a long tradition of scientists who have involved themselves in their own experiments in this way. One thinks of Dr. Barry Marshall, the Australian gastroenterologist who, in order to test his hypothesis that stomach ulcers are caused not by stress but by the common bacterium *Helicobacter pylori,* drank a mixture containing the bug and suffered gastritis as a result. For this discovery he later shared the Nobel Prize in Physiology or Medicine. Likewise, the eighteenth-century Scottish surgeon John Hunter deliberately gave himself gonorrhea in order to study a potential cure (unfortunately, the cure was unsuccessful, and as a result Hunter had to postpone his marriage), while Jesse Lazear, a U. S. Army surgeon, died of yellow fever in 1900 after allowing an infected mosquito to bite his arm. A more recent example in my own field is that of Professor G. S. Brindley, whose lecture on the efficacy of intravenous drugs in male erectile dysfunction was memorably described in the *British Journal of Urology:*

> His slide-based talk consisted of a large series of photographs of his penis in various states of tumescence after injection with a variety of doses of phentolamine and papaverine. After viewing about 30 of these slides, there was no doubt in my mind that, at least in Professor Brindley's case, the therapy was effective. Of course, one could not exclude the possibility that erotic stimulation had played a role in acquiring these erections, and Professor Brindley acknowledged this. . . .
>
> He indicated that, in his view, no normal person would find the experience of giving a lecture to a large audience to be erotically stimulating or erection-

41.3

There might have been no alternative to sleeping with Miss G., but that did not mean it would be straightforward. In fact, now that I thought about it, there was another, possibly even more insurmountable hurdle. Although polite relations had been restored, Miss G. was still being somewhat distant with me. I suspected that any suggestion from me that she and I go to bed together would now meet with a frosty response, not to mention accusations of hypocrisy.

It was imperative that I not waste unnecessary time in arguing with Miss G. about this. Turning to the internet, therefore, I googled "dating skills."

41.4

There were a huge number of sites to choose from—over two million, in fact. To take just the first few examples:

---

inducing. He had, he said, therefore injected himself with papaverine in his hotel room before coming to give the lecture. He then summarily dropped his trousers and shorts, revealing a long, thin, clearly erect penis. . . .

[Saying] "I'd like to give some of the audience the opportunity to confirm the degree of tumescence" he waddled down the stairs, approaching (to their horror) the urologists and their partners in the front row. As he approached them, erection waggling before him, four or five of the women in the front rows threw their arms up in the air, seemingly in unison, and screamed loudly. The scientific merits of the presentation had been overwhelmed, for them, by the novel and unusual mode of demonstrating the results.

Laurence Klotz, "How (Not) to Communicate New Scientific Information: A Memoir of the Famous Brindley Lecture," *BJU International* 96, no. 7 (2005): 956–957.

Dating Tips For Men

DoubleYour**Dating**.com. **Dating** Tips on How to Approach,
Meet & Date Any Woman You Want (sponsored link).

Social, Conversational, and Dating Skills— Psychological Self-Help

Social, conversational, and **dating skills** to relate better.
www.mentalhelp.net/psyhelp/chap13/chap13l.htm - 25k -
Cached - Similar pages

The <u>Dating</u> Academy

Professor Pickup shares scientifically proven secrets of seduction.
www.professorpickupsdatingacademy.com - 25k - Cached -
Similar pages

You don't get laid, I don't get paid!

Improve your **Dating skills** right now!
Tripod/psyhelp.htm - 25k - Cached - Similar pages

As you can imagine, I was relieved to find amongst the dross a
fellow academic who had taken the trouble to test and verify his
findings. I clicked on Professor Pickup's entry. It took me to a page
that read:

Discover the power of Advanced Neurolinguistic Programming!

Join Professor Pickup for his Seduction Seminar 101 and learn:

- How to Approach a Woman
- Using Fluff Talk to Elicit Her Values
- Kinaesthetic Techniques: Embedded Commands That Make Her Want You
- Patterning Her for Sexual Seduction
- and many other scientifically proven Techniques

Contact The Professor.

None of these terms was familiar to me, but as the subject was somewhat removed from mine I was not entirely surprised by that. I opened the e-mail link and wrote:

> Dear Professor Pickup,
>
> Forgive me for contacting you out of the blue. Like you I am an academic, although I confess that I am not familiar with your field of neurolinguistics. I now find myself in a situation where a research project I am engaged in requires me to go on a date with a young woman and, as unlikely as it sounds, to persuade her to have sex with me. Have you published any papers on this subject that might help?
>
> Kind regards,
> Steven Fisher PhD
> Oxford University
>
> PS: I am in a desperate hurry.

Barely half an hour later I received a reply.

> From: professorpickup@hotmail.com
> To: Fisher.S@nb.ac.uk
>
> dude,
>
> sure I can help you jus email me the money using Nochex or Paypal. It's $99 for three emails. You are so going to nail this chick.
>
> best,
> The Professor

The tone of this reply made me a little anxious. However, I was eager to find out about the professor's research, so I sent the payment and awaited a response.

It, too, arrived almost immediately.

From: professorpickup@hotmail.com
To: Fisher.S@nb.ac.uk

hey steve,

thanks for the $99. This is the first email, right? Here's how you're going to use Advanced NeuroLinguistic Programming (ANLP) to achieve your goals!

1. DON'T go on a date with this chick. Fact: chicks go on dates with men they're never going to sleep with. Dates are for schmucks (or as we Pick-up Masters call them, AFCs— Average Frustrated Chumps).
2. Get this chick to come along to something you were going to do anyway. Then here's how you play it.

There followed a detailed list of instructions which encompassed everything from the importance of Fluff Talk to the necessity of Keeping Away From Facts:

Facts BORE her! Get to the FEELINGS. Instead of saying "I like your perfume. What is it?" say "What's the STORY behind that BEAUTIFUL, SENSUAL perfume you're wearing?"

Then there was a section on something called Kinaesthetic Anchors:

> Mirror her Trance Words back to her in the same language she
> uses, while gently touching her on the elbow.

> What you're doing is linking that Positive Value to your touch,
> so that every time you touch her in the future she'll associate it
> with good stuff!

While the section on Embedded Commands was frankly revelatory:

> Use the power of the subconscious! Dude, if you talk about
> your "MASSIVE hapPINESS," her subconscious will hear
> "massive penis"! If you say "BELOW me," she'll hear "blow
> me"! This stuff really works!

Most of all, though, Professor Pickup wanted to impress upon me the Power of Patterns:

> A Pattern is basically when you TALK about GREAT SEX whilst
> PRETENDING to talk about something else. That way, you're
> putting the idea in her mind that SEX WITH YOU WILL BE
> GREAT!

He provided half-a-dozen Sample Scripts for me to memorize and signed off with these encouraging words:

> If you use these scripts properly I GUARANTEE that you will
> have sex tonight.

Even so, I felt uneasy. Much as I wanted to believe ANLP would work, I had very little confidence in my own ability to deliver some of the scripts without stumbling. And there were certain parts of the e-mail that looked suspiciously as if they had been cut-and-pasted from different sources.

I hit Reply and wrote:

From:Fisher.s@nb.ac.uk
To: professorpickup@hotmail.com

Dear Professor Pickup,

Forgive me if I query a couple of your points—the urge to double-check is, of course, the scientist's curse. Could you tell me which journals this study was validated in? May I have the references?

Sincerely,
Steven Fisher

_____

From: professorpickup@hotmail.com
To: Fisher.S@nb.ac.uk

Hey Steve,

It's Advanced NeuroLinguistic Programming, right? This stuff is scientifically PROVEN. There are plenty of references to it on the net, if you do a search.

Good luck,
The Professor

_____

From:Fisher.s@nb.ac.uk
To: professorpickup@hotmail.com

Dear Professor Pickup,

Could you at least tell me who awarded your Chair, and what professional bodies you are affiliated to?

Steven Fisher

From: professorpickup@hotmail.com
To: Fisher.S@nb.ac.uk

Hey Steve,

Chair? Don't follow you on that one, my man. I have a chair but it's just your basic Office World computer-desk model. It does have wheels, though.

That's your last email, officially, but seeing as how we've had a great chat, let me know if you need any more help and we'll sort something out.

The Prof

42.1

Despite my misgivings, I had little alternative but to follow Professor Pickup's recommendations. Even if he wasn't a real scientist, he almost certainly knew more about picking up women than I did.

I tried to think of something I could invite Annie along to that I would have been doing anyway. Then I remembered that the Campanology Society was planning a half-peal later that evening at St. Giles's, an event that would last about an hour and provide some interesting changes between different ringing progressions.

She wasn't in the lab, so I called her mobile.

"Oh, Steven," she said neutrally. "What can I do for you?"

"I was wondering—are you doing anything tonight?"

There was a slight pause. "Not much. Just writing up my notes on valency."

"I was wondering if you'd like to hear some church bells being rung." Even as I said it, I realized it wasn't the most exciting of invitations.

There was a long pause, and for a moment I thought Professor Pickup's advice must have been flawed.

"Well, okay," she said at last. "Why not."

"Great," I said, relieved. "Shall we meet at St. Giles's Church? They're planning to start at seven."

42.2

Hmm . . . Steven's asked me to some kind of bell-ringing concert. A little odd, perhaps, but I suppose he's saying that he wants to do something with me just as a friend. An olive branch after all the horrible things we both said a few days ago.

I'm still a bit cross with him about that, actually. But I also miss him terribly—miss talking to him in that open, easy way that we used to before the whole Richard thing happened.

So I'll go along. Even though bell ringing sounds . . . well, weird.

Although if this were some big Victorian novel, bell ringing would probably be another corny metaphor.

42.3

At ten to seven I was waiting in the church, along with a small audience of campanologists, mathematicians, and other interested parties. I had printed out Professor Pickup's e-mail for reference, and I passed the time memorizing his lines.

A few minutes later Annie turned up, wearing a lovely grey velvet scarf that set off her eyes. She slid into the pew alongside me.

"Hello," she said.

"Hello." We were speaking in whispers, as one does in a church. I cast my mind back to the professor's instructions. Step one: Fluff Talk.

"Um—what have you been up to?" I asked. No—damn—that was Eliciting Facts. But Annie was answering anyway.

"Quite a lot, actually. I've covered all of covalent bonds,

electronegativity, and the Pauling scale. Oh, and I rewrote an essay on ionic bonding."

"And how does that make you FEEL?" I whispered.

She gave me a puzzled look. "Well, it's not ideal, is it, but it's better than nothing."

"No, I meant . . ." I changed tack. "What's the story of that BEAUTIFUL, SENSUAL perfume you're wearing?"

"I'm not wearing perfume." She pulled the top of her sweater up to her nose so she could sniff it. "Do I smell? It's probably washing powder."

So far, I felt, Advanced NeuroLinguistic Programming was not proving much help. "If I were to ask you," I whispered, "what the most important thing in a relationship is, what would you say?"

She looked startled. "In *our* relationship?"

"No, um—just any relationship."

She thought about it. "I would say that different things are important in different relationships, depending on the other person. Why? Is it for a survey?"

"No," I said. "I was just wondering."

Now I had to Mirror her words back to her.

"Wouldn't it be nice," I suggested, "if you could spend time with a man who makes you feel differentiated? Whose voice intrigued and at the same time stimulated you? I get the feeling that this could happen to you right now, with me." As I spoke I touched her several times on the elbow.

"Steven, why are you poking me like that?"

"No reason." I cleared my throat. This whispering was quite hard work, and it was time to move on to a Pattern. "What do you really love doing, Annie?"

"Well," she said doubtfully, "work, I suppose. That's what I really like best—working."

"Work?" I repeated. Surely not even Professor Pickup could turn work into a paradigm of sexual intercourse. "Anything else?"

She shrugged. "Swamps and Sorcerers, perhaps. Why are you smiling?"

"I'm not smiling."

"You smirked," she said crossly. "And it's not a nice smirk. It's the same smirk you gave me the first time we met, when I asked you whether KXC79 was like Viagra. You think Swamps and Sorcerers is stupid, don't you?"

"No, I don't," I said quickly. Although, of course, there was something rather amusing about a grown woman playing fantasy games.

"Well, you should try it sometime. Instead of just sneering."

I almost made a smart retort. Then I recalled the Professor's instruction. "I'm curious. What is it about Swamps and Sorcerers that makes you love it?" I whispered. "What do you FEEL when you're playing Swamps and Sorcerers? What's it like when you're THERE NOW, Swamping and Sorcering?"

"Well, I suppose one of the things I like is that gender doesn't come into it at all. You create a character, and the character has certain powers, such as long-sightedness, indefatigability, or whatever, and then you roll the dice, and that's it."

Put like that, Swamps and Sorcerers also seemed unlikely to provide the opportunities I was looking for. I decided to move on to one of the Professor's own sample scripts. "You know that feeling you have when you get home after a hard day of work and all you can think about is STRIPPING off your clothes and SLIDING into a hot bath?"

"No," she said, somewhat shortly. "I shower. In the mornings."

At that moment there was a terrific din as several tons of iron began to peal above our heads.

I leaned towards her. "You know, I learned this amazing

visualization exercise that really helps you pick yourself up when you aren't feeling that great. Would you like me to show it to you, so that you too can do this and feel absolutely wonderful?"

She pointed to her ears and shook her head, frowning. "I CAN'T HEAR YOU," she yelled.

"IMAGINE YOU'RE HOLDING A FLOWER," I shouted.

"AN HOUR?"

"A FLOWER."

"WHAT KIND OF FLOWER?"

"THAT'S UP TO YOU. CAN YOU SEE THE BEAUTIFUL PETALS?"

"NO," she said. "WHAT'S WITH ALL THE PSYCHOBAB-BLE, ANYWAY?"

Above our head, the ringers effortlessly changed from Plain Bob Minor to Grandsire Triples. The members of the audience turned to each other, nodding and smiling. I glanced at Annie, but she was staring straight ahead with a scowl on her face.

It was fully ten minutes before Grandsire Triples changed to Cambridge Treble Bob. Annie was by now looking almost cata-tonic. With a sinking feeling I realized that I had invited her to something that was boring the pants off her—or rather, and far more problematically, boring the pants onto her. What on earth had I been thinking?

Eventually, after forty-five endless minutes, the ringers changed to a triumphant course of Plain Hunt, and thus to Rounds. After that the only sound was the echo of the bells' reverberations sub-siding gracefully off the stone walls. A little later the ringers them-selves trooped out of the tower, to be greeted by a smattering of polite applause.

"Well," Annie said, putting her scarf on. "That was, um . . . yes."

"Wait," I said. "Annie—I'm sorry—it wasn't very interesting."

"It was fine, Steven. Really."

"Annie," I said miserably, "you were bored witless."

"No, I wasn't," she said. She looked at me, and suddenly we were both laughing. "Though it was a little . . . repetitive at times," she admitted.

"It's one of those things you have to do for yourself before you can enjoy other people doing it," I explained.

"And then it's different?"

"Oh, yes," I said. "You see, ringing is all about making quite complicated mathematical patterns. You probably didn't even notice, but each one of those rounds—the peals—involved the ringers swapping places. Take Plain Major." I scribbled down a rough number line on a piece of scrap paper. "See? If you're the eighth bell—the tenor—every new peal puts you in a different position." (See figure 22.)

"So it must be pretty difficult?"

"That's the funny thing. When you start ringing, it's all you can do to keep the rhythm. You just heave on the rope when it's your turn, and hope no one notices the odd fumbled stroke. But once you get a bit more confident, you find yourself keeping track of the changes almost without thinking. Ringers call it bell sense—it's like a sort of intuition. Your arms seem to move of their own accord. And—it's hard to explain—somehow you're inside the pattern, and you don't have to plan what comes next at all. Instead of you pulling the bells, it feels as if the bells are pulling you. And that's when you relax and let the noise and the movement and the pounding of the bells just pick you up and take you away."

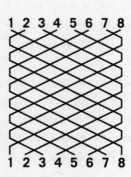

Figure 22: An eight-bell peal progression represented as a number pattern.

"Put like that, it doesn't sound quite so dull," she said with a rueful smile. "But I really do have to go now. I've got a paper to finish."

"Of course," I said.

"It was nice seeing you."

"Even though you were bored?"

She laughed. "Even though I was bored . . . some of the time." She leaned across and kissed me on my cheek. Above my head, the bells burst into an eight-bell descant. The planets themselves seemed to roar their approval as they whirled through space around our heads, singing the celestial music of the spheres. Every atom in my body seemed to have acquired a second positive charge and to resonate, thrillingly, with the force of the universe—

It was now or never.

"Annie," I said, "would you go to bed with me?"

She stared at me. The question, I could tell, had taken her by surprise.

"But I'm a research subject," she said slowly. "It's inappropriate, remember? Or doesn't that apply when it's you doing the asking?"

"Um," I said. Clearly I could not give her the explanation I had given myself without making her aware of the experiment I was now conducting. "Perhaps I was being a little overrigorous."

"Is this something to do with Richard?"

"Oh, no, not at all. Annie, I can't explain this properly. It's just that I need—in so many ways that I can't begin to describe—to hold you in my arms. But I can't tell you why. I can't even tell you why I can't tell you."

"You do find it quite hard to talk about your feelings, don't you?" she said, softening a little. "Look, Steven, it's just not really possible at the moment. There's a couple of complications I can't . . . And besides, the conference is only a couple of days away.

You're going to be famous. You'll have all the pretty female scientists in the world throwing themselves at you after that."

"No!" I said. "I really, really can't wait until after the conference."

"But I'm glad we're friends again. Let's face it, we're neither of us—well, you know. Sex would only complicate things, right?"

"Yes," I said numbly. "Yes, of course."

As she went she gave me a smile and a wave.

42.4

At home I wrote up my notes.

KXC79—Double-blind trial—test 2

Subject 2—Miss G.

Method and results

I attempted to establish a baseline without treatment. Miss G. showed no sexual arousal or interest, despite being exposed to a number of "chat-up" scripts containing proven neurolinguistic patterns. Thus a very different response to that exhibited by Subject 1 was established.

	Subject 1	Subject 2
Blue bottle (subject unaware of treatment)	Done	
Blue bottle (subject aware of treatment)		
No pill	Done	Done
Placebo (subject aware of treatment)		Done
Pink bottle (subject unaware of treatment)		
Pink bottle (subject aware of treatment)		

Figure 23: Updated schematic.

42.5

After I had written my notes, I fired off a rather curt e-mail to Professor Pickup.

> Dear Professor,
>
> I have to report that, far from "nailing" the young woman in question, the non-date was a non-event. Your scripts contributed remarkably little, and indeed were described by her at one point as "psychobabble." Do you have any further suggestions?
>
> Regards,
> Steven Fisher

To my surprise, he replied almost immediately.

> From: professorpickup@hotmail.com
> To: Fisher.S@nb.ac.uk
>
> Steve,
>
> Hey! Don't worry, we see the "psychobabble" block plenty of times. There are powerful, proven ways of turning it round so that she's jelly in your hands! These are, like, really advanced techniques so it's $199 for three more emails.
>
> The Prof

This time I did not respond.

My temper improved next morning, however, when I recollected that, whatever the results of these first two tests had been, I could reasonably expect them to be precisely the opposite when I swapped the pills over. That is to say, if the pills from the blue bottle had indeed been responsible for Susan's behavior, then giving them to Annie should have exactly the same effect on her. And this time, I decided, I would find a context for my experiment more conducive to romance.

Or would I? It occurred to me that, if I were to accurately gauge the effects of the pills on Annie, they should really be the only variable between the two events. Logically, I should take her to exactly the same bell-ringing concert all over again, repeat exactly the same chat-up lines, and only then determine what difference, if any, the addition of the pills made.

43.2

I was at the lab bright and early, waiting by the downstairs entrance for Miss G. to make an appearance.

"Good morning," I said, falling into step beside her as she swiped her security card. "I hope that on reflection you enjoyed last night."

"Oh—Steven. You startled me. Yes, it was interesting. Thank you for letting me come with you."

"Perhaps you'd like to do it again sometime," I suggested as we walked up the stairs.

"That would be nice," she said politely.

"Excellent. How about tonight? There's a rather interesting progression planned for a village a few miles away—a minor Surprise followed by Doubles. I think you'll find—"

"Actually," she said quickly, "I've already got plans tonight."

"Oh." We were by now in the lab, standing beside the strip of lab bench designated as her work area. By her computer was a large and expensive-looking bunch of flowers. They had clearly only just been delivered, as they were still wrapped in cellophane.[1]

"Those must be for Heather," I said, reaching for them. "I'll put them by her workstation." Then I happened to glance at the card.

Annie—Can't stop thinking about you—Richard

I put them down again. "They seem to be for you after all," I said stiffly. "From 'Richard.' Richard Collins, presumably."

"Presumably." She busied herself booting up her computer.

"He's your plan for tonight, I take it."

"No, actually. Tonight I've got a Swamps and Sorcerers game. It's been arranged for ages." She shot me a sudden look. "Why don't you come to that?"

"Oh, no," I said. "Swamps and Sorcerers isn't really my idea of a—"

"I mean it. You've been sneering at S & S for far too long. It'll do you good to see what it's really like. And I came to your bell ringing, so it's only fair."

---

[1] The biochemical symbolism, as it were, of cut flowers as a courtship gift is, now that I come to think of it, rather fascinating. Flowers are, of course, the sexual organs of the plant: once they are cut, their lifespan becomes even more limited than it was before. The giver is therefore reminding the givee that their own sexual organs will remain sweet-smelling for only a short while, before they too wither and die.

"I don't have a Swamp Character—"

"That's no problem. We could make one. I've got the dice right here." She pulled some polyhedral dice from her pocket. "Shall we do Armor first?"

It was clear that it was Swamping or nothing, so I took the first die and rolled it along the lab bench. "Fifteen points," I said.

"That's quite good," she said, writing it down on a scrap of paper. "And very useful in the Gorge of Darkwind. Some of the trolls down there have Weapon Abilities you wouldn't believe. Expertise?"

I rolled again. "Twelve."

"Which makes you a Storm Bringer. It's not the highest skill in the Wracked Isles, but believe me it's pretty handy when the Spider Hordes are on your tail. What about Fortitude?"

I rolled again. "Three."

"Oh, dear, never mind. Luck?"

"Twenty!"

"*Very* impressive. That means you get the Improbability Bonus. If you steal a Staff of Sorcery from one of the Wandering Wraiths, you could be a Seer by the end of the game."

I had forgotten how much fun Swamps and Sorcerers could be. "You have the Magus level?" I exclaimed.

"Yes, but that's advanced—it's only for those who have vanquished the hordes of Gorgoroth."

"As it happens, I have tyrannized the Gorgorothian Plains on more than one occasion," I said modestly.

She stared at me. "Steven Fisher—I knew it! You're a Swamper!"

I shrugged. "Not really. Well, perhaps a bit. A long time ago."

"But why did you stop?"

"You're talking to someone who used to be a Level 6 Dragon

Wrangler at school, and believe me, that can be pretty time-consuming."

"A Dragon Wrangler?" she said disbelievingly. "You're not saying you can speak the Old Tongue?"

"As a matter of fact, I can," I admitted. "Runish was a bit of a hobby of mine."

"Me too!"

"Oh. *Slub gratel mor wrasper?*"

"Mentas nord tangela!"

"Eta bentle? Tran farst can nazoor."

She frowned. "Shouldn't that be *'nazan'*? *'Nazoor'* means 'scarily hideous.'"

"Oh, yes. I was trying to say that you're *'nazan.'*"

She dropped her eyes. "Thank you."

There was a short but rather agreeable silence. "Well, anyway, I'll see you tonight," she said at last.

"Yes, I'll look forward to it," I said, going back to my own work.

43.3

"Steve?" It was Susan, standing at the door.

I glanced at my watch. Almost four o'clock. I had been so immersed in my own thoughts that the entire day had passed without my even noticing it.

"How's it going?" she asked, coming in and perching on the desk.

"Fine. Just a few last-minute things I'm still double-checking for the conference."

"It's not too late to cancel, you know," she said quietly. "No one will think any the less of you if you decide you need more time to refine the formulation."

I glanced at her, surprised that she had divined the reason for my unease.

"Steve . . . ," she continued. "You must have noticed that Annie's results have sometimes been . . . well, a bit odd."

"That's certainly true."

"I think you and I need to talk about it. Now. Before it's too late."

I sighed. "You're right, of course. I'll get us some coffee."

43.4

In the kitchen, I ground up two pills from the pink pill bottle and added them to her cup. One last experiment, before I decided what to do.

43.5

"To some extent I blame myself," she was saying. "I should have realized when she first put herself forward that she was completely unsuitable."

"Mmm," I said. I glanced at the clock. It had been eight minutes since Susan started drinking her coffee. And so far she was displaying no signs of behaving any more irrationally than usual. Quite the reverse, in fact. This was the most reasonable she had been in months.

I sighed. There seemed little doubt that whatever was causing the problem, it was in the blue pills rather than the pink ones.

"And then there are her latest tests. Steve, I'm certain she's stopped being orgasmic. Could the new formulation somehow be responsible for that?"

"But if you look at the brain-mapper scans there's nothing different," I argued. "Apart from this very faint activity in the anterior cingulate."

"Show me?"

I pointed to my laptop screen.

"Mmm," she said. "I do see what you mean."

As she leaned over my laptop I became aware of a faint but not unpleasant odor. Susan was wearing perfume.[2]

"Have you considered confounding factors?" she said, glancing over her shoulder at me. As if by accident one of her hands, dangling off the desk, brushed my knee.

"Of course. Observer bias, randomized selection—"

"I meant on her side."

"Such as?"

"Maybe she just gets off on all this."

I frowned. "In what way?"

"The machines, the pills, the equipment, scientists in white coats . . . Some people might find all this pretty sexy." Once again her hand brushed against my thigh. "I know I do sometimes."

I shot her a puzzled look. Unless I was very much mistaken, my colleague was again attempting to flirt with me.

Susan, meanwhile, seemed to take my silence as some kind of

[2] Given that man's olfactory receptors are no longer capable of detecting the sexual signals in female sweat, it might seem puzzling that women bother with perfume. However, further investigation shows that the picture is more complicated than it first appears. For example, it is well known that women in a closed community gradually synchronize their ovulations, the mechanism for which can only be airborne. Equally, the principal ingredient of perfume—musk—is obtained from a deer that is in season, while the secondary ingredients—flower fragrances—are the plant's own natural attractors to pollen spreaders. Clearly, there is some biosocial aspect to perfume-wearing that is not yet fully understood.

positive response. The hand traveled upwards, increasing its pressure.

This, of course, was most puzzling. Assuming that the pills from the blue bottle were the ones containing the active ingredient, she should on this occasion be behaving normally.

But then, I reflected, what *was* normal, for Susan? Given her behavior at SexDys, it might be that what I, or any sane person, would describe as erratic or disordered behavior was, for her, an everyday mental state.

On the other hand, my colleague had never before attempted—as she was doing at this precise moment—to drag the ends of her painted fingernails lightly up and down the inner surface of my thigh, whilst breathing heavily through parted lips.

Could I have got it wrong? Could the pills from the pink bottle, in fact, have been the ones containing KXC79? And if so, was I now witnessing a side effect of a magnitude that even I could not have anticipated?

Susan gave me a sultry look through her eyelashes. Then she gently but firmly swung my chair around to face her. Spreading my knees, she slid off the bench so that she was standing directly between my legs. Then she began gyrating her upper torso while simultaneously unbuttoning her lab coat.

"What are you doing, Susan?" I managed to ask.

"I'm taking my clothes off."

Her bra was red and black, festooned with tiny bows. But perhaps a sexologist has to invest in decent underwear.

"Yes, I realized that, but why?"

"It makes sex much easier." She swiveled her skirt round, undid a button, and stepped out of it. Then she reached up behind her back and unhooked her bra.

As her breasts—her surprisingly shapely breasts—swung free, I distinctly heard her mutter something that was even more surprising than her breasts. "I just hope this works."

Definitely a side effect.

43.6

As Susan was disrobing, I had a sudden thought about KXC79. It had just occurred to me where the difficulty might lie. Because KXC79 synthesized l-oxytocin from other peptides, the gain in oxytocin was matched by a potential loss of other neurotransmitters. It was as if I had turned all the buses in the city into taxis— there would be more taxis on the street, but no buses, so no one would be able to get to where they wanted to go.

Susan was by now crouching in front of me, undoing my trousers.

"Oooh," she said. "Nice."

If the other peptides—my buses, if you like—were having a previously unrecognized inhibitory effect on female behavior, that would explain why turning them into oxytocin had the dual effect of enhancing arousal *and* changing behavior. It wasn't an insurmountable problem, just a setback.

"It's not insurmountable," I said.

Susan started undoing my belt buckle. "Let's hope not."

"I need to send some of my taxis to their original destinations, and reroute some of my buses."

"You need to get out of these clothes."

"Susan, you don't understand. I needed to experiment—"

"Fine. Wear *my* clothes." Then she started doing something to me which was really rather pleasant. Mind you, I suppose a sexologist has to be good at that sort of thing.

Let me make something quite clear. When I conceived the double-blind experiment, I had absolutely no intention of letting things get this far. Unfortunately, though, my colleague seemed quite determined to continue.

"Susan," I said firmly.

"Mmnghf?"

"There's something I need to tell you."

"Hmmngh. Nndt gdtyh."

"Yes, now. The thing is—"

"Steve," she said, lifting her head, "shut up." Then she started to do something with the end of her tongue that was even more pleasant.

43.7

The mechanisms which control the human erection are quite interesting. Basically, there are at least two completely separate neural networks involved: the sympathetic and the parasympathetic systems. Nerve impulses are sent by the brain to the erection center positioned at the base of the spine. This causes the release of a substance called acetylcholine, which in turn causes the arterioles, or small arteries, in the penis to dilate. The parasympathetic system is the one which usually manages this process, with the sympathetic system acting as an override, for example in cases of fight-or-flight. Neither mechanism is under the control of the conscious brain—we can no more tell the penis to stop erecting than we can tell the stomach to stop digesting or the heart to stop beating.

Of course, what we do with our erections is a different matter; here the conscious brain does have a role. But the part of our brain used for conscious thought is actually a very small proportion of that organ: principally the outer part, which makes up less than 5 percent of the whole. It's a bit like the ocean: the surface may be where the fishing happens, but most of the really big, weird creatures live a long way below.

In those murky depths, not a lot of what we would recognize as actual thought takes place. In those deep, dark parts of the brain, in fact, lurk the shadowy synaptic remnants of all our forefathers: not just recent ancestors such as *Homo sapiens,* but the millions of generations which went before: Piltdown man; *Homo heidelbergensis; Homo erectus;* the prehuman hominids; the prehominid primates, *Dryopithecus* and his ilk; and further back still, eon after eon of mammals, fish, and various species of amoeba.[3]

And what every single one of those billions of ancestors was shouting at me now—either in my own language, or Indo-European, or cave-dwelling Neanderthal grunts, or the animal cries of the preplacentals, or even, perhaps, in the tiny squeaking urgings of amoebae—was this: "Do it, Steven! Do it!"

Goodness, she was certainly lithe.

43.8

Susan was evidently one of those people who like to talk during sex.

"In a minute, Steve," she said as she wriggled on top of me, "I'm going to tell you something."

If I replied at all, it was probably in Neanderthal.

"I'm telling you now," she said, grimacing as she pinned me to

---

[3] I choose amoebae as our ancestors here because it is the popular—albeit sentimental—choice. I am of course well aware of the controversy that surrounds this simple assertion, and that, in all likelihood, it may be more accurate to say "bacteria."

the floor with a particularly athletic squat-thrust, "because I know you're going to be angry.

"Furious, in fact," she added.

"The thing is," she said after a moment, "I've done something rather terrible."

"Urrgh," I said.

"And I want you to promise me," she said, looping her arms round my neck and throwing her head back and forth, "that when I do tell you, you're not going to overreact."

She paused to rearrange herself into a position redolent of the stretching exercises a jogger does at traffic lights.

"What you have to remember, Steve," she said with a catch in her voice, "when you do feel yourself getting angry, is that whatever I've done, I've only done for love."

"Love?" I said incredulously. "Love for whom?"

Susan did not answer this question immediately, and I did not press her, my own mind now being on other things.

43.9

We lay together on the floor, panting.

"So," she said eventually, "I'd better explain."

I sighed. "There's something I've got to explain first. Susan, I've got an apology to make. I'm sorry. I've been giving you KXC79."

She looked puzzled. "Why would you do that?"

"I needed to see what effect it would have. You see, I didn't really want to have sex with you at all. I just needed to double-check something."

Susan started to shake with laughter. She laughed wildly, madly, and without mirth.

"Oh, Steve," she managed to say. "You've been giving me KXC79. Of course you have. That is priceless. That is absolutely fucking priceless."

"I was worried about psychological side effects, you see," I explained. "And I was right. It has definitely made you irrational. More irrational, I should say."

That was an understatement, actually. It seemed to me as I spoke that Susan was by now quite hysterical.

She got up, fetched something from her desk, and threw it into my lap. Something small and white.

"It's all on there," she said. "You'd better read it."

I looked at the object. It was a memory stick.

"Steve," she said impatiently, "You really don't get it, do you? It's all bollocks. KXC79—it doesn't exist. It's a figment of your imagination. You stupid, stupid, stupid *arse*."

43.10

I looked at her pityingly. She really was behaving extremely irrationally.

"In which case, Susan," I said, "what have we been testing for the last three months?"

For a long moment she pressed the back of her hand against her forehead and closed her eyes, as if thinking deeply.

Then she opened them and said with a gulp, "Smarties."

"Smarties?"

"They're small candy-covered chocolates that come in an assortment of colors. Including pink."

"I know what they are, Susan. But why?"

She took a deep breath. "Because I'm in love with Heather,

that's why. Because I needed to steal the pills to persuade her to sleep with me. And because all the time she's been playing me for a fool."

"But I still don't—"

"It's all in there. Just read it." And, pulling on her lab coat, she hurried from the room.

44.1

I plugged in the memory stick. On it were a number of subfolders, labeled:

- Book Proposal ("My Life as a Sex Goddess: Inside the KXC79 Experiment," by Dr. Susie Minstock)
- Notes & diary
- Ibiza pictures (hot girl-on-girl)

I clicked on the second one.

44.2

June 12

I'm in heaven. This job is:

a. A job. At last! Luckily Dr. F. didn't spot the small gap on my CV. I guessed he wouldn't be too happy about my having spent a couple of years working on the phospheration approach, so I just skipped that bit.[1]

b. Fantastic. I mean, I'm in sole charge of the whole subject-selection side. Dr. F. just goes bright red and walks away whenever the subject of sexually

---

[1] I certainly wouldn't have been. The phospheration approach has been thoroughly discredited. Technically, Susan got her job on false pretences.

dysfunctional women comes up. Seems odd, really, that such a nerd would
end up working in this field.

I asked him yesterday if he'd tried KXC79 himself yet. He stared at me. "But
I'm a man," he said. "Oxytocin-derived enzymes are not a variable factor in my
physiological response."

"I meant, have you tried it with a girlfriend," I explained.

He looked even more confused. "You mean as an experiment? I don't think
that would be valid."

"Might be fun, though."

His frown deepened. "It could be seen as unprofessional. In any case, I don't
have a sexually dysfunctional girlfriend."

"Oh. Lucky you."

"I don't have a girlfriend at all."

Like I say, what a nerd. Can't wait to get my own hands on some of that
KXC79, though.

July 13

Getting some KXC79 is proving harder than I expected. Dr. F. keeps it all locked
in his fridge. But then he gives *me* the pills in a little paper cup, to give to the
subjects. So I switched a few with some Smarties, just before I passed them
on—the pink ones look just the same. Unprofessional,[2] I know, but I really need
to find out if this stuff works.

July 14

Hmm, interesting. I mean, obviously I'm only a sample of one, but I'd say that
on the evidence of last night, Dr. Fisher's certainly on to something. (Lasted for
ages, almost a multiple.) Haven't felt that good since Seville, and those three

[2] A better description might be "criminally irresponsible."

waiters. Which means . . . if this ever gets to market, I could make millions. Not to mention being the most famous sexologist in the world. Hooray!

I need to own this project. Have decided to flirt with Dr. F., just a little. He seems like the frustrated type, so he should be putty in my hands.

July 17

Flirting with Steve is harder than you'd think. He doesn't seem terribly interested. Could he be gay? That would be ironic, in more ways than one.

. . . On the other hand, he did tell me with a straight face that his last research project involved seeing whether female monkeys have orgasms. Apparently he had to "manipulate them digitally." Yikes—I'm sharing a laboratory with a man who's diddled monkeys for a living![3]

Mind you, all that practice on the higher primates should have done wonders for his technique. If only he wasn't such a stiff!

August 1

Summer vacation. Yay! Ibiza, here I come. I've built up a little stockpile of KXC79 to take with me, natch.

September 18

We've acquired a particularly gorgeous graduate researcher over the summer. Heather Jackson. Twenty-four years old, blond, blue-eyed, and cute as a button. But then you realize there's a little touch of mischief there as well. . . . Subtly

---

[3] This is a ridiculous slur on my reputation. Yes, I did study female monkeys to see if they could have orgasms, but at the time, so did a number of other researchers. See, for example, F. D. Burton, "Sexual Climax in Female *Macaca mulatta*," in *Proceedings of the Third International Congress of Primatology* (Zurich, 1970), 3:180–191; and M. L. Allen, and W. B. Lemmon, "Orgasm in Female Primates" *American Journal of Primatology* 1 (1981): 15–34.

brought the conversation round to "some bi-curious girlfriends of mine," and there was a definite flicker of interest. It's funny how one just *knows*. And to judge by the way she gave me a sideways glance from under that blond fringe, she knows just why I was mentioning it too. So now the chase is on. . . . This should liven up the autumn term.

September 20

Heather was cleaning out the lab cupboards today when she found some steel frames. They looked like orthopedic devices for straightening broken limbs.

"Do you still need these, or shall I throw them out?" she asked Dr. Fisher. "What are they, anyway?"

Dr. F. went bright red, although as that's something that happens at least once a day it took me some time to realize what his long-winded explanation actually meant. Apparently when he was diddling the monkeys, the monkeys didn't always like being diddled. So he had these frames made, and strapped the monkeys in before getting to work.

"Of course, this was at the beginning of the study," he said. "Later, as they came to associate my presence with pleasure, they actively sought out the frames. I had one particularly bright bonobo who learned how to strap herself in."

Yikes! I'm sharing a lab with a man who's into primate bondage!

Once he began talking about the monkeys, it was as if he couldn't stop. Apparently the very bright bonobo—Lucy, he called her—started out by biting him every time he came near her (he showed us the scars) but ended up by grooming him for fleas as a sign of her affection. And that, ladies and gentlemen, was what started him thinking about the role of neurotransmitters in female sexual dysfunction. (No, I don't understand the link either, but then I don't understand most of what Dr. F. says. The actual science of this project is way, way too advanced for me.)

Anyway, Heather—who is busy wrapping all the men in the Department round her little finger—asked him how the frames work, and under the guise of showing her how it all fitted together he was soon strapping her in and demonstrating where he used to stand to do his diddling—sorry, his *digital manipulation.* She looked at us from under her blond fringe and made a monkey noise. I swear, Dr. F. looked more excited than he has done in months. He had to go for a walk to calm down.[4]

So of course while he was gone I went and helped Heather out of the monkey frame. Except that before I undid any of the straps I thought I'd better make it quite plain that I wouldn't be letting her out at all unless she was a good little monkey. . . . And then the little tease started doing the same noises to me. "Ooo-ooo?" she said plaintively, opening her big blue eyes very wide. "Ooo-ooo-ooo?"

I couldn't resist it. I kissed her. Not her first girl-girl kiss either, to judge by her reaction. . . . Unfortunately Dr. F. came back, or we might have managed a bit more.

September 24

Nothing for the last few days . . . at least nothing *overt.* On the surface we're just being very cool with each other, very *matter-of-fact,* but the eye contact goes on just a fraction too long, and the body language is just a little more blatant than it should be. She'll smooth her hair back over her head, and I'll give a little stretch. . . . She'll fiddle with her necklace, and I'll touch my earring. . . . Oh, women are so *bad.* How can Dr. F. not have noticed? The air is thick with estrogen and female lust.

September 26

So today Heather wanted a guided tour of the testing room. I showed her the stimulators, of course, and there was a mock-innocent episode where I held a couple against her arm to show her how powerful they were.

Then she looked me in the eye and asked me if she could try some KXC79.

[4] This is, needless to say, complete nonsense. I had a bell-ringing practice to go to.

I explained it wasn't that simple—Steve keeps the pills locked up, and every single one he gives out is recorded in his lab notes.

"Please?" she said, fetchingly. "Pretty please?"

"Why do you want it, anyway?" I asked. "You're not going to tell me *you're* suffering from FSD."

She pouted. "Might be."

"Uh-uh," I said. "Though if you are, it could be because you've wasted too much time with men. It takes a woman to know what a woman needs."

"You're probably right," she agreed. "But some KXC79 would make the experience even better, don't you think?" More pouting. "*You're* the one who dishes them out. You could take a few when he's not looking, and replace them with Smarties."

Could she somehow have guessed I'd already done exactly that? The big blue eyes were giving nothing away. "But then Dr. Fisher would think he was giving someone KXC79, when he'd actually be giving them nothing at all," I pointed out.

"You could pull those results from the study. After all, it's not like we'd be talking about many pills. Just half a dozen or so."

"Half a dozen!"

"Some for me and . . . some for you?" A sly, wicked laugh in her eyes. "We could see which of us gets more out of it."

So that's the deal. She'll sleep with me if I get her some KXC79. Well, put like that, maybe a couple of duff results won't be that big a problem.[5] It's not like we're in a critical phase or anything.

I think I may be in love!

---

[5] I am absolutely astonished by the casual manner in which my colleague here reveals that she has, in fact, been undermining my project from the very beginning. This, it seems to me, is what comes of allowing sexologists into science laboratories—a total erosion of standards.

October 1

It's taken me a week to get the pills—I replaced them with more Smarties. I'm pretty sure Steve isn't suspicious. His mind's on next week's Sexual Endocrinology Conference and the paper he's giving about, I don't know, enzyme breakdowns or something.

So I told Heather I'd got the gear, and more or less suggested that we wait behind in the lab after everyone else had left to see what effect they had.

A frown. "Here? Here's not very *comfy*."

"Comfy? Who wants comfy? We're talking about a two-way trip to ecstasy."

Pout. "A girl can't just turn it on. I have to be in the mood. After all"—rolling her eyes at the lab—"this is where I *work*."

I refrained from pointing out that getting her in the mood was exactly what the KXC79 should be helping with. But I had already guessed what was coming.

"Of course," says the shameless little thing idly, "you and Dr. Fisher are going to that conference in Toronto next week, aren't you? Did you know it's at the Hilton?"

"So it is. But even if I wanted to take you, I couldn't. It's completely oversubscribed."

"You and I could share," she said. "No one thinks twice about girls sharing a room, do they? It could be nice . . . in all sorts of ways."

The thought of sharing a room with Heather Jackson at Sexual Endocrinology was, I had to admit, extremely tempting. After all, once we were locked in a room together for the night, the teasing would have to stop.

"You're an evil, manipulative hussy," I pointed out.

"I'm very, very bad," she agreed.

"And I won't be taking any nonsense from you at the conference."

"I probably do need firm handling."

"I'll tell Steve tomorrow that you're sharing with me."

October 20

Well, SexEnd is finally over, and I have to say that it didn't quite go as
planned.

For a start, when I imagined sharing a room with Heather, it was just that
I was picturing . . . the room, and the two of us enjoying a quiet (or, possibly,
a noisy) night in together. But it turned out that before we could get down to
business in the room, we had to hit the bar. And—Good Lord, what a surprise—
there were half-a-dozen people there Heather knew from previous jobs. (What
previous jobs? I must say it was news to me that she'd been working in this field
long enough to get to know so many people.)

When I say people, of course, I mean men.

In fact, I noticed that in our little group—our rather raucous little group—
Heather and I were absolutely the only women. When other females drifted in
our direction, an apparently chance remark from Heather would spin them round
and have them leaving us again.

Heather, I was coming to realize, is not the sort of woman other women like.
Unless, of course, they're bisexual and romantically deluded.

Round about midnight I noticed several other things, more or less
simultaneously.

a. We were now pretty much the only group left in the bar.

b. Heather had got out the little pill bottle containing the KXC79 I'd stolen.
She put one on her tongue, and held one up for me. I opened my mouth, and she
put it in. Then we swallowed together.

c. When she thought no one was looking, she passed the bottle to a man
who was standing behind her. I saw him take it without looking at it and quickly
put it in his pocket. Almost as if this was something prearranged. Something
they didn't want to draw attention to.

I said to the man I was talking to, "Who's that?"

He looked round. "Him? That's Paul Bryant. The sales director."

"Sales director of what?"

"Carvel Pharmaceuticals, of course. All us lot work for Carvel."[6]

"Not Heather," I pointed out. "Heather works for us."

"Course," he said vaguely. "Do you want another drink? It's a free bar."

"Did Heather," I said slowly, "ever work for Carvel?"

He shrugged. "Maybe. She had a summer job, I think. Very briefly." He handed me a mojito. "There you go."

I couldn't remember having ordered it, but I took it anyway.

Then at some indeterminate time I was in my room—our room—with Heather, and Paul Bryant, and three or four others, and someone had lit a joint. And whether it was the KXC79 or not I couldn't have said, but things were definitely getting out of hand.

Then Steve came to the door. He wanted some papers. And it was a funny thing, but I was almost pleased to see him. I thought, Good old reliable Steve, somehow he'll stop all this.

He didn't, of course. He didn't even realize it was happening. He took the papers and went back to his own room, oblivious as always.

When I went back inside, Heather was already naked, and most of the men were getting that way too.

With a sinking sensation I realized that, although I was going to have plenty of sex that night, it probably wasn't going to be with Heather.

October 21

Something else odd about that experience at the conference—I can't stop hiccupping.

---

[6] At this point in Dr. Minstock's account, I had to stop reading for five minutes while I threw up.

November 1

Heather's been avoiding me ever since SexEnd. But eventually she went into the testing room to hook up some new instruments.

"I've been wanting to talk to you," I said, following her.

She glanced over her shoulder. "Oh, it's you."

"You're an industrial spy, aren't you? For Carvel?"

"That's putting it a bit strongly. I'm just helping out some friends."

"How could you do this to us?" I demanded.

"It's entirely *your* fault."

"What do you mean?"

"Ever since I arrived," she said, turning those innocent blue eyes on me, "it's been clear to me that getting on here is dependent on giving you sexual favors."

"What?"

"I still haven't decided whether to make an official complaint. They take harassment quite seriously in universities these days, don't they? I should imagine that, for a sexologist, an accusation like that—particularly from another woman—would be quite a stumbling block in her career."

She turned and waved to Steve, who was in the control room, on the other side of the soundproof glass. "Just imagine if he could hear us now."

There was nothing I could say. She had me exactly where she wanted me.

"Oh, and another thing," she said. "If you were ever to tell anyone you'd been stealing KXC79 to assist you in your pathetic attempts to get me into bed—well, that probably wouldn't look very good either, would it?" She laughed. "Do you know, when I first came here, I assumed it would be Dr. Fisher who got me those pills. But I couldn't get anywhere with him. I was just starting to think I'd have to give up when you started coming on to me. Wasn't that a stroke of luck? My friends at Carvel are *very* pleased with me."

"What do you want?" I said.

"For the moment," she said, "I just want you not to do anything foolish, like tell Dr. Fisher that I ever had those pills."

"That Carvel has those pills, you mean."

She shrugged. The conversation was clearly at an end.

Oh, shit.

November 2

What do I do?

What do I do?

WHAT DO I DO?

November 3

Option 1: Tell Steve everything.

Option 2: Tell Steve nothing.

Option 3: Do something. (But what?)[7]

November 4

Option 1: If I tell Steve everything, he'll have me fired. My career will be ruined.

   Option 2: If I tell him nothing, Carvel will use the pills to scupper us. It won't be anything so obvious as copying our formulation—that would still leave them trying to catch up. More likely, they'll bring out a spoiler. For example, announce they've tried a treatment which just happens to be very similar to ours and discovered a nasty side effect. The only responsible thing to do, they'll say, is to abandon the whole approach. It doesn't have to be true: no one would let KXC79 go to a clinical trial with that hanging over it.

   Which leaves:

Option 3: Do something.

(But what?)

---

[7] It is, surely, obvious even to a retarded lesbian nymphomaniac what she should do, namely Option 1.

November 5

Heather sidles up to me. "I need some more pills."

"Why?"

"That last lot were no good, apparently—something to do with hiccups. But Dr. Fisher's been talking about a new formulation he's testing. So I need some of those, please."

Naturally I say, "Well, I'm not giving you any."

"If you don't get me those pills," she says sweetly, "I'll find some other way of getting hold of them." She looks across at where Wulf, Rhona, and Dr. Fisher are deep in conversation. "One of them will give me the pills. I doubt it'll take long. And then there'll be no reason for me not to get you fired."

Oh, shit.

November 16

So here's what I'm going to do: I'm going to replace *all* the KXC79 with pink Smarties.

This is not as stupid as it sounds.

If I replace the KXC79 with a placebo, it won't work. If it doesn't work, Steve (who, whatever else he is, is undoubtedly a genius) will assume that the formulation isn't right. If he assumes the formulation isn't right, he'll think of a different way of solving the problem—call it KXC80. Thus, when Carvel announces its spoiler, we'll be able to say it isn't an issue as we abandoned KXC79 ourselves some time ago.

Plus, even if Heather does get her hands on them, they won't be much good to her.[8]

---

[8] When I consider the utter, arrant stupidity of this plan, words simply fail me.

November 25

It's done. I got the key out of his lab coat when he went for lunch.

January 12

It seems to be taking a bit longer than I expected for Steve to realize that the pills aren't working anymore.

Oh, well. He'll get there in the end.

January 16

He still hasn't twigged. The main problem, actually, is that we don't have enough test subjects. Our small ad in the local paper ("Are you sexually dysfunctional? Female? Would you like to earn a little extra cash by helping out with medical research?") only ever seems to attract Ukrainian prostitutes.

I've told Rhona and Wulf to ask amongst their friends, with a cash bonus for every volunteer they deliver.

February 12

We have a volunteer at last. Annie G., a mousy postgrad who's clearly something of a geek herself (although she wouldn't actually be unattractive if she only did something with herself). Not an ideal test subject, by any means—viz. the following excerpt from her initial interview:

Susie: Could you describe a sexual fantasy, please?
Miss G.: I don't really have any.
Susie: You must have fantasies. Everyone has fantasies.
Miss G.: No, sorry.
Susie: [*Sighs*] Why do you want to take part in this project, Annie?
Miss G.: It sounds interesting, I suppose.

Susie: But you do want to become sexually functional?

Miss G.: Not really.

Susie: Then what are you hoping to get out of it?

Miss G.: I suppose I'm hoping that he'll stop getting cross.

Susie: Who are we talking about, Annie?

A little tea and sympathy, and it eventually all came out. She'd been having a relationship with her supervisor—or rather he had succeeded in seducing her, after a long campaign, only to become annoyed that she didn't enjoy his attentions as much as he thought she ought to. Annie is just the sort of person we should be screening out, but needs must. I tidied up her notes so that everything looked aboveboard and told her that the next stage would be for her to meet Dr. Fisher.

February 18

Steve has met Annie. It didn't go too well at first—Steve rather grumpily pointed out that we weren't meant to be recruiting any more volunteers. Then I had a brain wave.

"Anything you want to know about the science stuff," I suggested to Annie, "This is the man to ask!"

Well, of course Annie did ask him something, and of course Steve grabbed the opportunity to bore her rigid. Poor girl—I glanced through the lab door fifteen minutes later and Steve was drawing her a diagram of what her orgasms should look like.

Mind you, Annie didn't seem to mind too much. In fact, she seemed almost interested. And the test was excellent—by starting the program a bit early, I managed to contrive it so that it was completely uneventful for her. She actually went to sleep! If that doesn't alert Steve to the fact that his precious KXC79 doesn't work, nothing will![9]

[9] The notion that it is somehow my own fault that I failed to notice when I was being

February 20

This might be a slight problem—Trock wants Steve to deliver a paper on KXC79 at SexDys. I need to make sure he finds out that KXC79 isn't working in plenty of time to pull his paper, or we'll all be stuffed.

February 22

Annie's an odd one, actually. Every time Steve launches into one of his interminable scientific monologues she gazes at him adoringly. Steve, of course, shows no sign of noticing whatsoever.

February 25

Strike that last thought. Steve has taken to lending her science books and telling her that she has "a very fine mind, if I may say so."

He's never said that to *me*.

Annie is lapping it all up and pretending to have some vague clue what he's on about. Today I heard her hinting that she'd like to come along to one of his lectures "to find out more about neurotransmitters." Yeah, right. Luckily, he didn't take the hint.

February 27

Steve might not have taken the hint—but that didn't stop her from turning up at his lecture anyway. Hussy.[10]

---

hoodwinked by a duplicitous scheming virago is surely proof that here Dr. Minstock—who, I repeat, is not a real doctor but merely has a PhD in Applied Masturbation from the University of Sydney—has taken leave of her senses.

[10] A bit rich, considering who this comment is coming from.

February 29

This is getting stupid. Annie spends the whole of every session sighing and casting Steve longing glances. Whenever he's not around, it's Dr. Fisher this, Dr. Fisher that, when will Dr. Fisher be here, what does Dr. Fisher say about it, and—the really irritating one—you are so lucky to be working with Dr. Fisher, he's easily the cleverest man I've ever met.[11]

Hello? Can this be the same Dr. Fisher we're talking about? The one who saw a Valentine's card from Wulf on Rhona's desk a few weeks ago, looked puzzled, and said, "Why do they call it a love heart, when it's clearly an idealized representation of a vulva?"

The Steven Fisher who can't even tell that his bloody pills DO ABSOLUTELY NOTHING?

To make matters worse, I think Annie's started having orgasms. Steve hasn't noticed yet—but when he does, what if he thinks it's because of the treatment? He'll never abandon KXC79 if he thinks it's actually working.

Meanwhile Heather is prowling around the place in a cloud of fragrant CK One, like a cross between an albino panther and a heat-seeking missile.

March 6

God, so much has happened since I last wrote. Annie and her boyfriend have broken up . . . and Annie's persuaded Dr. Fisher to enroll her as a lab assistant AND teach her science AND let her co-write the paper. We're all furious, even Rhona, who's the sweetest-natured person in the world.

The only compensation is seeing how pissed off Heather is. She's just realized that she's got competition!

---

[11] Needless to say, this notion is just as ridiculous as every other deluded fantasy that inhabits my colleague's so-called mind.

March 7

Steven just assumes that we're all going to teach Annie A-level science for him. Which is a bit bloody much. Rhona says sarcastically, "Oh, it's not like we're busy." To which Steven nods and says, "Excellent."[12]

To begin with, I almost refuse out of principle. But then I remember that (a) she's only here because of me, (b) I can have some useful girl-chats with her under the guise of teaching her about sex, and (c) I don't really have any principles.

Later I spot Heather talking very intently to Julian Noble. It's soon clear why—she's found out that Trock has made Steven lock the pills in Julian's cupboard.

March 10

So now Heather is flirting with Julian Noble. There's a kind of terrible fascination, actually, in watching her at work. He doesn't stand a chance—it's like watching some doddering old fighter being demolished by some ruthless punk half his age.

March 18

Heather storms into the control room. "Very clever," she snarls.

"What is?"

"Those decoy pills. The ones locked in Julian's cupboard."

"Nothing to do with me," I say. "Must have been Steven, being careful."

"If you only knew what I had to do to get those pills," she hisses.

---

[12] This is not how I remember this conversation at all, incidentally. My colleagues were delighted to assist me with teaching Miss G., a task which in any case was—as I have related elsewhere—always a pleasure.

March 20

This paper seems to have acquired a momentum of its own. Richard Collins
even flies in ahead of the conference, to mark the project with his scent like
some snarling beast or something.

   This is getting desperate. Maybe I should just come right out and tell Steve
the truth? I can't let him make a fool of himself at the conference. Can I?

March 21

Annie and Richard Collins—who would have thought it? It was only the other
day she finally admitted to Rhona and me that she's totally got the hots for
Steve.[13]

   Still, there is a way in which this could work to my advantage.

   Methinks now might be a good time to have a go at Steve myself. After all, if
he sleeps with me himself he can hardly fire me, can he?

   First I just need to let him know about Annie and his mentor. . . .

March 25

Poor Steve. He's taking it pretty hard. In fact, I've never seen a man so deranged
by grief.

   For a moment I almost start to get cold feet about this. But needs must.

March 25

Heather sidles up after lunch. She looks unusually triumphant, even for her.

   "It's all over," she announces. "There's a side effect. I heard Steven talking
to Wulf."

---

[13] Ah. Well, if true—and we only have Susan's word for it—this does put a slightly different complexion on things.

"Meaning what, exactly?"

"Meaning that I no longer need those pills, of course. Either you'll pull the paper yourselves or—even better, from our point of view—you'll be stupid enough to go ahead and publish, in which case we'll trash Dr. Fisher's reputation forever."

Oh, shit. I can't let that happen.

I'm going to have to tell him everything.

And that's definitely going to be a conversation that'll be easier to have after I've just given him the best sex of his life.[14]

---

[14] If anything shows the extent of Susan's self-delusion, it is surely this comment. For the record, sex with her was like that famous description of life before the Romans—nasty, brutish, and short.

45.1

When I had finished Susan's diary I sat very still, thinking.

Then I went to the cupboard where I kept the KXC79 and unlocked it. Experimentally, I took one of the pills and put it in my mouth. The coating seemed unusually sweet, for a pill. I bit it in two.

The inside of the pill was chocolate.

I tried another. That, too, was chocolate.

45.2

Then I smiled.

Once again Susan had revealed herself to be completely deficient in simple scientific reasoning.

She had imagined I would be furious to discover that the pills contained chocolate rather than KXC79. *But exactly the reverse was true.* I felt a colossal weight lifting from my shoulders.

Now that I knew that Annie's results had nothing to do with KXC79, I was off the hook. We had reverted, in fact, to exactly the position we had been in before she first walked into the lab: twenty-seven sexually dysfunctional women had trialed the real KXC79, and twenty-seven women were now sexually functional. Our success rate was once more 100 percent. The launch of the paper could go ahead after all.

Heather, meanwhile, had been as misled by Susan's ruse as I

was, which meant Carvel would be under the impression that the treatment was sufficiently flawed not to require any further sabotage from them.

As for Annie, there was a simple explanation for her anomalous reactions after all.

And that very evening, I now remembered, I was due to be playing opposite her in a game of Swamps and Sorcerers—a game for which I was already a little late.

Everything was going to be all right.

The city was swathed in mist as I hurried through the medieval streets towards Annie's college. Streetlamps took on the soft, hazy glow of dandelion clocks. Only the occasional hiss as a student sped past on a bicycle reminded me that I was not completely alone.

At the Porter's Lodge I asked the porter where I would find the Swamps and Sorcerers. He tutted and shook his head.

"Not here, I'm afraid, young man."

"Not here?" I echoed, my heart sinking.

"There's been no swamp in this college since they made the lake, two centuries ago. As for sorcerers—well, there's some who claim that Elias Ashmole was an alchemist, back in the seventeenth century."[1]

I stared at him. It suddenly dawned on me that this oaf thought he was being funny.

"There is nothing remotely humorous about this situation," I informed him curtly. "Where is the fantasy society? It is a matter of great urgency."

He shrugged. "Turn left at New Staircase, straight ahead

[1] Elias Ashmole, 1617–1692, was a polymath who studied law, natural history, mathematics, and astronomy. In the Prolegomena to *Fasciculus chemicus* (1650), written under the pseudonym James Hasolle (an anagram), he defended alchemy against the charge that it is fraudulent. There are, he wrote, "many occult, specifick, incomprehensible, and inexplicable qualities" hidden in natural substances, waiting to be discovered. This assertion was, of course, exactly right, although it was not until the advent of biochemistry that we were able to prove it.

through Old Quad, turn left at the misty lake. You're then faced with a choice of two paths. Stop, roll a Decision die. . . ." He chuckled, but he must have seen my face because he added quickly, "Bear left and you can't miss it."

46.2

There were a dozen or so people in the room. Papers and dice were spread over the tables, along with the little plastic figurines that Swampers use to keep track of their position. Annie was wearing a metal helmet that curled down around her cheeks. I recognized it as the helmet of Azeroth.

"Annie!" I cried.

"Lady Maud," she corrected.

"Lady Maud. I'm sorry I'm late. But it's wonderful news. You never had a sexual dysfunction at all."

She turned to the others. "This is Lord Loroth, a disdainful tyrant and powerful adversary. We will need to pool our resources if we are to evade incarceration in the putrid recesses of his castle, where we will be forced to endure his every hideous whim."

For a moment I wanted to tell her everything, but then—with a happy sigh—I realized it could wait. There was a Level 3 adventure to be fought, with the prospect of ravishing Lady Maud in the Dank Dungeons at the end of it.

I held out my hand.

"Give me those dice," I commanded. "And prepare to flee from the wrath of Lord Loroth."

46.3

After the game we walked by the lake—the real lake, that is, the one in the college grounds, not the Sea of Silver Light.

"I haven't had so much fun in years," I said.

"Tonight was a particularly good level," she agreed. "Although I did think Willem was completely out of order, introducing salamander slime into your dungeon like that."

"We saw him off, though, didn't we?"

She nodded. "Or rather you did, when you proved beyond doubt that his salamander slime would be desiccated to powder by the unique atmospheric conditions of Castle Loroth."

We stopped, gazing over the lake. Mist drifted through the woods, enveloping us in skeins of muffled silence.

"Did you know," I said, turning to look into her eyes, "that a cubic mile of fog contains less than a gallon of water?"

"Yes," she breathed.

Just before our lips touched she said, "By the way, what was that you were saying earlier, about me not being sexually dysfunctional after all?"

"It can wait," I said.

46.4

"No, really. I'm curious," she said. "What was it you meant?"

"Oh. Well, in a nutshell . . ." And I told her about Susan, the substitution of the pills, and the fact that Annie had never been given KXC79 at all.

"I was worried about confounding factors, you see," I concluded. "Things like the placebo effect and so on. When all the time, it was the tomato effect I should have been thinking about."

She looked puzzled.

"When the tomato was first introduced to North America, scientists thought it must be poisonous," I explained. "It was only when they saw people cooking with it that they changed their minds. So we use the phrase 'tomato effect' when we fail to spot what's right under our noses. That's you, Annie—you're a big, red, juicy tomato."

She looked even more puzzled.

"Metaphorically speaking," I hastened to add. "What I'm trying to say is, that's the explanation for all your false tests, isn't it—you were simply too embarrassed to admit that it was *me* who was making the difference. Annie, that's the answer to everything: *You're in love with me.*"

She took a deep breath.

"A simple blood test could confirm it," I added.

"A *what*?" she said slowly.

"A blood test. You see, romantic attraction is associated with raised levels of phenylethylamine, or PEA. It's PEA that causes your heart to race when you see me, your breath to come faster, and makes you secrete almost imperceptible odors from your glands." I began ticking them off my fingers. "It's PEA that triggers a cascade of adrenaline, making you hyperalert, and another of dopamine, making you more receptive. It's the PEA in your system

Figure 24: A good example of observer bias.

that dilutes your natural levels of serotonin, the chemical associated with inhibitions and the control of impulses, making you do
crazy things and giving you a jittery feeling when you see the object
of your affection—that is, me. And it's PEA which makes you feel
those first irresistible stirrings of desire."

"But I still don't see why I need to take a blood test," she said.

"Ah." I was getting ahead of myself again. "Obviously, *I* know
you're attracted to me, and *you* know you're attracted to me, but
we'll need a higher level of proof for the conference."

"Conference?"

"Yes. Annie, don't you see? You're the best kind of evidence
there is. You're confirmation that where nature is chaotic and
muddled, science is ordered and logical. You'll be the climax of my
presentation—the ultimate visual aid! There may even have to be a
new formulation—KXC80—which builds on these findings." I was
gazing out at the lake, but what I saw in front of me wasn't water.
In the swirling mist I could see row upon row of people—my
peers, the greatest minds of my generation—clapping and cheering
me to the rafters. Some were even getting to their feet, giving me a
standing ovation. . . . And there, beside me on the stage, was Annie,
beaming proudly as she joined in the rapturous applause. . . .

I turned round. She was staring at me, and the expression on
her face was nothing like the proud, shy smile I had just been imagining.

"A 'visual aid'?" she repeated.

"Um . . . perhaps 'living proof' would a better description."

"I enjoyed this evening," she said slowly. "That's what makes
this even worse. I really, really enjoyed it."

"So did I—"

"No, wait," she said. "I'm trying to explain something. Something *important*. I enjoyed this evening because I thought it was
nothing to do with experiments, or measuring my responses, or

any of those other things I've had to do for the last six weeks. I thought, This is *fun*—almost like a normal date that normal people might have. But it wasn't, was it? All the time, you were watching me. Trying to work out if your theories were correct. Whenever we're together, whatever I do, to you I'm always just . . . data."

I opened my mouth to protest, then closed it again.

"You see, Steven, you are—as usual—quite correct. I do get the jitters every time I see you. My heart does race, and I do find it hard to breathe, and to concentrate, and all those other things you described. I didn't choose any of that. It just happened. But I can choose what do I now."

She looked at me, and I quailed under the ferocity of her gaze. "You know something?" she went on. "Sometimes those PEAs or whatever they are make the wrong decision. Well, now it's me who's doing the deciding, not them. And what I choose . . ." She swallowed. "What I choose, Steven, is that I don't want to be your lab rat anymore."

"But . . . ," I managed to say. "But, Annie . . ."

"But what?"

"But what about the conference?" I said anxiously. "You will be there, won't you?"

"I suppose so. I can't really let Richard down now."

"Richard? What's Richard got to do with it?"

She said slowly, "Because I'm going to be staying with him, of course. In his suite."

46.5

I stared at her, aghast.

"I thought you realized," she said.

I shook my head.

She shrugged. "He had to rush off from Oxford to Dublin last week. So we said we'd meet up at the conference."

"I see," I said, although in fact I could see almost nothing. Lysozyme, lipocalin, and lactoferrin pricked at my eyes.

"It's just bad timing," she added.

I nodded, unable to speak.

"So I guess I'll see you there after all." She let out a breath. "Anyway, it's good that you cleared up all the mysteries in time. I'm sure your paper will be a triumph. Just keep me out of it, all right?"

"Annie . . ."

"What?"

"Nothing," I said.

47.1

Somehow I packed my things for the conference. I assembled my slides, my charts, the spreadsheets breaking down our results by ethnicity, age, and every other variable known to science. I went through the presentation line by line, deleting every reference to Miss G. and her now-irrelevant results. Then I took Lucy to the lab, locked her in her cage with enough food and water to last her for the next few days, and caught the train to London.

At least, I suppose I did. Afterwards, I could remember almost nothing about those twenty-four hours. The only thing I can recall is that at some point I found myself staring at a train door, completely unable to remember how to open it. An elderly lady who was waiting on the platform to board had to remind me what to do.

47.2

Eventually I found myself in the vast lobby of the London Hilton, under a sign which said, in five languages, TOWARDS A SEXUAL-DYSFUNCTION-FREE FUTURE—TROCK PHARMACEUTICALS WELCOMES DELEGATES. In the distance I saw Richard, surrounded by a gaggle of admirers and the bright lights of a TV crew. Kes Riley was standing by the check-in desk, talking on his mobile.

"Steven. Thank God," he said, looking up and gripping my arm. "Where have you been? Got your presentation? Give it to the girls in the hall, they'll load it up for you tonight. Richard's going to introduce you—I've seen his stuff: it's quite a buildup. Not that the paper won't top it, of course. This is going to be *fantastic*."

"Actually, there are a couple of details I'm still polishing," I said mechanically. "I'll load it up myself, in the morning."

He looked anxious. "Nothing major, I hope?"

I hesitated. Then I said, "Kes, is there somewhere we can go? Somewhere quiet we can talk?"

47.3

The bar was full of delegates eagerly consuming Trock's special cocktails, wittily named KXC1. Eventually we found a quiet corner. Kes looked at me expectantly.

"The thing is," I said, "I'm having doubts about this project. Serious doubts."

His pale eyes didn't blink as he waited for me to go on.

"Oh, it's not the science—that all hangs together. It's just that I think the whole study could be based on a misapprehension. We've always assumed that women who can't have sex properly are dysfunctional. But what if the opposite is true? What if not being turned on is simply nature's way of saying something's wrong— something fundamental, something our treatment will mask instead of cure? What if by tinkering with sex, we're actually hastening the end of love?"

"'The end of love?'" he repeated, perplexed.

"It's a phrase of Richard's."

"Is this something to do with that research subject you were talking about? Your anomaly?"

"No. Well, yes. In a way. It turns out she was never part of the study at all—it's a long story. The issue isn't KXC79—that *works*, all right. But what does it actually *do*?"

"Steven," he interrupted. "You remember Wernher von Braun, the German rocket scientist?"

"Of course."

"He was asked once about the damage his rockets did. Know what he said?" Kes leaned forward, tapping my knee with his finger for emphasis. "Von Braun said, 'My job is to send the rockets up. Where they come down, that's someone else's department.'" He nodded. "You've done your job, Steven, and done it brilliantly. As for the rest—that's someone else's department."

"Yes. Yes, of course," I said numbly.

"Look, you're apprehensive. Of course you are: it's a big day tomorrow. A day, dare I say it, that will change both our lives. Get a good night's sleep. And tomorrow, let's make history."

He slapped me on the back, and then he was gone, his hand raised in greeting to a delegation of Chinese endocrinologists.

47.4

I sat in my room, my head in my hands.

The acclaim of my peers—the prize I had pursued for so long—was within my grasp.

And now I knew that I did not want it.

There was only thing I really wanted, and that was the one thing I had ensured I could never have.

47.5

What I had described as the truth—that Annie was romantically attracted to me—was actually only half the truth. What I had failed to say—failed even to acknowledge to myself—was that I felt exactly the same way she did. That my own pulse raced when I saw her; that I too knew the sweet agony of phenylethylamine coursing through my veins; that I felt the vagus nerve twitch in the pit of my stomach whenever I thought about her, which was all the time. I hadn't told her that the thought of kissing her, of holding her in my arms—of simply being close to her—made me weak with pleasure; or that when she was near me my inhibitory serotonin levels were so nonexistent that I had to restrain myself from turning cartwheels and bursting into song, just for the pleasure of seeing her smile.

I had treated Annie like a problem to be solved, when all the time I should have treated her like a person, to be loved.

Why had I not realized what these things meant? Why had I not admitted them to myself?

Because I'm a fool.

Because denying my feelings had become a habit.

Because years of trying to be a good scientist has made me ashamed of the irrational, flawed, emotional human being I really am.

47.6

As I sat there, there was a knock at the door. I rushed to open it, hope and phenylethylamine surging through my veins.

But it wasn't her. It was Wulf. He had Rhona with him.

"We need to talk to you," Wulf said quickly, pushing past me into the room. "Don't say you don't want us to, because we're coming in anyway."

47.7

"What's going on?" he demanded. "Why are you sitting up here on your own?"

So I told them. Susan. Heather. KXC79. The experiment that never was. The irrelevant results that, the more I thought about them, were more relevant than anything else I had ever done.

When I had finished explaining Wulf looked at me and said, "Well, okay. But you know, Steven, people make mistakes."

47.8

It was such an inadequate response to the situation that I almost laughed.

"Wulf," I said, shaking my head, "your gift for understatement is almost as brilliant as your work."

"No," he said doggedly. "Listen to what I'm saying. *People make mistakes.* That's what science is all about—trial and error. Take radar. Robert Watson-Watt, the man who invented it, was actually trying to invent a death ray. Or take Alfred Nobel. He said, 'My dynamite will lead to world peace sooner than a thousand world conventions.' Lord Kelvin, probably the greatest British scientist of the nineteenth century, thought airplanes were a hoax. Thomas Watson of IBM believed there was a world market for no more than five computers. Aristotle thought the function of the brain was to cool the blood. James Watson and Francis Crick's first attempt at a model for DNA was so hopelessly implausible that they were actually forbidden from working on another one. Galileo, Einstein, Newton, Bohr—they all cocked up, time after time. And time after time, they picked themselves up and they *tried again.*"

"I know all that. But this is different. Annie isn't a piece of science. I blew it with her—I can't just have another go. And now I have to decide what to tell this conference."

Rhona said slowly, "You could tell them the truth,"

"The truth? Hardly. The truth is that I've been a complete and utter idiot."

"But isn't that what science is, really?" she said. "Just a series of hopeless failures, and the occasional chance to learn from them? Isn't that the only responsibility we have, as scientists—to tell the truth, however stupid it makes us look?"

"And it seems to me," Wulf added, "that you need to decide what's really important here—your career, or Annie."

They sat on the bed, hand in hand, watching me. "But what you seem to forget," I pointed out, "is that I've already lost Annie. My career is all I've got left." I sighed. "Look, I appreciate you coming, but you'd better go now. I've got to work out how I'm going to play tomorrow morning."

47.9

As I unzipped my laptop from its case something fell out of the side pocket. Something bulky and rather battered. A book.

Collected Poems of W. B. Yeats. I must have put it there and forgotten about it.

Picking it up, I began to turn the pages. As I did so I thought about that man—that shy, studious, stammering poet, who knew that he was never going to be the kind of person whom Maud Gonne would love, and who poured his sorrow into creating these poems instead.

Yeats had told Maud Gonne how he felt. It made no difference, in the end, but at least he had told her, in poem after poem and rhyme after rhyme. Even if she had told him to stop, he would no more have been able to than if she had asked him to stop breathing.

And then I thought, If Yeats had been given the opportunity I'd been given—if the woman he loved had so nearly loved him too—would he have sat in his room writing poetry, or would he have done everything in his power to win her back?

Well, of course, he was a poet, so perhaps he would have chosen to write beautiful poetry after all. But I was not a poet. I was a man of science.

And scientists, as Wulf had so rightly pointed out, are not deterred by a couple of trivial mistakes.

47.10

Throwing W. B. Yeats to one side, I booted up my laptop and deleted the presentation I had been planning to give.

Then I began to construct a quite different paper.

This paper.

The last paper that I will probably ever be asked, or indeed allowed, to give.

The paper in which I will finally admit—to Annie, to myself, to all of you—the truth.

48.1

Downstairs, as I write these final words, over five hundred delegates are busy collecting their name tags and their Welcome Packs from Registration. They are milling in the bar, drinking their complimentary rum punches, exchanging nods and handshakes and gossip.

Here in my room, though, it is very quiet. Occasionally I hear sounds from the corridor, knocks on doors, voices raised in genial greeting. As the night has worn on the knocks have become more furtive. The voices speak in whispers, the doors open and close more softly, as the parabola of human encounters proceeds to its inevitable conclusion. Strangers, male and female, catch sight of each other for the first time, exchange a glance, look away, then go back for a second glance. Strangers who before the night is out may yet become lovers.

Who knows.

My paper—how will it go? I wonder. By the time I reach this last section, how will you all be reacting? Stravinsky's *Rite of Spring* famously provoked its first audience to a riot. But we in the field of sexual dysfunction are a more subdued lot. There'll have been some murmuring, I'll guess. Many of you will have exchanged looks ranging from the baffled to the outraged, rolled your eyes, snorted disbelievingly. Perhaps you will even be putting me through the ultimate indignity as one by one you get up and leave the hall, either in protest or in perplexity, until all that remain are those who indulged themselves too freely the night before.

What shall I say to you few who are left?
Two things.

48.2

If, as Professor Collins has so brilliantly suggested, you think of sex as a parasite which needs human beings to propagate, then you can see that in recent centuries the parasite probably thought it was doing rather well. Its host population had been growing at an astounding rate; the forces of repression appeared to have been all but vanquished.

And then sex hit a problem. Chemistry.

The discovery of norethynodrel, the first contraceptive pill, meant that, in evolutionary terms, sex was effectively neutered. People might be having more sex, but suddenly sex wasn't making more humans.

So sex hit back. Sex used every means at its disposal. Because for sex, this is always a total war—a fight to the death, if you like. And, since the sex-parasite has successfully taken over people's brains as well as the rest of them, it was able to use books and films and magazines and the internet to pump out the same propaganda, over and over: *Have more sex! Have more sex!*

But propaganda wasn't enough. Sex needed to use the same tools that had stopped it in its tracks. Sex needed *chemical weapons*. So—lo and behold—suddenly, from nowhere, an industry appeared that whispered, *Take this pill, and have more sex.*

Oh, I know that our treatment will initially be for those with sexual problems, and it will undoubtedly make a great difference to these people's lives. But do we really think that it will be used *only* by them? It will be a massive social experiment—an experiment in which there is no control group, no antidote, and no going back.

Not a single person in this industry—not the scientists, not the pharmaceutical companies, not the sexologists—can tell us what life will be like when feeling desire, or even lust, is as simple as popping a pill.

48.3

There is one other thing I want to say. You will recall the legend of Pandora, the first woman, created by the gods and given by each of them a gift to make her more beautiful. Jupiter, who was angry with mankind, sent her a box, along with instructions not to open it. The box contained all the pestilences of the world. But it also contained their cure, hope.

I think we, like modern-day gods, are in the process of making another Pandora's box. In that box there are many kinds of desire. But there is also love.

Sex and love—it has only just occurred to me how very different they are. Sex says spread your seed as widely as possible. Love says put all your eggs in one special basket. Sex says me, me, me; love says you, you, you. Sex says muscle in on the best-looking genes you can find. Love says search for that one unforgettable face.

Sex says move on, find someone new. Love says don't let anyone or anything take her away.

Sex says it's all about the species. Love says it's all about the one.

But one man loved the pilgrim soul in you.

Sex, you see, is biology. But love is chemistry.

48.4

I don't know exactly what will happen after I say all this, apart of course from the spectacular implosion of my career. But I know what I want to happen—what I can *imagine* happening.

I will look up and see her, standing at the back of the by-now-almost-empty hall.

I will say into the microphone, "Annie . . ."

And if she gives me any sign or encouragement at all—a smile, a gesture, a nod—I will run from the podium and make my way towards her, knocking the papers from the lectern in my haste, a confetti of notes tumbling in my slipstream, diagrams and data dispersing on the drafts of that vast auditorium. . . .

Is that how it will be?

I have just rolled the dice on Luck, and it looks as if I still have the Improbability Bonus.

So.

Who knows?

REFERENCES

Allen, M. L., and W. B. Lemmon. "Orgasm in Female Primates." *American Journal of Primatology* 1 (1981): 15–34.

Belzer, E. G., Jr. "Orgasmic Expulsions of Women: A Review and Heuristic Inquiry." *Journal of Sex Research* 17, no. 1 (1981): 1–12.

Burton, F. D. "Sexual Climax in Female *Macaca mulatta*." In *Proceedings of the Third International Congress of Primatology*. Vol. 3, Basel: S. Karger, 1970.

Carmichael, M. S., R. Humber, J. Dixen, G. Palmisano, W, Greenleaf, and J. M. Davidson. "Plasma Oxytocin Increases in the Human Sexual Response." *Journal of Clinical Endocrinology & Metabolism* 64, no. 1 (1987): 27–31.

Chevalier-Skolnikoff, S. *The Ontogeny of Communication in the Stumptail Macaque (Macaca arctoides)*. Vol. 2 of *Contributions to Primatology*. Basel and New York: S. Karger, 1974.

Darling, C. A., and J. K. Davidson. "Enhancing Relationships: Understanding the Feminine Mystique of Pretending Orgasm." *Journal of Sex and Marital Therapy* 12, no. 3 (1986): 182–96.

Dunn, K. M., L. F. Cherkas, and T. D. Spector. "Genetic Influences on Variation on Female Orgasmic Function: A Twin Study." *Biology Letters* 1, no. 3 (2005): 260–63.

Elkan, E. "Evolution of Female Orgastic Ability—A Biological Survey." *International Journal of Sexology* 1:1–13 and 2 (1948): 84–93.

Fox, C. A., and B. Fox. "Blood Pressure and Respiratory Patterns During Human Coitus." *Journal of Reproductive Fertility* 19 (1969): 405–15.

———. "A Comparative Study of Coital Physiology, with Special Reference to the Sexual Climax." *Journal of Reproductive Fertility* 24 (1971): 319–36.

Goldfoot, D. A., H. Westerborg-van Loon, W. Groenveld, and A. K. Slob. "Behavioral and Physiological Evidence of Sexual Climax in the Female Stump-Tailed Macaque (*Macaca arctoides*)." *Science* 208 (June 1980): 1477–79.

Kohn, I., S. Kaplan. "Female Sexual Dysfunction, What Is Known and What Remains to Be Determined." *Contemporary Urolology* 11, no. 9 (1999): 54–72.

Phillips, N. A. "Female Sexual Dysfunction: Evaluation and Treatment." *American Family Physician* 62, no. 1 (2000): 127–36, 141–42.

Singer, J., and I. Singer. *Types of Female Orgasm.* In *Handbook of Sex Therapy*, edited by J. LoPiccolo and L. LoPiccolo. New York: Plenum Press, 1978.

Slob, A. K., W. H. Gronveld, and J. J. Van der Werff ten Bosch. "Physiological Changes During Copulation in Male and Female Stumptail Macaques (*Macaca arctoides*)." *Physiology and Behavior* 38 (1986): 891–95.

Zumpe, D., and R. P. Michael. "The Clutching Reaction and Orgasm in the Female Rhesus Monkey (*Macaca mulatta*)." *Journal of Endocrinology* 40 (1968): 117–23.

EDITORIAL

International Journal of Submolecular Biochemistry, June 2008

The furor, if that is the right word, over Dr. Steven Fisher's paper at the Trock Sexual Dysfunction Conference continues to dominate these pages. In this month's issue is a response by Ms. Heather Jackson, one of Dr. Fisher's former colleagues. "It saddened many of us," she writes from her new position at Carvel Pharmaceuticals, "to see this once-promising scientist reduced to spouting wild conjecture and rambling anecdote. In his defence, I would point out that for many years Dr. Fisher has labored under enormous professional and personal pressures. No one could ever have driven him harder than he has driven himself. Of course, I accept my own share of the blame for not noticing sooner the strain he was putting himself under. I only wish he'd had the courage to ask for help."

Other correspondents have highlighted the continuing difficulty of defining what female sexual dysfunction is, and therefore what scientists such as Dr. Fisher are actually trying to cure. "Until we understand what constitutes 'normal' female function, what does 'dysfunction' mean?" asks one. "And what makes us think these women even want a treatment for it?"

However, the letter from Kes Riley, Trock's director of marketing, stresses that Dr. Fisher's treatment was "only one of a number of possibilities we have been pursuing in this area. In fact, we had recently informed Dr. Fisher that his program was to be wound up owing to lack of progress, coupled with some very exciting and positive outcomes from a completely different approach we have been funding elsewhere, of which you will be hearing more very shortly. Had we known that this news would add to the personal burden under which Dr. Fisher was already laboring, we would have offered him counseling. The welfare of our employees and colleagues is always our top priority."

We also print a letter from a Dr. Jay, who was actually present at Dr. Fisher's presentation. He points out:

> If every scientist who now claims to have been there really had been, the room would not have held us all. The truth is, I don't suppose there were more than a hundred in the audience at the start, and by the time Fisher finally wound up there were only eight of us left. I myself only stayed because I fell asleep around ten minutes in. When I woke, I found to my surprise that, according to my watch, more than two hours had passed. I was about to follow the others out when I realized he was almost done—he was rambling incoherently by this time about chemical weapons and sorcery and someone called Miss G. Then he peered towards the back of the room and started calling "Annie? Annie?" in a querulous voice. Well, we all looked round—but there was absolutely nobody there. After that the wind seemed knocked out of him, and he got his things together and left. I've heard since that he was supposed to be frothing at the mouth, or that he started manhandling the security staff, saying they must have stopped this woman from coming in, but I certainly never saw him do anything like that. He looked perfectly calm to me, almost dignified, although of course you can never tell with mad people.

Whatever the truth behind Dr. Fisher's behavior—and it now seems likely to be the subject of an investigation by the authorities at his university—it is certain to raise further issues about the governance and regulation of research studies dealing with female sexual function.

Congo Blog

Hey ho, here we are on Day 5 already. I'll try to post yesterday's photos on Flickr when I get a chance. (Most of the places we stop off only have generator power, so I'll wait until we reach something resembling civilization before I risk an upload.) Today has been spent paddling slowly upriver, first through the mangrove swamps, then through proper rain forest. Funny, after spending most of my adolescence in a Swamp, to actually see one for real at last. It's nothing like the Blood Swamps of Azeroth, of course. For one thing, we never had to worry about mosquitoes in those days. Here the little beggars are everywhere. Hope the malaria tablets are working. (They make me feel terrible, so they're obviously doing something.)

And—ah, dammit. Here we go again. I'm crying.

It still creeps up on me at the oddest times. Just then it was because I wrote that stuff about taking the malaria pills. Suddenly I was back in the lab, swallowing my KXC79. With Steven.

Will this ever go away?

It will. Of course it will. Already I'm not crying more than, I don't know, six or seven times a day. Six months ago it was, oh, seven or eight.

Six months ago. It feels like another lifetime.

I didn't go to the Trock conference. I still wonder if I should have done, whether everything would have been different now if I had. But at the time I just couldn't face it. The thought of being stared at by all those scientists while Steven explained how my infatuation with him was going to be the basis of a whole new treatment for sexual dysfunction wasn't terribly appealing, somehow. Not to mention the awkwardness with Richard . . . So, like an idiot, I decided I'd wait until after the conference was over, when maybe there'd be an opportunity to have a proper conversation with each of them.

But there wasn't. Suddenly all hell was let loose. Steven was suspended, and there were demonstrations outside the department building—it was the animal rights people, mainly, who'd got wind about Lucy, with a few feminists and anti-Trock protestors thrown in for good measure. Simon Frampton even popped out of the woodwork, making heinous—and entirely hypocritical—allegations about Steven and me, which whipped up the university authorities even more. So then there was an investigation, and somehow it was all Steven's fault, the attitude of the university authorities being much the same as Tennyson's:

> Weakness to be wroth with weakness! woman's pleasure, woman's pain—
> Nature made them blinder motions bounded in a shallower brain. . . .

Even so, with no supervisor, no thesis, and no job, I was pretty much persona non grata too. Then, just as I was considering my options, as they politely call it, I got a call inviting me to apply for a Richard Collins Scholarship at Harvard.

Which was pretty surprising, because after Steven's paper and my no-show I'd imagined that Richard wouldn't want any more to do with me. But they paid for me to fly out there, and there was round after round of psychological tests—well, I walked those, of course: one of the few good things to come out of the whole KXC79 debacle is that I now know exactly how to tick the boxes on a Myers-Briggs. And eventually there was an interview with Richard himself. At which, inevitably, we started talking about Steven.

"Have you heard from him?" Richard wanted to know.

I shook my head. "Not a thing."

"I'm just wondering . . ." He hesitated. "Was there anything left after the project was wound up? Papers, perhaps? Computer discs? Anything he gave you for safekeeping?"

"Nothing. But that whole approach has been discredited now, hasn't it? Most of the new FSD trials seem to be looking at the testosterone approach."

"Yes." He nodded impatiently. "But did he ever—that is, I'm working on a small project about hiccups. And Steven—I have a vague idea that he might have looked at that area too, just in passing. On my behalf. I thought perhaps he might have left some notes. . . ."

"You mean, how to replicate the effect of orgasm on intractable singultus?" I said.

"Yes!" He looked at me, his eyes suddenly alight. "Did he ever say what the mechanism was? He'd made some progress—I know he had. But there are so possible candidates—the amino acids, oxytocin, phenylethylamine, the peptides. . . ."

"He did mention something about hiccups, yes," I said slowly.

"What?" he demanded.

And I seemed to hear Steven's voice, very clearly, in my head, saying, *"I got as far as working out it was one of the chemicals being released during orgasm—oxytocin, was my guess. . . ."*

I shook my head. "Sorry. Can't remember."

"Well, I'm sure it'll come back to you. Look, Annie, we want to give you this scholarship."

"That's wonderful—"

"And on a personal level too, it will give me great pleasure to have you here. Hiccups—singultus—could be your own little project. Reporting directly to me, as your supervisor."

"But I thought there was no money in it?"

"No money in hiccups!" he said, astounded. "Whatever gave you that idea? It's one of the most common maladies in the world—almost as common as sneezing. Imagine if a drug company could bring out, I don't know, a little one-dollar nasal spray, or something you squirt down

326 ANTHONY STRONG

your throat. Every mother in the USA would want one of those in her medicine cupboard."

"But Steven said . . . ," I began.

And then I began to see what had really happened.

"That's what this was all about, wasn't it?" I said. "Hiccups."

His face darkened. "I don't know what you mean."

"Please, Richard. Let's not insult each other's intelligence."

For a moment he looked almost guilty. Then he nodded.

"It was five years ago," he said. "I'd already published by then. Three best sellers, one after another. But not actual science. Books of *ideas*. Then a young postgrad applied to be supervised by me. A complete geek. And, unquestionably, the most brilliant student I had ever had. Cleverer . . ." He swallowed. "Cleverer than I was."

"But not so clever that he could see his supervisor stitching up his career."

"I wasn't stitching it up. Not exactly. Just . . . applying the brakes a little. To make sure that I stayed involved in his projects." He groaned. "But I was hardly ever there. My books . . . It was a constant round of interviews, PR appearances, self-promotion. It was hardly surprising there was no time for real research. I was living my life on airplanes. Every time I came back to Oxford there'd be some new breakthrough— some new avenue Steven was already exploring. And each avenue was leading to more avenues. He was like a one-man research institute, spilling ideas in every direction."

"That was when he started looking at hiccups."

He nodded. "I realized straightaway he was on the verge of a massive breakthrough. And once that happened, he wouldn't need me as his supervisor anymore. He'd have his own fame, his own funding—"

"So you switched him to FSD."

"It was a joke!" He closed his eyes wearily. "God. It was just a joke. I passed him on the stairs and said something about why couldn't human females have as many orgasms as his blasted bonobos. But Steven doesn't do jokes."

"He took you seriously. And started thinking about it."

"Which could have been perfect. I thought if I helped get him funding for the FSD project, there'd be no time for hiccups. I never imagined—never in a million years—that he'd crack FSD as well."

"If that's what he did."

"If that's what he did," he agreed. "I doubt if we'll ever know, now." He looked up. "Are you sure there's nothing? No mention of a neurotransmitter, perhaps, or a hormone?"

I shook my head. "I can never quite remember the difference between those two," I lied.

Then, at the end of the chat, Richard suggested that we continue over dinner.

"Is that part of the interview?"

"Of course not," he said. "It's just that . . . Annie, ever since we . . . ever since that amazing afternoon in Oxford, I haven't been able to stop thinking about you. Don't get me wrong," he added quickly. "You passed the selection process here fair and square. With, I might add, flying colors. But I suppose I'm hoping that if you and I see each other more often . . . well, that something else might develop."

"I see," I said. "Well, that is unexpected."

Flying colors. For some reason, out of all the things he had just said, it was those two words that were going round in my head. That's what I always pass with, isn't it? Flying colors. I've never failed at anything.

I don't deny that the package Richard Collins was offering was an attractive one. A scholarship from an Ivy League university. Supervision from one of the most famous scientists in the world. Who also happened to be sweet on me. My own, funded, research project. And the knowledge—the hint—that oxytocin was the chemical involved, which would give me a head start. . . .

"I'm flattered," I said, "but I should probably explain something. That time I slept with you in Oxford, I was faking it." That was when I started to have my own suspicions that there was something funny about KXC79, as a matter of fact. That it wasn't everything Steven thought it was. Which in turn was why I suddenly felt . . . *responsible* for what I was doing.

Richard looked at me doubtfully.

"Thanks for the offer, Professor, but I'm going back to England. Somewhere will take me, in the end. And after that, I'll be a proper scientist."

And that's pretty much how it panned out. Eventually I managed to get a place in a biochemistry course at Oxford Brookes, which is one of those establishments that call themselves universities but which academic snobs still refer to as polytechnics. And it's great—absolutely great. Quite apart from anything else, I've met a nice bunch of people.

Though I doubt if any of them would know the chemical composition of tears.

Would I have done anything differently, if I'd known what I know now? Funnily enough, the one thing I don't regret is having walked out on Steven, that time by the lake. My whole problem was that I'd been behaving like some swooning Victorian heroine, drifting along, being wooed, letting everyone else tell me what to do. Even when I played Swamps and Sorcerers, I was letting the dice make the decisions. But sometimes you can't just roll a polyhedron and let it decide your fate. Sometimes you have to make a plan. And telling Steven to get lost was the start of that.

Admittedly, the bit in between Richard and starting at Brookes is all a bit of a blur. That was the beginning of a slightly mad period. Not that I regret any of it, necessarily, but it wasn't really me. Call it making up for lost time. I even surprised myself by becoming a bit of a slut for a while . . . until I realized that the only person I wanted to be a slut with wasn't there.

I'd lost touch with the others in the lab by then. Although I did glimpse a couple of things. There was an article in the *Daily Mail* about some new sex toy. Apparently it uses miniaturized biofeedback software "based on the technology used in professional sex research laboratories." According to the newspaper, the young couple who invented it, Rhona and Wulf Sederholm, are on track to become multimillionaires.

And then one day during my first term I was buying *New Scientist* in W. H. Smith when I looked up and saw a paperback called *Sex Goddess: Inside the KXC79 Experiment,* by Dr. Susie Minstock. On the cover was a full-length picture of Susan looking sexy. And a publicity quote from Professor Richard Collins, best-selling author of *The Evolution Revolution*: "Full of mystery, humanity, laughter, and sex."

Meanwhile, I've been going on these field trips with the guys from my course. Like this one. Well, when I heard it was about bonobos, how could I not sign up for it? Plus, it sounds like we might actually do something useful. Bonobo numbers have been shrinking over the last ten years, apparently, but without accurate tagging it's impossible to say how much or why—everyone's pretty sure it's the destruction of their habitat, but the data to prove it haven't been collected. So that's what we're going out to do. Though—secretly—we're having a good time too. Today, for example, I found myself sitting in the middle of a mangrove swamp, eating grilled river perch, arguing with Melissa about who's cooler, Leela or Trinity.* How much fun is that?

---

* Well, duh. Despite all her awesome powers Trinity is clearly only in the movie as eye candy for the boys, whereas Leela is a Strong Woman in her own right. Plus her relationship with Fry always makes me cry, and no one could say that about Trinity and Neo.

Urlgirl67@hotmail.com

"There are only ten kinds of people,
those who understand binary and those who don't."

Day 6. Today we pushed the last sixty miles upriver to the camp. Nice place—basic but friendly. Ben, our group leader, has been here before, and the local people greet him effusively before unloading our stuff and carrying it into the huts. And—hurrah!—there's even broadband access, a really ingenious rig that uses a router hooked up to a satellite phone that's connected to some toll-free number in Mexico. . . . Hence the blog update.

After supper we get a brief introduction to bonobo culture. I know most of this, of course, but it's always interesting to hear it from an expert. Except that as Ben explains about how bonobos use sex for conflict resolution I feel the familiar pricking behind my eyes, because talking about bonobos reminds me of Steven. Oh, dear. That was something I hadn't factored into my packing—that I might end up blubbing every half hour. The nearest supply of Kleenex is six hours away.

And I'm crying so hard, and trying not to let anyone see it, that I almost miss the reference to someone called Fish.

Fish is their tracker, it seems, a man who understands bonobos so well he can follow them through the rain forest and find their camps. Fish can almost *talk* monkey. Fish has even rigged up webcams in the jungle to send pictures of bonobo gangbangs back to UCLA.

Just for a moment, I think: Fish? Could it be him? I mean, the monkey connection makes sense, but—no, it can't be.

Six months ago I thought I saw Steven Fisher on every bus I stepped on. Once I even went up to a total stranger and started a conversation about peptides. So although when I hear the name Fish I have a great surge of euphoria and excitement, a miserable crashing of my expectations follows as I realize that once again I'm just being stupid.

"If you've got any questions about bonobo social organization," Ben says, "he's the man to ask. But you may have to wait a few days. We've got a hunting party of chimps in bonobo territory." It turns out, you see, that bonobos and ordinary chimps don't mix. Although bonobos are vegetarian and peace-loving, regular chimps aren't, and occasionally they organize raids into the bonobos' territory to steal their babies and eat them.

"Which, of course, poses a dilemma for us conservationists," Ben adds. "Do we intervene and save the young bonobos from their predators, on the basis that their numbers are so depleted they need our protection? Or do we simply observe? It may be that when predators take the weaklings, they actually end up strengthening the herd. If we intervene, we run the risk of upsetting the evolutionary balance."

"What does Fish say?" someone asks.

"Fish says . . ." Ben pauses. "Well, Fish has a slightly unorthodox perspective. Fish says we can never be just observers. He says we're part of the experiment, like it or not. So that's what he's doing now— guarding the bonobo kids."

Someone prepares some food, and as the sun begins to set the Africans in the camp start to sing, a lovely mournful sound. That sunset— it's a real Congo sunset, the sun pumped up into a great orange egg yolk that seems to swell until it fills the whole sky, before slowly squashing itself down against the horizon, and finally breaking in a gush of red and yellow into the swamp. The forest goes quiet, and the heat of the day dissipates so fast you can actually feel the sluggish air draining from your skin. Then, from the forest, comes a whole series of unearthly shrieks and calls.

"Bonobos," Ben says.

I lean against a tree trunk and watch the sky as it turns a rich, streaky red, only half-listening to the conversation around me. I hear someone say, "What a beautiful sunset," and then a different voice says, "Yes. It's the refraction that does that, of course. The longer wavelengths of the sun's rays are filtered by the atmosphere of the earth."

I know that voice.

I look up and—

He looks so different. For one thing, the jungle clothes really suit him. He's wiry and lean and completely at ease. But that's not the most striking thing. With his long hair, and that wild beard . . . he looks an awful lot like Chewbacca.

How come I never noticed that before? He was a clean-shaven Chewie, all the time.

He sees me too, and he hardly seems surprised. Like he's been waiting for me to turn up.

He nods, slowly.

"Annie," he says simply. "You're here."

Of course, with everyone else milling around, it's some time before we get to talk to each other alone. But eventually he stands up, and I stand up, and then somehow we're walking away from the fire together.

"Come with me," he says, heading into the forest.

"Where are we going?"

"Shhh. I'll explain later." And I follow him down a moonlit path into the forest, wondering about snakes.

Eventually we come to a clearing. He stops and peers into the gloom.

"There," he whispers. "See them?"

It takes my eyes about a minute to get used to the near-darkness. Then I spot them. About half-a-dozen bonobos are rolling around on the floor of the clearing, having enthusiastic sex. In the foreground, a big male is squatting on his hind legs thrusting away at a female who's lying back and eating a bamboo shoot. Another female comes up and squats over her face. Then a second male comes over and takes care of the second female, helping himself to a mouthful of bamboo as he does so. More join them. They stop, start, break off, swap round, and occasionally pause to pelt each other with fruit. When they finally finish, the males lie back, pleased with themselves, passing a piece of bamboo around like a cigar, while the females groom each other for fleas and indulge in a little surreptitious extra sex play.

"There's Lucy." He points to where a knot of simian polyamorists are clustered around one especially tireless female.

"You remember me saying that no one knows what the female orgasm is actually for?" he says, still speaking quietly so as not to disturb the bonobos. I nod. "Well, I have a new theory about that. I think it might be related to mate selection. If females gravitate towards males who have the ability to make them climax, it would favor more intelligent, dextrous, empathetic males, and ultimately enrich the gene pool. That would explain why female orgasms are apparently random and elusive: it's a kind of compatibility challenge."

"So nothing to do with neurotransmitters after all?"

"That's the interesting thing. How does a female know in advance which male is clever enough to make her orgasmic? Guesswork? Romance? Trial and error? There could be a role for some kind of chemical messenger after all."

I nod. Then, because I realize he won't be able to see me in the near-darkness, I say, "Agreed. But the trouble with messages is that they can be so hard to read. Even chemical ones."

"Almost impossible," he agrees.

"Take you and me. How wrong did we get those signals?"

"Exactly." He pauses. "Just to make absolutely sure that neither of us is misreading them now, shall we double-check our reactions against each other?"

"Good idea."

"For a start," he says, "I'm feeling a little unsteady on my feet. Almost as if I want to fall into your arms."

"Check," I say. "Which is probably due to a rush of dopamine, increasing visual attention but impairing fine motor coordination."

"You've been doing some science?" He sounds impressed.

"Biochemistry. A degree course."

"I'm also feeling intense gratification at your presence, akin to a deep-seated hunger that's finally been satisfied," he says.

"Check. That would be the effect of opiate-like beta-endorphins creating addiction-and-reward pathways in the brain."

"Now I'm feeling an overwhelming urge to touch you."

"Check. Caused by oxytocin, elevated levels of which are associated with cuddling, breast-feeding, and other attachment stimuli. You can if you want."

"Can what?"

"Touch me."

He takes me in his arms. "I'm feeling good about myself—"

"Check," I say, a little breathlessly. "Which is due to cascades of serotonin, a powerful mood enhancer."

"—excited yet calm at the same time—"

"Check. A cocktail of epinephrine, which causes the excitement, and its sedative counterpart, L-dopa."

"—dizzy—"

"From the intoxicating effects of norepinephrine."

"—but also strangely focused. As if there's nothing outside this place, this moment, just being here with you."

"Our old friend the dopamine again."

"I'm breathing somewhat heavily."

"Me too," I breathed. "Prostaglandin."

"My lips are tingling—"

"As if they're dying to be kissed."

"In fact," he says, "I think it might be a good idea to do just that."

So he kisses me, and then he kisses me some more. First on the lips, and then the neck, and then the ears and the eyelids and the throat, before going back to the lips again. For one endless, ecstatic minute, time pauses while every single cell in our bodies jumps up and down and applauds.

"I'm pretty sure our chemical messengers are reporting an

exceptionally high level of compatibility," he murmurs, breaking off.

"Possibly. Although the view that kissing has any such function is regarded by many as overly sentimental," I tell him sternly.

"What's not in doubt is that I'm becoming somewhat, ah, vasodilated."

"I'd noticed."

"Sorry."

"Don't be. It's a relief to know you won't be needing Viagra. Plenty of nitric oxide in the old corpus cavernosa."

"Exactly. Accompanied by a giddy mixture of melting tenderness and ferocious lust. On the one hand, I want to hold you in my arms like some delicate precious flower. On the other, I want lay you down and pound you senseless."

"The luteinizing hormone, LH, is probably playing havoc with your testosterone levels. On the other hand, you're also sloshing with oxytocin. Thank goodness. I'm not sure I'm quite ready for the pounding bit. Or, indeed, the senseless."

He kisses me again, more deeply. I sigh and wriggle further into his arms. "Mind you," I admit, "I am starting to feel a little giddy myself. And a certain amount of vasodilation may well be taking place, less obviously of course. But there's a definite feeling of wanting to melt into your arms like a swooning Victorian heroine."

"That would be the vasopressin."

"I'm also getting a strong urge to take all my clothes off."

"Me too. Hardly surprising, with all these chemicals reacting inside us. First law of thermodynamics." Then as he kisses me again he slips his hands a little higher, inside my shirt, where he does something clever with his thumbs, and I'm reminded that what this man doesn't know about sex probably isn't worth knowing.

Then, unexpectedly, I hiccup.

"Better do something about that," he says without missing a beat. "And I think I know just the thing."

After that, rational thought becomes pretty much redundant. A few minutes later one of the bonobo females looks up, sees us, and chatters. For a moment the other monkeys regard us curiously; then, as if we've given them the idea, they get back to doing what they were doing before, which is pretty much the same as us.

Posted to:

The Ringing Tower (Web site of the Oxford University Campanology Society)

Events: We are pleased to report that a quarter peal was rung on Saturday last to celebrate the engagement of Steven Fisher, PhD, and Ms. Annie Gluck, MSc, both currently research fellows at the University of Mombasa, Kenya. The peal was made especially noteworthy by the fact that both parties participated, Dr. Fisher on the number eight bell and Ms. Gluck at number four. Despite Ms. Gluck's being a relative newcomer to ringing, several impressive changes were achieved, including a Jarrock's Surprise, ten rounds of Triple Hunt, and an unusual grand finale of Splendid Bob and Rounds. The happy couple, who are in the country for only a short while, also attended a celebratory gathering of the Swamps and Sorcerers Society, of which they are both active online members.

From: *Fisher.A@momb.ac.ky*
To: *Fisher.S@momb.ac.ky*
Subject: **FW: FW: FW: FW: FW: Funny**

>>>A boy was crossing a road one day when a frog called out to him and said, "If you kiss me, I'll turn into a beautiful princess."

He bent over, picked up the frog, and put it in his pocket. The frog said, "If you kiss me and turn me back into a beautiful princess, I'll stay with you for a week and be your girlfriend."

The boy took the frog out, smiled at it, and returned it to his pocket. The frog said, "Look, let me make this deal clear. If you kiss me and turn me back into a princess, I'll stay with you and do *anything* you want—anything—for a whole week."

Again the boy took the frog out, smiled at it, and put it back into his pocket. Finally the frog asked, "Look, what is it? I've told you I'm a beautiful princess, that I'll stay with you for a week, and that I'll do anything you want. Why won't you kiss me?"

The boy said, "Look, I'm a geek. I don't have time for girlfriends. But a talking frog is really cool."

The End

Acknowledgments

The scientific papers referenced by Dr. Fisher come from many sources. Some of the more interesting can be read at his Web site, www.chemistryforbeginners.com.

So far as I can ascertain, Dr. Fisher's own science is accurate, although I have not corrected a few statements which, I am told, most biochemists would consider fanciful. I am indebted to Dr. Cynthia Graham, research fellow at the Kinsey Institute for Research in Sex, Gender, and Reproduction, senior research fellow at Harris Manchester College, University of Oxford, and research tutor, Oxford Doctoral Course in Clinical Psychology, for reading through the manuscript. Dr. Fisher's mistakes are in no way hers.

My thanks too to Ileen Maisel who, in developing the film adaptation, offered many ideas which found their way into the manuscript; to Tom Vaughan and Peter Friedlander, who championed it from the beginning; to Tim Riley; to Danielle Friedman at Touchstone, for her suggestions during editing; and to Louise Lamont, Judith Evans, and Elinor Cooper of AP Watt, for loving Dr. Fisher as much as I did.

Chemistry for Beginners

For Discussion

1. Did you expect Susan, Heather, or Richard's betrayals? How did you react to the discovery of their ulterior motives?

2. Discuss the many sexual relationships in the book (Richard and Annie, Wulf and Rhona, Annie and Simon, Steven and Annie, Susan and Heather). Were they all dysfunctional? How did sex affect their work environment? Similarly, discuss the romantic relationships throughout the story (Annie and Simon, Steven and Annie, Julian and Heather). Were any of them what they seemed?

3. How did the inclusion of Miss G.'s blog help to frame the story? Did hearing directly from her enlighten you and add to the story, or could you already adequately determine her perspective from the main narrative?

4. Richard Collins states, "For every action there is a chemical reaction" (page 33). Discuss the cause and effect of a few actions (and subsequent reactions) within the story. Consider the revelation of Susan's diary, Steven and Annie's awkward dates, and the slow unraveling of the KXC79 project.

5. In Section 47.8, Rhona asks, "But isn't that what science is, really? Just a series of hopeless failures, and the occasional chance to learn from them?" (page 310). Do you agree with this sentiment? Does it hold true for more than just science?

6. Why do you feel that Steven repressed his feelings for so long? Does science get in the way of emotion?

7. Do you consider FSD a problem to be solved or an evolutionary message?

8. Were you surprised by Steven and Annie's reconnection in the Congo? Discuss their jungle consummation.

9. Is Annie a true scientist by the story's end?

10. How did you perceive the role of fantasy throughout the story? (From sexual imaginings to the dragons and battles in Swamps and Sorcerers). Which do you find more fun?

A Conversation with Anthony Strong

Some of the scientific theories in the book are incredibly complex. Do you have a background in biochemistry or any other area of science?
Sadly, no. When I had this idea—and I originally thought of it as a short story, or possibly a novella—I was a complete ignoramus about science. But I have a child who has an unusual medical condition, and in the course of trying to research possible treatments for it I struggled through a vast number of scientific papers with the aid of a science dictionary. I was struck by the way they're written, which of course is usually very dispassionate, but sometimes you get these little glimpses of passion or excitement. . . . Somehow the idea of writing a love story about a scientist kept growing, and then finally I had the thought of writing my whole story as a paper. After that Steven's voice just appeared on the page, and before I knew it I had fifty thousand words, then eighty thousand. . . . But doing the

research was incredibly hard, particularly as I set myself the goal of getting the science 99.9 percent right—the missing 0.1 percent being where I deliberately distort it for comic effect. So almost all of the science papers I reference, for example, are genuine—you really can go online and look up peer-reviewed papers about neurotransmitter cascade in the orgasm of the female bonobo, or whatever.

As a literary writer, do you think that there's merit in a scientific approach to poetry?

I think there's much more merit in a poetic approach to science. Albert Einstein once said: "The most beautiful thing we can experience is the mysterious. It is the source of all true art and all science. He to whom this emotion is a stranger, who can no longer pause to wonder and stand rapt in awe, is as good as dead: his eyes are closed." That seems to me to be very close to a poet's view of the world. And of course, however logical scientists try to make their discoveries seem, really great science—the science of an Einstein or a Newton—is about genius, insight, and inspiration. Scientists are actually the most passionate of men: they just have to hide it behind the language of academia.

Is Steven meant to be as romantically naïve as he seems? Does science interfere with love on a basic level?

Well, love is science. And at the moment, with all these popular evolutionary thinkers around, there are plenty of people who explain things like love *only* in terms of science. I wanted to show that there's an opposite point of view—that we're much more than the sum of our evolutionary influences: that chemistry is as important as biology.

In a way, I'm not sure Steven is naïve. Repressed, yes, blinkered, self-deceiving . . . but it's almost as if he knows too much rather than too little. I have to say, I like him. But then, I'm probably quite similar to him.

What made you decide to include varying narrative formats, such as Annie's blog and the editorial bit at the end of Steven's "paper"?
Originally, it was just for the plot—the little revelations that need to be explained somehow. But as I developed those bits, and particularly Annie's blog, I was struck by the way that having more than one perspective on an event goes right to the heart of what the book's about—that truth is more complex than science sometimes acknowledges, particularly when it comes to the different ways men and women view sex. And it allowed me to break up Steven's scientific language with something a bit more immediate. It's easier to root for Annie if you've been inside her head.

Why do you think Steven is able to keep his composure after the discovery of his colleague's duplicity?
Well, he does throw up! But of course the fact that the pills are placebos neatly solves the problem of Annie's anomalous results. So in a way it's a big relief for him.

Was there a method behind when you referred to Annie by her name or as "Miss G.?"
A little. We get the sense that Steven is using her real name in conversation but not in the paper. Then, at moments of intimacy or crisis, he forgets himself and calls her "Annie."

Have you ever played any game like Swamps and Sorcerers?
Nope—not Dungeons and Dragons, World of Warcraft, or any other fantasy game. But I love the language they use. And I wanted the book to celebrate geeks, not to satirize them. It was very important to me that Annie isn't just a love object. She's someone who, at the

start of the book, has a real need to find her inner geek, even though she hasn't realized it herself yet. Her love of Swamps and Sorcerers is just one of the ways that the reader knows before she does that she's destined to be a scientist.

Which definition of "plasm" do you prefer?
Funnily enough, I was never a big fan of *Lady Chatterley's Lover* until I reread it on Annie's behalf. Then I realized what a wonderful, sensual, mystical writer Lawrence is about sex. So I'd probably choose his definition—not that he really defines what plasm is.

Are you planning on writing another book? Will science be involved?
Definitely another book—but whether science will be involved I don't know. It's all about finding the characters, really. And I like the notion that romantic comedies can be set in quite unusual worlds. So the next one might be another surprise. . . .